Remembrance

a novel

also by velda BROTHERTON

Sexy, Dark, and Gritty.

TWIST OF POE MYSTERIES

The Purloined Skull

The Tell-Tale Stone

The Pit and the Penance

THE VICTORIANS

Wilda's Outlaw

Rowena's Hellion

Tyra's Gambler

THE MONTANA SERIES

Montana Promises

Montana Treasures

Montana Dreams

OTHER TITLES

Beyond The Moon

A Savage Grace

Once There Were Sad Songs

Stoneheart's Woman

Wolf Song

Remembrance

a novel

VELDA
BROTHERTON

FOYLE PRESS

AN IMPRINT OF
OGHMA CREATIVE MEDIA

ISBN: 978-1-63373-225-4

Interior Design by Casey W. Cowan
Editing by Gil Miller

Foyle Press
Oghma Creative Media
Bentonville, Arkansas
www.oghmacreative.com

For Iva Dell.

My lifelong best friend who introduced me to life on Monkey Island one bright summer weekend and who always told me when she grew up she wanted to be just like me. We were ying and yang and possessed a rare love for each other. I will always miss her.

Acknowledgements

It's often difficult to acknowledge properly all those whose influence and help contributed to a novel like *Remembrance*. Though inspired by a true story, the characters all sprung from my own mind. I'm always grateful to my expert editor Gil Miller and publisher Casey Cowan, for without their assistance this and other of my books would remain in boxes under the bed. The support of my family—especially my daughter Jeri—and my many friends keeps me creating even when the going gets rough. And I'm always grateful to all my fans.

If you would like the true story of my discovery and visit to Monkey Island go to my website www.veldabrotherton.com and leave your email address with request code MKIS on my contact page and I will send you a free PDF.

"And he took bread, gave thanks and broke it, and gave it to them, saying, 'This is my body given for you; do this in remembrance of me.'"

Luke 22:19

One

Tiny bits of daylight dribbled through gaps in the ivory drapes. Groaning, Becca fumbled around on the night stand, knocked something off.

Pills.

They rattled from the bottle when it hit the carpet. Zoloft? Valium? Morning again. Dear God, when would it end?

When she had the courage to make it end, that's when.

If she didn't wake up, he would still be alive.

No good. She had to move, function. Open one eye, then the other. Blink. Wait for the devastation to hit.

Downstairs the phone rang, and she stared at the muted instrument beside the bed.

Go away. I'm not home. Rebecca Kraft is out. Gone. Left. She doesn't live here anymore.

After a while the ringing stopped. She swung her legs from under the sheet, felt hard little cylinders underfoot. Capsules filled with blessed oblivion. Another groan.

God, she was pitiful. Pathetic.

There was nothing for it but to get out of bed. Eyes squeezed shut, she staggered into the bathroom, pulled up her nightgown, and plunked down, landing precisely on the commode.

Getting better at that all the time. Could be blind and get along just fine. Could be dead and get along better.

Finished with that chore, she moved in front of the mirror and eased one eye open, then the other. Opened her mouth and stuck out a coated tongue.

You're a mess, Becca. What would sweet Jeremiah think if he could see you now?

Tear-filled, bloodshot eyes stared from the glass. How long had she made it this time without thinking her son's name? Two minutes, three? Maybe she'd get a stopwatch, start timing it. Write it down.

Hell, after four-hundred-sixty-nine days, you'd think she could manage five or ten minutes without…. If it's four-hundred-sixty-nine days, why then it must be April 12.

That's it, girl, hang in there. Dredge up all the silliness you can.

Forget. *Forget.*

Brush your teeth, wash your face, comb your hair. Do something besides… die. She made her way through each task murmuring the mantra over and over.

Teeth, face, hair. Teeth, face, hair.

Teeth, goddammit. Face, goddammit. Hair, goddammit.

The phone rang again.

"If you want to talk to me, Jonathan, then come to the house. Don't keep calling me 'cause you're too much of a coward to face the mother of your dead son."

You bastard.

But he wouldn't. Hadn't been out here once all winter, not even for the anniversary of Jeremiah's death.

Someone banged on the front door.

Dammit!

The room tilted... whirled.

When she opened the door there they were. Two of them. Detectives, they must've been, because they didn't have on uniforms. One a woman. She flashed the badge, the man didn't... wouldn't look at her. Stared over her shoulder into the house, still decorated for Christmas. Lights gleaming, the heated aroma of the huge pine tree seeping around her shoulders into the brisk, cold night.

"Mrs. Kraft?" The woman asked, pity softening her official tone. "Do you have a son... Jeremiah?"

They knew she did. Of course, she did. Well, she had, anyway. Until they came to the door. For an instant there, she'd thought it was David they were talking about, off in Europe bumming around. David who had stepped in front of a car, or fallen in with bad company, or been shot by some Irish Catholic soldier.

Would it have been worse, better, or the same, had it been her other son who died that night?

Dear God, how could she even wonder such a thing?

Downstairs, someone banged again, then leaned on the damned doorbell. She looped an arm over her head to stop it exploding.

"Go away, go away." The shout only added to the painful cacophony.

Not the cops, surely. Come to tell her Jeremiah was dead all over again. She wanted to scream, but instead staggered across the bedroom and opened the door. Glanced down at herself. Dirty gown, nipples like matching pearls beneath the stained blue satin.

Who the hell cared, anyway?

Gripping the balcony rail, she skidded down the carpeted stairs, rather proud that she didn't tumble head over toenails. The drugs made her dizzy, but by God, she'd take them if she wanted to. Shuffling through the hallway, she grasped the cold knob in the center of the wide door and swung the pretentious thing open. Hanging on. Peering out.

A young man stood there, sandy hair windblown, scowling furiously, holding out a rolled newspaper.

Jeremiah? My baby.

For a moment, a flickering moment, she'd thought—but, no.

"Mrs. Kraft?"

"What?"

"Mrs. Kraft, it's me, Len. Ma'am, you haven't picked up your papers in a while. Uh, I thought maybe, uh, ma'am, are you okay?"

She leaned against the jamb, squinted at him. "Why would I be okay? Of course I'm not okay. Stop bringing them, then. I don't need them."

He shrugged, continued to hold out the folded paper.

With a hand that shook, she took it, just to get him to stop poking the damn thing at her.

"I'd be glad to gather these up for you, ma'am. Put 'em out in the trash." He had begun to look at her as if he expected some insane reaction, eyes jittering down to her breasts, then away, like he didn't want to look but couldn't help it.

"Do what you want with them."

He didn't move, continued to study her tits.

"What?"

He jerked his eyes away. "If you want me to cancel delivery, I'll leave a bill. You can pay it by mail."

"Fine."

"Mrs. Kraft?" He caught her glance with embarrassed eyes.

"What?" Why couldn't she stop saying that, like a dog barking over and over at some damned shadow?

"I'm sorry, I mean, I was sorry about Jerry. I never got to tell you that."

Jerry. Don't call him…. A whimper started deep in her belly, the pathetic wave of sound that erupted every time someone said they were sorry. A choking that kept her from speaking. This boy… this boy was alive and he *dared* tell her he was sorry Jeremiah was dead? Dared call him—call him *Jerry*.

She leaned against the door frame clutching the hard roll of newspaper and watched Len write out a bill and rip it from a pad. When she didn't take it, he shrugged again and, leaning forward, gently tucked it into the paper she held. He exuded a whiff of dusty weeds and sweat and something sweet like grape or strawberry, maybe that goop boys spiked their hair with.

What a beautiful boy. So full of promise. God, how she wanted to gather him into her arms, tell him to be careful. There he stood, unaware of all the horrible things that could happen to him.

She blinked, stepped back.

"Len? I think I remember you. He was older than you, my Jeremiah. Yes, I remember you. I wish…. Oh, do be careful. Don't let anything." Her throat closed over the words, her eyes filled.

In silence he studied the littered ground. Without looking at her again, he quickly gathered the mess from the porch and walked away, shoulders squared, all long legs and big, sneakered feet. How old? Fifteen, sixteen?

How old had he been when he'd known Jeremiah? They'd played baseball together. Basketball, too, maybe. Len looked like he was just now reaching Jeremiah's age. An age her son would always be. Forever, into eternity, he would be fifteen years, eleven months, and fourteen days old. And she would never see him again. Never.

All the kids in Chota went to the same school, so they all knew about the boy who carried a 4.0-plus GPA, who was a math genius and a star basketball player. A boy who laughed easily, whose eyes were blue as periwinkles and twinkled as if frosted. The golden boy who once swam around the tip of Monkey Island to impress little Jillian Wentworth, whose parents owned three banks in Tulsa. And then she'd gone out with his best friend and broke Jeremiah's heart, for all of two days.

A boy whose heart would never be broken again.

There it came once more, the dreadful moan from out of the darkness of her soul. She backed up, closed the door, and leaned against it for a long while, staring through tears into the desolate bowels of the house. Listening to the echoes of her grief.

Much later, when she could breathe again, she put on a pot of coffee and dragged open the ivory drapes to let in the morning sunlight sparkling off the lake beyond the sweep of deck. Bright, shiny, as if nothing bad had happened. Could happen. Not in a place like this. It was too early in the season for water sports, but a few boats plowed the surface, mostly fishermen. In another month or so families with summer homes along the lake shore would begin to arrive. Kids would water ski and swim, houseboats and cabin cruisers would form a crisscross of white wakes over the cobalt water. The smell of barbecue and hickory smoke and the sound of laughter would feather through the warm air, drifting from shore to shore.

And she would spend another summer without Jeremiah. Without Jonathan. Without anyone.

Maybe she'd call Christi, see if she wanted to come out for a few weeks when school let out. David was still off somewhere in the Middle East, living there now, in a place called Bazratain. No, that wasn't right. Something Bazra. Digging wells, building huts, doing God knew what with those mysterious women who covered their bodies from head to toe, dark eyes peering out like trapped, frightened animals. He'd flown home for the funeral, then right back out, square jaw clenched against the pain of losing his younger brother. But did he cry? Not on your life. Too much like his father.

Father of Jeremiah who'd made it very clear that she had to get past her grief before he'd come near her again.

"Face it, Becca," he'd said. "It's the way life is. You take your lumps and stand up again. Stop moping about and get busy. Go back to work with Lorraine. You always loved the coffee house. RainTree is your creation. For God's sake, do something. You can't expect to get over this until you work through all the stages of grief. You can't stay stuck in the middle the rest of your life. It's been nearly a year, for God's sake." This at Christmas, the last time she'd seen Jonathan.

As if a year were the time allotted to recover. Stages of grief. How like him to say something like that. She'd wanted to hit him, just haul off and beat on him until he came to his senses. But she didn't. That would've taken a passion she no longer possessed.

"You may be able to forget our beautiful son and act like nothing ever happened. I can't. I won't. You and David and Christi, all of you, just go on like he never existed."

He'd taken her by the shoulders then, gently, because Jonathan was never a violent man, though he could clench that granite jaw when the occasion called for it. "Oh, Becca, that's so unfair. We loved Jeremiah. We'll *always* love him. But he wouldn't want us to give up the rest of our lives to mourn him. He wouldn't. You've got to get hold of yourself, love. You shouldn't live this way and I can't. I won't. Not anymore. It's killing me. Killing *us*."

All but struck mute by his words, she managed, "God forbid you do something you don't want to do. Go. Stay in Tulsa and work and have lunch with clients and forget all about what happened. That's about all you ever did anyway."

He gazed at her for a long while, hazel eyes forlorn, then rubbed a thumb down her cheek. "That's not true. You know it isn't." Then he'd kissed her in the same spot where he'd touched her, lips so cold they branded her with his betrayal.

Without another word, he turned and walked out the door, closing it oh, so softly. Just like him.

She raced across the room, flung it open and shouted at him. "Why don't you get mad, Jonathan? Slam the damn thing." And she'd done just that, so hard the crystal porpoise David had sent from London for her forty-eighth birthday this spring fell from the corner shelf in the foyer and shattered into jagged pieces across the ivory terrazzo stones.

That had been the day after Christmas and just before the anniversary of Jeremiah's death, December 29th. Jonathan hadn't been back since, though he called at least twice a week. Sometimes, like today, she didn't answer. But she knew it was him, same as she knew her life was over.

She hadn't seen David since he stalked away from Jeremiah's funeral, shoulders hugged up to his ears against the bitter cold wind.

In spite of what she'd said about Jonathan's never being there, she missed the times they had spent together. Mornings sitting on the deck drinking coffee and eating those gooey sweet rolls he loved so much, and never gained an ounce from. Still looking his old sturdy self and handsome as that boy she'd met in college and fallen for almost before they exchanged a word. And all those years later, sitting together, laughing and discussing the kids while a gentle breeze off the lake tousled his silver-streaked auburn hair so he looked young again. Where had it all gone? Why couldn't they have held on to it through the tragedy? Lent each other enough support to struggle through.

Because he knew, that's why. He knew that not all the support in the world would have gotten her through Jeremiah's death. Jon was right. She was stuck as if in quicksand, could do nothing about it. Each time she considered the idea of stepping out into the sunlight, offering her flushed cheeks to the wind's caress, heading with purpose to the silver Nissan in the garage and driving into Chota to RainTree, she fell into an even deeper funk.

Sighing, she poured coffee and sat down, hands wrapped around the mug as if they were cold. Dead. The newspaper she'd brought in lay open on the table, and the name in a headline caught her eye. Letting go the cup, sloshing liquid everywhere, she pawed at the pages, squinted at the headline—*PELL RELEASED TODAY.*

Flattening the paper under both palms, she smoothed down the dampened wrinkles with fingers that shook as if palsied. A dark arrow of pain shot through her heart, making her gasp. Blood roared in her ears. Darkness threatened her vision until she could scarcely read the small print under the headline.

Didn't want to anyway. Wanted to burn the damned thing, make the reality go away. But she had to know. Picked it up. Read.

Lucas Pell reached the age of accountability today and was released from Juvenile Detention where he has been held since December of 2008. Because Pell was a juvenile at the time of his arrest, no details were available as to the charges, but Pell said that he would continue to live in Chota where he grew up.

"Everyone in town knows what happened," he told the Sentinel. "It's a joke to say different. And I'm so sorry for causing those good folks grief. I will do anything to make up for what I did."

Pell spoke to this reporter candidly, saying that he hopes the community will understand how he feels about what he did and forgive him.

"I would like a chance to make up for what happened," he added. "Especially to that poor family. I did a terrible thing to them and I hope to make it right."

Becca clawed the paper into a ball, threw it across the room. "Little bastard. Make it right."

The telephone rang and she stared at it through half a dozen long tones, then picked up.

"Becky?" Lorraine. Her best friend.

"Yes, it's me."

"Did you hear that Lucas—?"

"Yes. I read it. Raine, how could they let him out? He killed Jeremiah. Got drunk and climbed in a car and ran him down."

"I know, sweetie. Lord, don't I know. I'm sorry. I just wanted to make sure you're okay."

"Well, I'm not. Of course, I'm not."

"Honey—"

"No, don't worry."

"I can come over if—"

"No, you have to get to the shop. Please, I'll be fine. Go to work."

Silence, then, "I'll call you later. Why don't you come down? See what we've done to the place. It's yours too."

"Not today." Not today. Not tomorrow. Not the next day. Not ever. If she held herself very still, didn't venture out of the house, maybe she wouldn't shatter into a million pieces. Maybe she'd heal, if only she never moved again. She felt like a broken china cup mended with glue that never dried. And everyone kept pouring her full of water, but it drained out through the seeping cracks.

"Okay, but, well, I'll talk to you soon."

Oh, Raine, I'm so sorry. Please understand. I don't know how to explain it.

Becca hung up without saying goodbye. Sat there for a long while as coffee grew cold in her cup. Then stood. There were ways to get back at Lucas Pell for what he'd done, and if the law couldn't do it, she damn well could.

She went to the island in the center of the kitchen, yanked open a drawer, and pawed around till she found a small notebook and a pen. Perching on a walnut stool, she made a list of all the ways she could get back at that little killer for what he'd done to her and her family. He wouldn't get away with serving a lousy year and some few months in a sissy home and getting out so he could go about his business.

Sitting there, thinking and writing, the pen point cut deep into the paper. Something infinitesimal glowed deep in her gut, like a fanned coal in the ashes of a long ago fire. She felt alive for the first time since that night she'd swung open the door and found two harbingers of death standing on her door stoop.

All she had to do was find Lucas Pell and make him pay for murdering Jeremiah. Then everything would be all right. She wrote it down with big, broad strokes.

MAKE HIM PAY.

Two

The Cherokee Motel, on the northeast side of Chota, though several decades old, offered Spinner a comfortable place to stay while he counseled Lucas Pell. Built in his favorite style. Cheap with no frills, the one-story affair had a dozen or so units that opened on the parking area. True, the rooms had an odd ancient odor to them, but he'd smelled a lot worse in his time. Good to be able to come and go as he pleased without trudging through a lobby past a curious clerk. The fact that it was named for his people notwithstanding, it was not much of a place to set up an office, even a temporary one. What the hell? It beat driving back and forth for the time it would take to get Lucas settled.

A small round table served as a desk and there was no Internet service. Every time he scooted back from his work, he banged an elbow on the wall. Two slightly wobbly, straight wooden chairs weren't much to brag on either. Wishing for the reasonable comfort of his office in Vinita, he studied Lucas.

The boy slouched in a chair across the table from Spinner, who more than took up the other. Lucas made every effort to appear iced, but Spinner wasn't fooled, not for a minute. Poor kid might as well be hanging from a precipice by the tips of his fingers. Buck naked. In a freezing wind. He'd seen them before, these pathetic, self-destructive monsters in the making. Most of them beyond help. Some had slipped from his grasp, until it was getting so he doubted his ability to drag yet another from the terrible place where their minds took refuge.

Not good. For him or this poor kid. Yet, if he lost his confidence, he might as well go to work flipping burgers. Somehow he would find a way to help this one.

The kid stared at the toes of his dirty, worn sneakers. Spoke into his worn shirt. "I need to tell them I'm sorry, man. Everything'll be okay if I can just say I didn't mean it."

Where did anyone get this idea that a few insincere words could mend a destroyed life and make everything all better?

"You can't just walk up to someone and tell 'em you're sorry you killed their son. What do you think? They're going to pat you on the head and say it's okay, go forth and sin no more?"

The kid squinted a spiky blue gaze through a fringe of dishwater hair and gnawed at a dirty thumb. "Why not? It's one of the twelve steps… admit you done wrong and seek forgiveness."

Under Spinner's nervous fingers, the red pen rotated on the battered table top, and the kid stared at it. "True, but this isn't AA, and it's not ever that simple. Besides, I thought that approach didn't work for you. They kicked you out for—"

"They said I was disruptive when I tried to speak my mind. Thought that's what I was there for." He scowled, slouched lower, and stretched jean-clad legs. Knobs of pale flesh stuck from the thin fabric, worn through at the knees.

A wry grin tugged at Spinner's mouth. Disruptive. A mild word to use for this boy's unruly behavior. But they must've said it. He'd never have come up with it himself.

"They were being kind, Lucas. Disruptive doesn't begin to explain tossing chairs around and kicking over a table. That temper of yours explodes like a load of fireworks struck by lightning."

Lucas smirked as if proud of his reputation to go off, jerked his head to toss lanky strands of hair from his face.

Should make these boys keep their heads shaved while they were in juvie, save everyone a lot of trouble. Probably save everyone more trouble if they died at birth.

Subconsciously, Spinner touched the thong that tied back his long, black hair and sighed. He had to get out more, have some fun. This job was getting to him. "You have a lot to do before you're ready to meet up with the dead boy's family. You have to face that it may never happen."

A tic twisted Lucas's narrow mouth. "Oh, it's gonna happen. I'm gonna make it happen. And you don't have to remind me all the time I killed him."

"Someone has to. It's called facing the truth. But here's another truth. You need a job, a place to live, a plan."

"Ain't nobody gonna hire me. Everyone in town knows what I did. It's a joke to say the records are sealed 'cause I was just sixteen when I done it. It wasn't my fault. I was drunk."

Spinner smacked the table with the flat of his hand, the sound echoing like a backfire.

Lucas jumped and his eyes widened.

Spinner softened his tone. "I think you missed a step. Take responsibility for your actions. You were drunk because you chose to be. And by God, it was your fault you killed that boy."

Lucas nibbled at his lower lip, mumbled something Spinner didn't understand.

"What? I didn't hear you."

"I said, okay. It was my fault."

"It'd help if you believed that."

A silent shrug was his only reply. The boy was more than half right. The fault went way back to those perverts who raised this kid, feeding him whiskey from the time he was a toddler so he'd do the terrible things they demanded of him. Renting him out to other sickos who got their rocks off "playing" with kids. If anyone was to blame it was the adults around him, but Lucas had to seek his own atonement, stand up and fight back in his own right. Couldn't let him think he could lay it all off on someone else every time he chose to do something bad.

If he didn't stop doing that, and soon, he was doomed.

Spinner played with the pen some more, glanced past the boy out the motel window. Pretty day. He ought to be fishing. Sparse traffic on the highway that dead-ended at the tip of Monkey Island.

"You could go someplace else. There are other counselors. I could hook you up with someone. Get you settled. Maybe in Muskogee or even Tulsa. I'd look in on you from time to time. Might be best."

Lucas picked at a loose thread on the arm of the worn chair, didn't look at him. "Wouldn't be no different. S'matter, don't want to help me?"

"Come on, boy. Get up on your hind legs and help yourself out of this mess you're in."

"I can't go someplace else."

"Why?"

He glared. "'Cause, I ain't, that's all. Just 'cause."

"There's nothing here to keep you. No family, no friends. Do yourself a favor and start over somewhere besides Chota, Oklahoma." Do me a favor too, he almost said, but bit back the retort. This had everything to do with saving a kid and nothing to do with what he might want.

It was more than the belligerent attitude that tagged this one as damaged beyond repair. Hell, they were all belligerent when they came out of juvie, the majority damaged beyond his ability to do anything for them. Yet, a few were salvageable, and there was something here that told him he might save this one. Damned if he knew what it was, just a feeling was all.

He pushed aside the obvious. That the kid reminded him of himself at that age. Something promising hid behind the tough defiance, the sullen outlook, the refusal to face up to his problems. He ought to know what it was, he'd possessed it himself. Obviously. He had survived, with help. He owed at least as much as he'd got.

He fingered the thick file under his hand. Sooner or later they would have to get into all the ugly stuff. His father's abuse, his mother's indifference and drunkenness, their coupled perversions that dragged this boy into hell before he was old enough to go to school. But not now, not this day. Today was for setting him straight. Showing him that whatever else he did, he wouldn't fool anyone, he wouldn't get away with anything, he wouldn't pull the wool over Spinner's eyes. Spinner was tough, Spinner was mean. Meaner, by God, than Lucas ever thought of being.

He rose, addressed the glowering boy. "Come on."

"Where we going?"

"Got you a place to live. It's not much, but it's a start. There's a fella at a garage other side of town who needs a gofer, he's willing to give you a try, long as you behave. Friend of mine, so you damn well better."

Lucas popped out of the chair, fists clenched at his sides, pasty complexion flushed. "Why didn't you tell me you done all this? Let me think you was gonna send me away."

Muscles tensing, Spinner faced the lanky kid whose body language telegraphed an imminent attack. He might have to take him on right here.

"Wanted to make sure you really wanted to stay. Take it easy, kid. You go off every time someone does something you don't like, you won't be out long. And next time it won't be a stroll through juvie. They'll send you to play with the big boys."

"Yeah, well, that's where I'll be anyway. Sooner or later. So what? I've been beat on and worse by the biggest and toughest." All the fight drained out of him. "No one's gonna leave me alone."

"Maybe not, but you have to learn that if you go back in there it'll be your doing, not someone else's. Only you can decide your own fate."

And if the kid believed that, he'd show him a flock of flying pigs. Even if it wasn't necessarily true, he had to make Lucas believe it, otherwise he'd just give up without a fight, and he damn sure wouldn't get anywhere that way.

Only those who stood tall and tough and got up every time they were knocked down made it in this world. God, how he knew that. And he had to make this boy a believer if he were to have a chance to survive. A plea in the boy's eyes told Spinner that if he couldn't help this one, it would sure as hell piss him off.

A long time ago Gano Burke had helped him when everyone else gave up on the alcoholic Cherokee boy who'd cut loose on a man in a bar when he was only thirteen. A man who looked and acted like his father, a man who would sit in a wheelchair the rest of his life because of Spinner. A man who'd spit on him when he tried to say he was sorry.

If Lucas's conscience bothered him about killing the Kraft boy, he didn't show it. Only hostility surfaced when he talked about facing the family and asking for forgiveness. That might just be bluster, though.

Spinner led Lucas down the stairs and out onto the street to his vintage Chevy Nova. "Get in. We're gonna get you a haircut before I take you over to Hank's and introduce you, then we'll get you something to wear besides those…."At a loss for words, he gestured at the worn, baggy jeans, and faded blue tee shirt.

Lucas eyed the rusty right front fender of the car. "Nothing wrong with these or my hair. Ain't got no money. Don't look like you do either."

Good. Interested in something besides himself.

"I like old cars. As for clothes and a haircut, the state pays. Come on."

"I can buy my own. You can't take me shopping and pick out something like I was your kid. I ain't nobody's kid. Ain't never been. And what's this shit about a haircut? Nothing wrong with my hair." He fingered the stringy mass out of his eyes.

"I got the money, here in my pocket. You can pick out your own clothes, long as I approve. As to the haircut, that's my say. Now get in."

"Shit." The boy yanked at the door handle. When it didn't open, he kicked the side panel and shouted the expletive over and over.

Spinner took him firmly by the shoulders, felt like he'd grabbed two handfuls of wild mustang. The boy had a lot of pent-up fury, but he held on till Lucas settled down.

Opening the door, he gestured. "Get in and close it, nice and easy."

Heated anger flowed from Lucas into Spinner, igniting emotions he usually kept in check. His heart went out to the boy. He wanted to smack him, or take him in his arms, hold him till all the filth spewed out, but neither would work with this one. There'd come a time when a hug would be just what Lucas needed, but not until he burned off the bitter outrage and fear that rode him. Not until he learned to trust Spinner. Not until he knew Spinner wouldn't do vile things to him. As for smacking him, Spinner would never, had never, hit a kid. Would make him too much like his own dad.

Lucas slammed the door so hard the half-open window rattled, then stared through the opening, jaw set in an expression that dared Spinner to do something about it.

Opting to cool down himself, he took his time circling the car before climbing in the driver's side. He keyed the ignition and glanced at the boy.

"Well, I guess you showed me. Do you feel better? Feel ready to go out into the world and make good? Feel all grown up?"

"None of the above," Lucas said, then fell silent.

Glancing over his shoulder, Spinner pulled out into the empty street. "Do you have any idea why?"

No answer.

Hanging a right at the first corner, Spinner headed for Len's Barbershop, where the old man who owned the place still charged only $5 to buzz off a head of hair.

The small, gloomy place was empty of customers, weak sunlight probing through windows covered in years of murk. Lucas bit his lip and squenched his eyes shut while Len ran his clippers through the thick hair until it carpeted the tile floor. He said nothing when the old man finished, just got out of the chair and stomped to the door, flung it open, scuffled down the sidewalk, and climbed in the Nova.

Next stop, Hank's garage. Spinner glanced at the sullen boy. "I don't advise you to get in a fight with this guy. He'll clean your clock for you."

No answer, but at least Lucas glanced at him with a look in his eye he couldn't quite read and said nothing in reply.

"You want this job, Lucas?"

With a grimy nail, the boy traced around a tear in the dashboard. "He wants to beat on me, tell him to come on. I've been beat up on plenty. Won't be nothing new."

Spinner shook his head. Telling the boy that Hank would clean his clock might have been a mistake. Sometimes he wondered if he was truly suited for this job anymore. He took it on 'cause of what he owed Burke. Besides, there was nothing else he could do. Nothing else he wanted to do. He lived only because of a man who cared more for helping a mean little Cherokee heathen bent on destruction than he did about money or fame. Sounded corny, but it was true. It was payback time, and would be for a long, long while.

The worst part of that was Burke would never know he'd succeeded. Some bastard had knifed him in a beer joint down in Tahlequah last year. So Spinner wasn't sure who he owed what anymore. He just couldn't seem to stop lunging at the traces.

"And do you want the job?" He prodded Lucas with a harsh glare.

"If I don't take it, you'll figure a way to send me back in. So yeah, I want it." Begrudgingly, but there it was. The first sign of capitulation.

Spinner wanted to shout with joy. A small victory, but a victory, nevertheless. Without signaling he hung a left into the drive in front of Hank's Garage.

Shoving down his red-hot anger, Lucas rubbed his bristly head and glowered at the dilapidated building with its dirty windows and flaking paint. Three bay doors stood open, with a car inside each. Some more waited in the lot. The place smelled of grease and the searing tang of a welder. A pair of feet in new work boots stuck out from under one side of a bright red Corvette, and his heart kicked at his ribs. What he wouldn't give to get his hands on that ride.

But this guy had said gofer, so he probably wouldn't get to go near the cars or talk to the mechanics.

Every night for sixteen months he'd wanted to jump off that hard cot in juvie and bust his way out, but he hadn't. Every day he'd wanted to beat somebody's head in, but he hadn't. Something crawled around under his skin, beneath the scars on his back. A thing that crept up his throat and spewed out as terrible words that sent people scurrying. And he knew, deep down inside himself, that he had to stop whatever it was, dig it out and cast it aside. Wasn't sure he could, though.

Even after all this time, he craved a drink of whiskey to get him past what was coming. Yearned to get so drunk he didn't know where he was and couldn't remember what his life had been like or worry about what it was going to be like. They'd told him in AA that it would always be there, that thirst, that hunger to drink. Said he would never be able to take even a sip or he was doomed. If he squenched his eyes up real tight he could see the fires of hell waiting for him to mess up. Sometimes, most of the time, he didn't care, though he'd never tell this big, mean Cherokee that. He just might scalp him.

Spinner opened his door. "Come on, get out, we're here."

The Cherokee was a big man, tall and broad, with skin the color of smoked copper, and straight hair so black it shined blue. He wore it to his waist, but tied back with a leather thong. He had high cheekbones and a broad face and eyes as black as bottomless pits. Caves, man, where boogers lived. But Lucas wasn't scared of boogers. Was he?

When Spinner'd grabbed him by the shoulders back there, Lucas sensed the man could break him in two with one hand, but he wasn't about to let him know. And if he tried it, why then Lucas would go down giving as good as he got. No one on this fucking earth was ever gonna pound on him again, no matter what he had to do to stop it.

One hip cocked, he stood in the open door and eyed the man who rolled out from under the Corvette. He was a damned Indian too, but then you had to expect that around here. Indian Territory, man. Unlike Spinner, this one was squat and thick through the chest and arms. And darker skinned. His hair was short, buzzed, and when he reached out a hand to shake with Spinner, Lucas saw grease beneath his fingernails and across the palms.

"This the boy?" These Indians, they spoke English, but the words didn't sound the same. Almost like they were singing a song.

"Yep. This is Lucas Pell. Lucas, this is Hank Sitton."

Lucas hung his thumbs in his pockets and nodded.

Spinner elbowed him. "Shake the man's hand."

"He's got grease all over him." Fully expecting Spinner to smack him one, Lucas stuck out his chin and refused to remove his own hands from his pockets. He was shocked when the two men laughed.

"Well, boy, you sure you're ready to go to work where you might get your hands dirty? I'll see if I can find you work in the office filing papers away, if that's the case."

"No, that's okay," Lucas muttered, but he still didn't shake hands.

Spinner and this Hank fella eyed each other, then turned their backs on him to talk. Discussing what ought to be done about this little pisser, no doubt. He didn't much care, and wandered off to inspect the tools hanging along one wall. No use in getting accustomed to the place. He wouldn't be here long. Just as soon as he found the family of that dead kid, told 'em he was sorry, he was lighting out.

The burning came up out of his gut again, and he screwed his eyes shut, clamped his lips tight. Ain't nobody said this would be easy, but he'd done lots of stuff that was worse than this. He could do it. Just do it man, and get it behind him. Then the nightmares would go away and he could stop seeing that twisted body, all that blood, those eyes open and staring at him. That's all he wanted. He didn't believe any good would come of it otherwise, but he could handle all that other shit. It was this one thing that had come up on him and wouldn't let go. This dead kid who walked through his head all the time.

He had a long list of people he hated, a long list of people he would kill if he ever got the chance. But this, this killing, he could not get past.

And so, he would find the family. There was a mother and father, a sister and brother. He would find them all, no matter who did what or who said what and, no matter what he had to do, he would make them forgive him.

Three

Becca stepped from the shower, wiped steam off the mirror and stared at herself. Turned away in disgust. She looked like a reanimated mummy. Wrapping a towel around her wet hair, she walked on trembling legs to the closet. She would do this. Had to do it.

The first thing she touched, a denim blue pantsuit with red piping, would do. Red shoes to match.

Impossible. She could not do this. Could not. Her hands shook and she dropped everything on the unmade bed, sagged to the mattress, and stared through tears at the pills scattered over the cream carpet.

Again and again and again she had imagined the screech of brakes, the terror slamming through Jeremiah when he saw the car hurtling toward him. Would it never end? Would she never stop wondering how long he had suffered, if he had called her name? Why hadn't she been there? Done something. Helped him, for God's sake.

Within the darkness of her mind, earlier resolve flew apart. Dropping to her knees on the floor, fists clenched to hammer on her head.

"Damn you, damn you. How could you do this to me? Is this how you show your love? Take my baby from me?"

The addressed deity did not answer. To Hell with him.

Clawing at the scattered pills, she filled both hands. Cursed under her breath, cried until she couldn't take a breath, shook until she couldn't find her mouth. Finally, she crammed the pills between her lips, emptying both hands. Quickly, before she could think, she washed them down with lukewarm water from a glass on the table. It didn't matter what she took, or how many. Drugs were drugs and would accomplish her goal. Oblivion.

The telephone rang and she snatched it up, wiping water from her chin. Time to talk to Jonathan, before the pills dumped her in an apathetic pit of dysfunction. Maybe she could probe deeply enough into his cold, uncaring world to get a rise out of him. Surely he'd be incensed that Lucas Pell had been released.

"Yes?" she said after a moment of listening to his breathing.

"Hi, love. Did I wake you?"

"No." His falsely bright question told her he knew, wanted to make sure she hadn't done something foolish.

"What are you doing?"

"Not cutting my wrists, if that's what you mean. If I could get that little prick in my sights, though—"

"Becca, I'm coming out."

"Oh, don't do that. Why ever would you want to do such a thing as that?" Was that her voice? That snarling, nagging, vicious voice?

How much she loved him. Hated him. It seemed like she'd always loved him. Where had the hate come from?

Her baby's death, that's where. And him not giving a damn.

"Don't, please."

"Don't," she mimicked. "I don't want you to come, Jon. Not just because of this."

After a short pause, "Tell me, what would make you want me to come?"

A bit dizzy, she lay backward on the bed. "Nothing. Forget it. It's too late anyway."

"It's not too late."

"I'm thinking of calling Christi, seeing if she'd like to spend a week or two here at the lake when school is out." Why had she said that? Just idle chatter. Something to say so he wouldn't guess about the pills.

Another pause, then, "She's going to Australia."

The world around her whirled, turned blacker. Losing them all. Forever. "Why?" The question croaked from her searing throat. If she were dead, what difference would it make that they were all gone?

"Some sort of student summer exchange thing. She'll be gone all summer. Well, our summer. It's winter down there."

"And she couldn't be bothered to call and tell me? How could she do this, so soon after her brother's death?" There it was again. That hated shrill sound fighting its way into her words.

"Christ, Becca. Do you want her to die too? It's been over a year."

"Ah, yes. I forgot. The magic number. A year. Why, everyone should be sufficiently recovered to go on with their lives after a year. I don't know why I didn't realize that." Her tongue felt funny, the words slurred. How many pills had she taken? She couldn't remember, wasn't sure she'd counted.

Tell him goodbye, do it now. He won't have time to stop you.

"Becca, I have to go. There's a meeting, and we have this job coming up that's important."

"Aren't they all?"

"Well, they do keep you under a roof out there, don't they? Have to keep those pills coming."

"I guess it is my fault you have to work so hard."

His voice took on an edge. "Sorry, Becca, have to run. Talk to you soon. Take care of yourself."

"Oh, sure, you bastard," she muttered after he hung up. Tossing aside the blue pantsuit, she dropped to her knees, scrounged around on the carpet, found the vial, tapped out more pills, swallowed them with the last of the water. With legs and arms trembling, she crawled onto the bed and rolled into a ball.

She opened her eyes to a dark, quiet room. A small light glowed on the wall. A fire burned in her throat and she couldn't swallow. Her stomach was a great empty vat slowly filling with lava. From somewhere off in the distance came a soft, monotonous pinging.

What was that? Who was she?

Oh, yes. Calistra Rebecca Cannon. No, no. Just Rebecca. Dropped Calistra a long time ago, prior to college before adding Kraft. Okay. Rebecca Kraft. That's it. Somehow, the decision soothed her a bit. Who would name their child Calistra, anyway? Her mother, her crazy, sweet, loving mother. Long dead, long gone to her reward after one too many trips on LSD.

Stop the mind babble. Concentrate on moving, on rolling the head. Pain. Not good. Don't do that. Listen to murmurs, laughter, the pinging that wouldn't stop. Touch the skin to make sure she was still in it. Couldn't do that either. Nothing worked, or at least was allowed to. Arms, legs, body. Couldn't move them. Tied down, strapped. Afraid to open the eyes, afraid of what they would see.

Where had she left off in that other world? Taking pills. Too many pills. Nothing unusual in that. Had she died this time? One constant remained crystal clear. Jeremiah was dead. Yesterday? Last week? Last month? Did it even matter?

"Welcome back," a cheery voice piped, jabbing pain through her throbbing head. Fingers wrapped her wrist. A touch at once firm and gentle. At least she was still inside her own skin.

"Help me," she said, comprehending the plea perfectly inside her brain, but her ears heard only a dry squawk.

"We'll get that tube out soon," the same voice said, and something cool and wet touched her lips. "Sorry about the restraints. Can you open your eyes?"

Weren't they open? Screwing her face around, she worked at lifting each eyelid. It was like picking up Jeremiah's barbells. Impossible, until he leant a hand.

"Mom, let me help you. Those're too heavy for you."

His broad, strong fingers closing over hers.

A whimper worked its way from her constricted throat.

"Oh, let's not cry now, it'll only make matters worse." That damned cheery voice again.

"Then take this fucking thing out," she shouted somewhere down inside her gut.

Of course, no sound emerged, but she did manage to open her eyes thanks to Jeremiah's help. Confused, she gazed around trying to find him. He'd been there a moment ago, but there was no sign of him. He was gone, leaving only a pale glow.

Nearby a cute little thing in a white uniform. A room painted puke green. A bed with rails, holding her in. All she could see without moving her head, and that wasn't possible.

Well, I guess you've done it now, Becca. They'll have you in a strait jacket in a padded cell. Locked away for your own good. Or better yet, for everyone else's good. Still, she couldn't quite remember what she had done, or where she'd been or how she got here.

"Your sister is here to see you, but only for a minute."

"Sister? I have no sister." The words came out gurk and gawk.

"Don't try to talk until we remove the tube, okay?"

Cutie-Pie moved away and another face took her place. One she knew. Name. Give me a name.

"Hi, Becky, sweetie. I'm so sorry. I should've guessed. I should've come out to be with you when you found out." Lorraine. Raine—that was it—leaned down and kissed her forehead, smoothing strands of damp hair from her cheek. "Sorry, I had to say I was your sister. They said only immediate family."

"And my family isn't here, are they?" Another mass of gobble-de-gook.

"Sorry, sweetie, I can't understand you. Just rest now and forget all about this. It'll work itself out, you'll see. They said you'll be getting some counseling. Take my advice and—"

Becca turned her head so she didn't have to look at her friend, but the rest of the sentence followed. "—take their advice." The movement brought the walls and ceiling caving in and a pitiful sound boiled from her aching heart.

"Okay, Becky. Don't get upset, I'm sorry. I'll be back in the morning. You'll feel better then and maybe we can talk."

Suddenly, Becca didn't want her friend to leave. Hospitals were such lonely places. Perky nurses with their well-trained voices and caring attitudes only made them more so. Yet, she could do nothing, for another Cutie-Pie, this one with dark hair, opened the door and beckoned to Raine.

Becca wanted to look out the window, but the blinds were closed. That didn't stop the fog from rolling in, covering her, smothering the next breath, the next thought.

"Cough," someone said from far away.

She obeyed, then gagged out the tube.

"There, that's better, isn't it? Open up."

Dragging her lids open she peered into a sunny room and yet another face. Lord, what a bunch of cute little things they had around this place. A hand held out a spoonful of ice. Eagerly she took it into her parched mouth, opened up for another. Like a helpless baby bird. After a while she felt a little better. Realized that she was no longer tied to the bed. A tube ran into a needle in the back of her hand.

From outside the door, she heard a familiar masculine voice. "In here? Thank you."

"Jonathan?" Christ, she still sounded like a chicken squawking.

"Rebecca. How are you this morning?"

He didn't approach, but stood at the foot of the bed, condemnation clear in his expression.

"Oh, just peachy. Who called you?" The words, though crackly, were understandable.

"The hospital, of course. They know the number by now."

"Well, you may go. I don't need you, I don't want you here."

He did a strange thing then, and it confused her need to hate him. Face clothed in sorrow, he took hold of her blanket-covered foot and rubbed at it with his thumb. "Goddammit, Becca. Why do you keep doing this?"

"This?"

"You know good and well what I mean."

"Get out, Jonathan. I can die without your help."

"Obviously not. If you wanted to die, I should think you'd be dead by now. What is this, five, six times you've swallowed too many pills? Can't figure out yet how many it takes?"

"You bastard. Don't you care at all that our son is dead and the man who killed him is free?"

He should've been accustomed to her asking such questions, but he blanched as if she'd slapped him, his eyes going all shiny.

"I care a great deal. And something else I care about is I've not only lost my son, I've lost my wife as well. Why don't you do us both a favor and get it over with?"

He looked about to cry, but it must be the lighting. Jon never cried.

"Well, Jonathan, it's good to see you in such rare form." Raine stood in the open doorway. "Your usual bedside manner at work, I take it."

"Hello, Lorraine. Good to see you, too. Since you're here, I'll be going. I have a meeting and it's a long drive back to Tulsa."

"Then you'd best be on your way." Raine stepped into the room and moved aside so he could leave. "Lowlife son of a bitch," she murmured after him, not caring if he heard or not.

"It's okay, Raine. Don't be upset with him. I'm not. What he says is true, I'm just too much of a coward, I guess. Or maybe I really don't want to die, I just want some relief once in a while."

Raine drew up a chair and took Becca's hand in her long-fingered grasp. She always appeared so cool and collected, her angular features made up with such perfection you noticed nothing but that she was gorgeous, her black hair styled in a shiny, unstirred cap. Her svelte figure was clothed in a long-sleeved blouse the shade of ripe peaches and a brown skirt short enough to show off shapely knees and calves. Leather shoes hugged feet a bit small for her elegant height, and a scarf green as jade covered her throat and the scar her ex had left there. One would never guess she was in her forties, except for the fine crow's feet at the corner of each chocolate brown eye.

Raine understood better than anyone, and Becca loved her like the sister she'd earlier claimed to be. Even managed to grin at her despite the situation.

"I didn't mean to do it," Becca finally said, nervous at being studied so closely. "I remember taking some pills, then getting really upset and taking some more. I guess I forgot to pay attention."

"I'm sure you didn't mean it, honey. But you've got to do something about this. One of these days, they won't get you back."

"How did they? I mean, I was alone in my bedroom the last I remember."

"I got worried about your tone when I talked to you and when you didn't answer the phone came on over. Good thing I did or this might've been the last time. Honey, won't you at least talk to someone? Try to get some help? You need to get beyond this, somehow. I know you'll never recover from Jeremiah's death. No mother would. But you have to get through the stages and restructure some sort of life for yourself."

Becca stared at her friend for a long while. "They turned that bastard loose, Raine. How could they do that? He killed Jeremiah, and he's walking free. I can't stand it. I just can't."

"Oh, I know. I know you're hurting and this just makes it worse, but you can and you will. You have to."

"Everyone says they know, they understand. But they don't. No one could. Not even Jonathan or Christi or David. But I'll tell you something, Raine. This was an accident, with the pills. I did not want to die. For the first time since Jeremiah was killed, I have a reason to live. And that will keep me going."

"Honey, I don't know what you mean."

"I'm going to see that boy is punished for what he did. If it takes me forever, I'll see him punished."

"Sweetheart...." The beautiful features clouded.

"I mean it."

Inside the door of Craig General Hospital Spinner checked a note he'd jotted when the call came in from the sheriff's office. Room twenty-nine. One of his boys caught robbing a Mini Mart and shot in the arm for his trouble. At Craig County Hospital in Vinita. Could he come talk to him?

He headed down the hallway, shoes squeaking on the shiny floor. Hospital smells had become such a part of his job he hardly noticed them anymore. To his left an elegantly striking woman came out of a room and closed the door softly behind her. The expression on her face was one of despair, and he felt bad for her. Must be someone she loved dying in that room.

He halted, nodded as her gaze swept quickly over him. She returned the nod, stirring her cap of dark hair. Flecks of green sparkled in her brown eyes. Interesting. Yes, indeed, but too rich for him. Besides, the only women who appealed to him anymore were one-stop-shopping ladies, and this one was definitely not that. The outfit she wore had come out of a fancy boutique and did a good job showing off her figure. No skinny model type, this one. The shoes alone cost more than he made in a month. At her throat she wore a filmy scarf that reminded him of fields of grass.

Unwilling to lose the opportunity to hear the sound of her voice, he said, "Could you tell me where room twenty-nine is?"

She glanced over her shoulder. "This is eighteen, but I don't know which way is up. I mean, which direction."

He smiled widely. "I sometimes don't know which way is up, either."

Her return smile lifted his heart, and, stupid as he was, he took another chance. "Spinner," he said and stuck out his hand.

"Sorry?" Even though she posed the query, she gave him her graceful fingers, the skin starkly white against his own.

A light sexy fragrance tickled his nose. "I'm Spinner."

"I'm Raine."

"Good," he said. "I mean, good to meet you. Family? A friend?" He nodded toward the closed door behind her. What in the hell was he doing?

"A friend. She'll be okay. Friend, family?" She tipped her head at the slip of paper he held.

"Client."

She cocked her head and the sleek black hair swung away from one ear revealing a tiny dot of turquoise in the lobe. "You're an attorney?"

His laugh caused a nurse down the hallway to stop and stare at them. "No, I work with, uh, troubled kids."

"Ah, a psychologist."

"Closer. Yes, that's actually it, I suppose."

"You aren't sure what you do?"

He still held her silken-skinned hand, one finger lying along her wrist so he could feel the rhythm of her heartbeat. A genuine good feeling ambushed him, and he grinned down at her. "Sometimes I wonder if I'm sure of anything."

Walk away now, fool. He shivered and tried to let go her hand. No dice.

"Well, dealing with kids will do that to you."

"You a teacher?"

It was her turn to laugh. Christ. Dimples and incredibly white teeth. Jesus, what was going on here? This was only a woman, after all. He still held her hand and wasn't about to let go.

"No, hardly. I'm… I own RainTree, in Chota. It's a gourmet coffee shop. So you see, not a professional at all. I just cater to them."

"You mean, you make all that fancy, foamy coffee that costs five bucks a cup?" He ran a thumb over the back of her hand, watched her eyes spark bits of green fire.

For fuck's sake, he was actually trying to *flirt* with her.

"Seven-fifty, actually. Yes, that's what we do there. My friend, inside there, Becca, is my partner. We see that everything runs well. Promote the place, search for new products, keep everything moving. At least, until she…."

He was disappointed when she stopped. "Until she?"

"I'm sorry. I don't know what's making me rattle on so. You aren't interested in her problems, or mine." She regarded him once again with that intriguing, quizzical gaze. "You must be one hell of a shrink, the way you have me opening up to you."

She slipped her hand from his, and he felt like he'd lost something.

Dumbass.

"Come by sometime, try one of our specialty drinks. We're on the corner of Cherokee and Main, just off the square."

"Cherokee and Main. I just might do that. Thanks. It was nice to meet you, Raine?" He hoped she'd fill in her last name, but she didn't. So, he supposed if he wanted to see her again, he'd have to go into that fancy coffee shop.

He could do that. He could even spring seven-fifty for something he wouldn't even drink just to sit and watch her. Way too damn late to back off. She had him like a fly in her web.

"See you, Spinner." Spoken so softly he almost didn't catch it, then she was gone. She moved away, her stride like that of an athlete.

"Yes, indeed you will." Spoken under his breath.

For a long while he hadn't believed in much of anything, and especially not in how he felt this very moment. She'd reached inside him and touched a place hidden for a long while. Yet, he was nine kinds of fool for reacting to that touch. Women and love would never again hurt him. Pulling his gaze from her disappearing figure, he went in search of room twenty-nine and the unfortunate boy who would probably end up in jail in spite of anything he could do.

Most of the kids he dealt with did wind up back inside, and he wondered again if he was trying to beat back a wildfire with a wet bandana.

Raine turned to watch the tall Cherokee negotiate the hallway. That was interesting. There was something different about him. Not like the men who moved in her circle. Might be the faded jeans and tee shirt, both tight enough they left little to the imagination. She seldom met a man who caught her interest, had recently come to the reluctant conclusion that she would never marry again. Maybe never have a satisfactory affair. If indeed she knew what that was. But meeting Spinner, well, he was definitely a possibility. And his eyes revealed he felt the same.

With trembling fingertip she touched the scarf covering the scar on her throat. Called up the vow she'd made. Best if she steered clear of this man, yet she had a deep down feeling that she wouldn't and it terrified her.

Four

Lucas stood at the dirty window and stared into the night. This place was a funky dump. On the wrong side of town. All he had to look at was some old broke-down boats sagging on their chocks. But what'd he think? For sure he wouldn't get put up in one of those fancy shacks along the lakeshore.

The idea made him snicker. He'd ask Spinner about that next time he saw him, see if he could swing him a deal with one of those rich slobs. What a joke. Besides, he wouldn't see that Indian again. He'd done his job, such as it was. Got him a nowhere job and a worse than nowhere hole to live in. Bought him a couple pairs of cheap jeans, some tee shirts, and no name shoes at the local mercantile. And, oh, yeah, six pairs of jockey shorts. Earlier he unwrapped the plastic and spread the jocks out in the middle of the narrow bed. First time he'd ever had new undershorts that he could recall. Damn, but they were white, laying there against the gray sheet.

Standing at the window, he glanced at them again. Even in the dim light of the bedside lamp, the fuckers glowed like great white birds.

"Shit," he muttered, and went back to staring out the window at the scattering of lights that marked Chota and the shoreline of Monkey Island. Not an island, really, just a jag of land sticking out into Grand Lake O' The Cherokees.

He sneered. What a hoot. That O with an apostrophe stuck on its end. Leave it to the rich. Indians probably had nothing to do with naming it.

He wanted a cigarette, he wanted a can of beer, he wanted a long, deep draw from a bottle of bourbon. The burn and the kick, the smoothing out. Just so he never had to sleep again. That dead kid ganged up with other monsters in his dreams, proving there was something out there even more bad-ass than his past.

When the demons came he couldn't tell if he slept or if he was awake. Sometimes there was no line between the two.

The man who called himself his father appeared to stand over him, and that was a clue right away he was dreamin'. The son of a bitch was dead. Course him killing that kid and everything from then on could be a dream and this nightmare visit the real thing.

The stench of fear, the grinding of his teeth, the knot in his belly, all told Lucas this was real. The dead boy, taking the place of the others who usually came to do terrible things to this helpless child who lived inside his skin.

His old man took the money and the devil came at him, undoing his pants. Lucas clenched his fists till the nails bit into his palms, swallowed hard to keep from gagging, and fell to his knees. This one liked to use a lash on him and it came down with such force across his thin shoulders that he howled, a grievous sound cut off as the man shoved into him. A great, long, hard rod, straight from the fire. His attacker all mixed up with the boy he'd killed. And didn't he deserve that?

The sky glowed like burnt silver when Lucas jerked awake, wringing wet and slumped against the wall under the window. Whimpering, crying, shaking. Expecting more monsters. Yet, there was no one in the room but tendrils of the fading nightmare. And himself. Lucas Pell, in sweat-soaked, dirty old clothes that raised a stench to rival the room where he cowered.

Dragging himself upright, he waited for the trembling to cease. Was that the nightmare? Or this? Hard to tell, but it mattered little.

Had to take a piss. For the first time in memory he had a bathroom to himself, if you could call it that. And real or not, he would use it. A shower in one corner with a mildewed curtain, a commode and sink, both streaked by rust stains that looked like dried blood. When he screwed the taps real hot water came from the shower head, and he peeled out of his clothes, took a leak, and stepped under the spray. He stood there for a long time while it beat down on his head. Feeling good despite everything. A sliver of cracked soap swam in the dish, and he scrubbed himself from the top of his head to the tips of his toes, rubbing between each with a finger. The water cooled before he could drag himself from under it.

Shivering, he waited for his body to air dry beside the open window. Damn, he'd have to get a towel. Maybe he wouldn't be here long enough to bother. Once he found the dead boy's family and told them he was sorry he was gone. Shouldn't be so hard. They lived on Monkey Island behind one of those iron gates, or at least they had when he ran over their son in that fancy car of his. The dumbass should've learned to drive better. Spinner told him to forget that part of his life, to go to work and make something of himself. When he'd asked like what, Spinner only gazed at him with that scary look in his cave-dark eyes. Stuff lurked in there it wouldn't do to stir up.

There would probably be a phone book at the garage, and when he went to work he could see if the Krafts were listed. A place to start. He would do this, if he did nothing else. Something had to chase away that dead boy. Hell, half the time he couldn't even think straight for remembering standing over the broken body, watching those terrified eyes leak their last moments of life into the night. He'd seen lots of stuff, but never had watched anyone die before that. If it'd been one of those dudes that messed with him all the time, maybe killing him wouldn't've mattered, but this was different.

For a long time he tried to tell himself that, given the chance, Jeremiah Kraft would've treated him the same as everyone else. Then he'd have deserved to die. Even that didn't work anymore.

With a plan of sorts in place, he slipped on a pair of new jockey shorts. Snapping the elastic several times, he jiggled his balls into a nest in the double thick pocket in front. For a long while, he stood in the middle of the room, bending over, stretching, taking a step this way and that to check out the fit. Wished he had a mirror so he could see if he looked so fine.

They felt good. They felt damn good.

Finally, he unfolded a pair of the stiff new jeans and slipped into them, put on the blue tee shirt, a pair of new socks, and his shoes. Starting over, fresh and clean. He almost hated to go to work and get grease and sweat on them.

It was only three blocks to the garage and, walking along the cracked, weed infested dirt path next to the pocked street, he remembered the red Corvette he'd seen on the lift the day before. Maybe it would still be there. He ached to run his fingers over the soft leather upholstery, palm the steering wheel, maybe sit in the seat and play his feet over the pedals. Imagine racing along the Cherokee Turnpike with the top down. At juvie they'd had a copy of that movie—he couldn't think of the name—where the guy was driving the car cross-country and all the cops was after him, but everyone else was cheering him on. Then, at the final roadblock, when it came clear they was gonna get him, he couldn't get away, he just jumped that car—what was it? A GTO?—way up in the air, sailed over all those cop cars and those cops with guns, and faded away. Gone. Disappeared to some other place where no one could follow, and he could just drive all day and all night, do whatever he wanted. No one would stop him. Ever again.

Lucas struggled with a deep longing to do just that, moved across the concrete apron where the garage and his job waited. Just drive that Corvette out those double doors and sail off into space and disappear. What if he went somewhere else? Snap. Like that. And none of this had ever happened.

Even if he could, it wouldn't do no good. Things would just get all fucked up again. Besides, there was still the dead boy following him around.

"Hey, Lucas," Hank Sitton shouted. "You're early. That's good. Come in the back, I've got you some coveralls to put on before you start re-stocking."

And his day had begun. He hadn't disappeared after all. He was going to work for a man who would clean his plow if he didn't do as he was told. Nothing new there.

Jonathan sat immobile in his Mercedes outside Craig General until the warmth from the morning sun reminded him that he needed to move on. From her bed up there behind those windows, Becca's last words echoed in his throbbing head. Of course he cared that his son was dead, cared even more that the little beast who killed him was today walking free on the streets of Chota. If he thought he could, he would find him and drive back and forth over him until there was nothing left but a bloody puddle. There was something to say about being too civilized to give in to such urges, but he wasn't clear exactly what it was.

"Christ." Head buzzing, he keyed the ignition and drove from the lot, turning on the air conditioner before he reached the interstate.

The cell phone buzzed and he plucked it from its holder.

"Jon, this is Celie. When will you be in?"

"Take me an hour or so. I just left the hospital in Vinita."

Silence just long enough to show disapproval. Then, "Bill Thornton called. Said he has a crisis, wondered if you could stop by there before you come into the office."

Anger at Becca unloaded on this idiot of a client. "Thornton has an ongoing crisis because he won't listen. I'm paid to consult, not to hold his frigging hand. Call him back, tell him he has my report, he needs to follow through on it." Warm sunlight flashed over his face and he drew in a deep breath. "Oh, never mind. I'll call him myself. Not your problem. Is the Cox Group meeting set for one? I want to stop and have lunch first."

"Yes. How's Rebecca?"

Jon gritted his teeth against the answer he wanted to give. She's a pain in the ass, is how she is. That wasn't really fair, and certainly none of Celie's business.

"She's okay, I guess. You know."

She certainly did, and he was damned sorry about that. One slip and him acting like a fool, touching her, breaking down and crying in her arms. One thing leading to another, and she knew more about him and Becca than he wanted anyone to know. And he refused to fire her because he couldn't keep it in his pants. It was his stupidity not hers. Besides she was damned good at her job, at keeping him focused when all he wanted to do was fly into a million pieces. So good at running his part of the business when necessary. No, he wouldn't fire his red-haired, outspoken assistant, just because they'd fucked once on the couch in his office. It wouldn't happen again, and they both knew it.

Her voice gathered him from his rambling. "Everything's ready for Ewen Cox. Your presentation is on your desk, I've reminded Josie and Clay that they are to sit in to back you up. And don't forget you have reservations at the ballet for eight o'clock tonight with Mark and his wife."

"Thanks, Celie."

"As always." He sensed her tight little smile before she hung up.

Clicking off, he punched in Thornton's number. Out the side window, sunlight shimmered off the lake's surface. Along the shoreline, amid thick trees, the private homes of the rich and the near rich hid dark secrets. Were any of those people truly happy with their boats and cars and diamonds, their misbehaving children and drunken wives and husbands who worked day and night to pay for it all? He sure as hell wasn't, but he couldn't stop the rush to earn more, buy more. It was like an addiction, or a runaway train with no brakes. What could he do but hang on for the ride?

If only he could take Becca somewhere far away, live in a cabin in the woods where she couldn't get her hands on pills and he didn't have to leave her every day to pay for all the stuff they no longer wanted. He pictured their place, hanging out over the bluff beyond the first copse of jade trees along the shoreline of Monkey Island. Below the deck, accessible by a long curve of stairs, the dock and tied to it the boat they'd christened *Dream Kraft*. Neither he nor Becca had set foot on board in too long a time to count. He'd loved it all once. So had Becca. Things had gone wrong long before Jeremiah's death. He needed to call someone. Sell the damned boat, before it rotted away from neglect. And if things kept going the way they were, sell the house too. What the hell did they need with it, anyway?

He'd let her have the condo, set himself up in new digs where no memories of that long-ago happiness lurked to torture him.

Shaking himself back to business, he replied to Thornton's assistant, who put him through immediately. Swallowing his anger, he went over his earlier instructions yet again. The man was a genius but possessed absolutely no acumen for running his own business. Jon never told him, but probably should, that he ought to go to work for IBM or Microsoft.

By the time he hung up, he had left Grand Lake behind and was speeding along the Will Rogers Turnpike headed for Tulsa, the matter of Lucas Pell and Becca stored in the back of his mind. Concealed so as not to drive him insane with its probabilities.

Raine took Becca home from the hospital. After assuring her friend she was okay, a relieved Becca watched her leave for the shop. She needed to be alone, to plan, to think. Before she could do so, the phone rang.

"Mom, you okay?" Her daughter Christi.

"Of course." Becca tried to keep the edge from her voice, but couldn't. This was the child who was running away too, just like Jon and David, and Jeremiah too. Leaving her completely alone with her grief.

"Dad called, said you, uh, you tried to—you took too many pills."

"It was an accident, Christi. You and your father might get your stories straight before you go behind my back to fix things. And by the way, I hear you're going away this summer. I was hoping you'd spend some time out here with me." God, did that sound like a whiny, complaining mother, or what? She really did want Christi to have a life, it just seemed so unfair that she was willing to go so far away at such a time.

Christi was so quiet, she feared she'd hung up. "Honey, you still there?"

A big sigh. "Yes, Mother. I'd like to come out, spend some time with you. I really would, but I have all these last minute things to do. Exams to take. Shopping for the right clothes. You know."

"How about coming Sunday for dinner, then?"

"Mom? Oh, okay. What time?"

"One or two. Doesn't matter. I want to talk to you about something."

"What?" Reluctance colored her tone.

"That boy, the one who killed your brother. He's out of jail."

"Mother, please don't do this. Don't. It's over. I don't want to talk about him or what he did. Couldn't we let Jeremiah rest in peace? Nothing we do will change things."

Her voice broke, and Becca ached to take back the whole thing. She really didn't want to see Christi suffer, if only her daughter would allow her more time to get over this.

Yet Becca couldn't stem the rising tide of her resentment. Once it flowed, it was as if the hurt and despair and loss poured forth in words that turned her into some kind of foolish, crazy harridan. "Jeremiah won't rest in peace until that boy pays, dammit. I won't let this go. Not until it's finished. For good."

"Oh, Christ! What are you planning now? Mom, please stop this. Stop it before it's too late for us all."

"What do you mean by that? Too late for us all?"

"You've driven Dad away, David won't come home, and I can barely stand to—"

"That's not true. I didn't."

No reply.

"Well, it isn't." A still small voice deep in her soul whispered that it was indeed true. She was losing her entire family, and could do nothing about it. Nothing at all. Soon she would lose herself as well.

"Honey, will I see you Sunday?"

Another sigh. "Yes, Mom, but promise me we won't talk about this. If you start, I'm leaving."

"Okay, we won't talk about it. We'll talk about your trip. You can tell me all about your plans. What would you like to eat?"

"Oh, something easy. Don't go to any trouble."

"Okay, I'll think of something. I haven't cooked in a long while. It'll be nice to plan something for just the two of us."

And God willing, she'd allow it to be just the two of them. Keep the subject of Jeremiah closed for this final afternoon with her daughter before she too fled a crazed and demented mother.

Why couldn't she be who she once was? A happy, contented mother and wife. Involved in her children's lives, and the one she enjoyed with Jon. She'd try to do better. Forget the pills and the bottle. Get back to work with Raine and spend time with Jon. Let this matter with Lucas Pell alone. She really would.

The buzzer on his phone sounded and Jon punched at it without looking up. "Yes, Celie."

"Your daughter on line two."

"Thanks." Jon smiled and hooked the phone up, leaned back in his chair and rubbed at his temples. "Hi, sweetheart. Whazup?"

Laughter. "No, Dad. It's 'sup. Just sort of let it fall out of your mouth without forming much of any sound at all. And it's not really a question, you know?"

"Whazup? Zup? Ah, well, too old I guess."

"Cool beans, Dad."

"Now, that's more like it. That I understand. How's it hanging?"

More laughter. He hated letting her go off to Australia like this. As if he had any say in it. She was twenty-one. He truly was so happy for her, so goddamned happy that her life was on track and going the way she wanted it to.

"Hanging, Dad? It's hanging way out there. I called Mom."

"Oh. And?"

"She wants me to come out Sunday for dinner. A chat." A hesitation he didn't fill, then, "Dad?"

"I know, sweetheart. Please do go. You can put up with it, for her sake, for mine, can't you?"

"She wants to talk about that—"

"I know. Lucas Pell. He got out and she's fit to be tied."

"Do you blame her?"

"No. I'd like to kill the little son of a bitch myself, but let's face facts."

"Why is he staying in Chota? Do you have any idea?"

"No, I don't. And it doesn't matter, Christi. Nothing about him matters. We have to forget about him, not think about it. We have to survive this, honey, the only way we know how. We can't go around trying to avenge your brother's death. It won't solve anything."

"I know. Suppose you were to meet him face to face? Then what?"

Jon pinched the bridge of his nose and frowned against a hammering in his temples. "Christi, I don't want to talk about this and neither should you."

"I don't, it's just that I… I'm so glad I'm going away for the summer. If this opportunity hadn't come up, I think I'd have found something else. Anything, just to get away from him and Mom and…."

"So, will you spend the afternoon with your mother? It's not much to ask, is it? She *is* your mother."

"It's a lot to ask. But I need to ask something of you."

"What?" He was afraid he knew.

"Come out too, Dad. Join us. It'll be easier all around."

His mind raced in an effort to come up with a plausible excuse for not going to Monkey Island Sunday. This was his daughter, for Christ's sake, how could he even think of lying to her? But he did not want to spend any more time with Becca. He couldn't stand it. Absolutely could not stand to watch the woman he'd adored most of his adult life living as a mass of quivering, useless, self-pitying.... Besides, she'd probably be drunk or stoned before—

"Dad?"

"What time?"

"Oh, thank you, thank you. She said two or so. She's cooking. Will you call her and tell her, or shall I?"

He knew damn good and well what the answer to that had to be. "You call her, sweetheart. She'll be more receptive than if I call and say I'm coming out. Then she'll think we're conspiring against her."

"She'll think that anyway, but I'll call her. Love you, Dad."

Yeah, sure, kid. Got your way with me again, didn't you? As he hung up, he grinned. Christi always could wrap him around her little finger.

God, he was going to miss her. David gone, now her. And Jeremiah.

Something tore through him, so quick, so hurtful that he gasped. A tear rolled down his cheek, and for a moment he lost it. Fists clenched and stomach roiling, heart hammering as if trying to burst from his chest.

How the hell do you expect me to live the rest of my life without him? But the question went unspoken. He shook away the desolation and went back to work.

Five

Clipboard in hand, Raine left the office cubicle and moved behind the counter, inhaling the heady aroma of freshly ground coffee blends. The hiss of the latté machine mingled with muted conversations from the small tables scattered among huge pots of ficus, dumb cane, and monkey trees, all of which lent the RainTree its tropical forest ambiance. Diffused pink and gold lighting added the aura of a sunset eve. Fountains gurgled and splashed. Windows that would have looked out on the street were covered with murals of waterfalls and wild animals. Customers might well believe they sat on the lawn of a South American plantation sipping coffee grown and picked on nearby mountain slopes.

Everything about the place made Raine happy, except the absence of the one most responsible for its existence. Her best friend Becca. She missed her as if she had died, and felt so helpless to remedy the situation.

Together they had been quite a pair. Locating this empty, hopelessly shabby building, they birthed RainTree, nurtured it, watched it grow. Scrubbing, plastering, painting, refinishing the stained wood flooring, spending endless weekends shopping at flea markets and antique shops for the perfect old tables and chairs that could be renewed. It had all been so damned much fun, so like starting a new life after her disastrous marriage. She could scarcely bear to think of the tragedy that had befallen her best friend. Becca should be here to share its growing success with her.

She could close her eyes and see her, patched jeans and old tee shirt, a red bandana covering her blonde curls, speckled with paint from head to toe. The two of them laughing and falling down hysterically over some silly thing one of them had done. How long had it been since she'd seen Becca laugh? Even smile? Much, much too long.

Though she had little use for Jon and the way he was handling Becca's breakdown, he had consulted with them as he would have the highest priced client to ensure the business end of RainTree was expertly handled. Now he did nothing but complain about his wife's inability to get over their son's death. Sometimes he acted as if it hadn't bothered him at all, was merely an inconvenience to be worked around. That was probably unfair, though. She wasn't privy to his private life. People mourned in different ways.

Raine couldn't imagine anything worse than losing a child. Losing one in the womb had almost destroyed her, but the circumstances had been much different.

Russ kicking her around the apartment, telling her he didn't want kids. Who the hell did she think she was? Kicking her again and again, until he accomplished what he'd set out to do. Killed their baby. Then expecting his naive little wife to welcome him with open arms when he apologized. After all he had rescued her from poverty. She refused, and given time and plenty of love from good friends, Becca and her family in particular, Raine had recovered. So how could she offer any less to Becca than complete understanding and support? It was simple. She couldn't.

"Raine, you okay?" Cherry's pert young features twisted in concern.

"Of course. Sorry. Just woolgathering. Everything under control?"

The pretty young girl fairly danced with delight. "Perfect. I just love working here, you know that. Do you need me to do anything? I mean, in back, with the stock?"

"No, you stay out here and wait on customers. They like you. You have a way with them."

The girl blushed. "Okay. Thank you, I will."

And do twist that lovely butt. Raine had to admit she envied the shapely girl her ability to wear anything and look cute. At first she'd worried because most of their clientele were women, and Cherry dressed like most kids in low slung tight pants and hi-slung blouses that exposed not only a bare middle but the ring in her belly button. Oddly, customers seemed to get a kick out of her shenanigans. Perhaps some secretly yearned to return to their own youthful days. For that reason she'd said nothing about her clothes. But if those pants got any lower or the tops cropped any higher, she would definitely rein her in.

Amused, Raine turned to the shelf behind the counter and counted the bundles of coffee mixes, each sealed packet individually wrapped in bright cotton fabric and tied with a ribbon. These were sold to customers who wanted to enjoy RainTree's special blends at home.

A shiver skittered down her spine. No one spoke, yet someone watched her, and the feeling was familiar. She hadn't expected him quite so soon.

Carefully, she laid down the clipboard and turned. "Well, glad you could come. Spinner, isn't it?" She knew damned well it was.

He grinned like he knew she knew. "This is quite some place you've got here. A nice surprise to step off a street in Chota, Oklahoma and end up on a South American coffee plantation. Clever."

"Thank you. Would you like to try one of our special blends?"

"I'm used to my coffee hot and black. Just what do you have in mind?"

"Oh, we have that too, if you're afraid to be adventurous."

"I haven't been afraid of anything in a long time. Tempt me."

She flushed, cheeks heating. It scared her that she'd be more than happy to tempt him—and not with coffee, either. The last thing she needed was a man in her life. Since Russ, she'd struggled to avoid any serious relationship. Why was she always attracted to the scary ones? The obvious answer—that she secretly liked danger—she didn't care to contemplate at the moment.

A retort to his request flowed smoothly, though she had no idea how. "I thought perhaps an almond and vanilla latte with a dollop of thick, sweet cream."

"Only if you'll join me," he said.

The way he stared at her with eyes so black the pupils melted into the irises, she'd have joined him anywhere. Only a formidable man who exuded such self-assured tenacity could rouse sexual desires in her, for she wanted no more of mealy-mouthed men who hid their violence behind a facade of kindly lies. A man like Spinner need not beat a woman into submission, nor would he ever be so cowardly as to try.

How dare she be so sure of that? She knew better. You couldn't spot the dangerous ones that easily. Fear niggled her into submission. Be nice to him, but set the limits and stick to them. She knew nothing about him, nothing at all. And shouldn't want to.

She smiled, wiped her hands on a paper towel. "I'd be glad to join you. Anything to please a customer."

"I'll make a list," he said.

"Excuse me?"

"Of things you can do to please this particular customer."

Damn. She'd been cloistered too long. No man had ever talked so boldly to her. Was this the way it was done now? This mating game? Maybe she ought to check out some books on the subject, catch up.

She studied his lean, graceful body, poised in the wait mode, relaxed and loose so he appeared to have all day, yet ready to pounce should it be necessary. Patiently waiting to see what she'd say, waiting to touch her elbow, to lead her across the room. Waiting to jump her bones.

Feeling like bait, she moved from behind the counter. He cupped her elbow with firm fingers, went with her to a table in the far corner behind draping fronds of banana palm. An odd sensation embraced her, that of being controlled, and it terrified her, caused her to stiffen under his touch.

Like an old-fashioned gentleman, he held her chair, then sat next to her, dark gaze holding hers. "Now, about that list."

Confused for a moment, she felt knocked off balance. "Sorry, I...?"

"Anything to please a customer?" A corner of his mouth tilted, his eyes sparked.

"I amuse you?"

"You do a lot more than that, but amused will do for a start."

A seething terror surprised her in its intensity, and the short hairs on the back of her neck prickled. *Run far, run fast,* urged a little voice. Annoyed, she brushed it away, and forgot her snappy comeback. Probably just as well, she never was good at perky repartee. At that moment Cherry appeared.

"Now, you look like the black coffee type," she told Spinner, eyes on him as if they were alone in the room. "I'll just bet you'd be up for something different."

The girl was a born flirt. "He'll have—"

"An almond vanilla latté with lots of cream," Spinner said. "And bring her one too. On me." He grinned widely at Cherry, who appeared hypnotized by his gaze.

Strange, he had pointed incisors like a wolf. Not surprising, the wolf part. Though he appeared to be quite civilized. You could pen wolves up. You could even pet them, but you'd better be damned careful when you did. She'd do well to keep her distance.

Cherry stirred, glanced at Raine, her expression one of confusion. The girl was never at a loss for words, nor did she normally stand around stupefied.

Spinner's peculiar charm cast a wide net.

"Honey, that's all," Raine said softly.

"What? Oh, yeah, sure. Okay. Two almond vanilla lattés with lots of cream. Would you like an éclair or cheese Danish?"

Spinner raised his eyebrows in Raine's direction. Unable to find her tongue, she shook her head.

Spinner replied for them both. "No, not today. Thank you, Honey."

Both Raine and Cherry gasped at the politically incorrect *faux pas*.

"What? You called her Honey. I thought that was her name."

"You did not," Raine said.

He held up a hand. "I swear, I did."

"My name is Cherry."

"Oh, that's much better than Honey." Pause for a beat while his dark eyed glance slid toward Raine. "Isn't it?"

Cherry sidled away, and Raine was sure she was laughing, though she couldn't see her face.

Everything the man said stirred a buried passion that alerted her senses. Had she been overpowered by some chemical explosion over which she had no control? If so, she ought to run. Now. Her butt stuck firmly to the chair. To keep from looking him in the face, she watched his graceful brown fingers drum silently on the tablecloth and tried to curb her riotous imagination.

"Well," she said, and immediately felt foolish.

"Well?" he asked gently, as if it weren't really a stupid thing to say.

"How long have you…?"

"I would've been here sooner…."

Utterances that came out one over the other.

"You go first," he said.

"I was just wondering how long you've lived here."

"I live and work in Vinita, but I'm not from there. I work for the Department of Human Services. One of my kids needs some special attention right now, he's, hmm, he's a special case. And that's why I'm here in Chota for a while. However, I would've come over here sooner had I known this was here." He gestured to include her.

"Oh, yes, you're a counselor." All she'd remembered about their first encounter at the hospital had nothing to do with his occupation.

"I guess you could say that."

"Forgive me, but you don't look like a counselor. More like a—"

"A convict?" Again, the feral smile.

"Uh, no, I wasn't going to say that. Either. Exactly."

Cocking his head, he waited. "You were, and I do."

Fortunately, Cherry brought their coffees in time to save her further embarrassment.

Before she could do anything else dumb, she lifted her cup and sipped the rich concoction. He continued to stare at her.

"Aren't you going to try it?"

"I imagine I will." His gaze dragged somnolently over her before he glanced at the steaming offer. "Oh, the coffee."

Over the lip of his cup, Spinner eyed the tiny mustache of creamy froth along her upper lip. Damn, he'd always liked women who blushed every time they had a naughty urge. She'd been at it since he walked in, and he'd give a silver dollar to have a list of those thoughts.

Oh, well. Some other time. Flirting with her was enjoyable, but that's where it would end. He had no intention of getting involved with anyone, especially someone like Raine. She would demand too much. He tried the almond vanilla latté. Made a face.

"How is it?" She took another sip and wiped her mouth with a napkin.

His glance followed the napkin over her full lips. "Well, if you forget it's supposed to be coffee and think of it as melted ice cream that ought to be sweet, it's fine. I wouldn't want to be in need of a cup of coffee and this be all I could get. I'd like to put sugar in it. Whip it up. Freeze it. Eat it with Oreos."

She laughed, and he enjoyed that almost as much as her earlier blushes. It wasn't put on or affected in any way. Just pure delight. And he had a feeling she was as surprised as he.

Changing the subject was in order.

"Your friend," he managed. "How is she?"

"Who?"

"At the hospital. Where we met. The first time? You remember."

"Of course, I was still with Oreos in a frozen latté. She's fine… well, not really, but they let her go home. Nothing serious. At least, nothing life threatening. At the moment."

Ah, a place we won't go. Deep, dark secrets. Well, everyone has them. He certainly had his share.

"A good friend."

"The best."

"Good. Everyone needs a best friend, especially when they're in trouble."

She studied him so closely, he fidgeted. "What's makes you think either of us is in trouble? Do you always get this personal with someone you've just met? Or is this just a pickup line?"

She had him there. He wanted to know more about her, but she wasn't having any of it. He shrugged. "Well, I tried. Next time, maybe."

"I don't think so."

Wow, he'd chipped his way through some cold ice before, but this one was on freeze. He stood, fished his billfold from a hip pocket, took out a twenty, and laid it on the table. "Is this enough? I have to go. It's late and I have an appointment."

She stared at the bill, refused to even glance at him. "Come back. You can have plain black coffee, if you'd like."

Without replying, he nodded, then got the hell out of there. What he had in mind she definitely wasn't interested in, and he didn't want to make a fool of himself.

After he left Raine went over their earlier conversation. Chota was a small town. This man Spinner had come here to counsel someone. Who might that be? One of his kids, he'd said.

"Sort of a good-looking guy," Cherry said at her shoulder.

"What? Oh, him. Wouldn't go near him if he had wings."

"Too bad he didn't make much of an impression. He's hot."

Raine rung up his bill. "I didn't notice."

Cherry laughed heartily. "Guess you're blind."

After they finished cleaning the shop, Cherry went on her way. Raine lingered a while, enjoying the ambiance of the place. It was literally all she had in this world except her friendship with Becca. And she wanted it that way. With a sigh, she pulled the door closed, checked the lock, and headed for her car. Another lonely two days in the offing. Maybe she'd go to Tulsa, take in some music shows and visit a museum.

Six

A storm blew in Saturday night, a real Oklahoma thunder boomer. Becca hardly slept, huddled under the covers flinching at every flash of light and drum of thunder. Childish to continue to fear thunderstorms. She'd hated them as far back as she could remember. Lying awake in the Volkswagen bus beside her young parents, who'd lived their entire lives on the road as flower children, she'd been terrified the lightning would rip open the roof or the wind pick them up and blow them away. And she'd never quite gotten over that fear. Jeremiah being killed during a storm added hatred to her terror.

Then she remembered something else, something she hadn't thought of in a long while. Jon holding her close while a storm lashed the windows of their first apartment. Their passion growing, hers fed by the danger she imagined, his because she clung to him so fiercely, until they made mad, crazy love, their orgasms matching the ferocity outside.

Now, alone in her bed, she could only hug herself and tremble.

By the time she crawled wearily out of bed Sunday, the storm had settled to a steady downpour. She staggered into the bathroom, turned on the shower, and ducked under without removing her gown. The walls whirled around her, and she leaned against the cold tiles until the world righted itself.

God, she was tired of feeling this way. No more pills today. Not one, well, except maybe a Prozac to raise her spirits. The drug of choice this week. She'd been really careful the night before to swallow only enough Valium to soften the edges. Today, her family was coming for dinner and she wanted… no, had to show them she was doing okay.

The telephone rang while she sat on the edge of the bed, working up the energy to find something to wear.

No, please. Not Christi, saying something had come up. Please.

After the fourth ring she picked up the instrument.

"Yes?"

"Mom?"

Oh, sweet Jesus. "David? Is that you? Where are you?"

"Here, Mom. I'm in town. I wanted to come out, but… well, I couldn't reach Christi or Dad and I wasn't sure if you—"

"Oh, well, of course. Please do. Christi and your Dad will be here for dinner. This is wonderful. Can you come, too? Everything would be so like…." She let the thought drift away, held her breath for his reply.

"Dinner?" The incredulous question cut at her heart. His broken family, actually gathering in the same house. She heard the implication as if he'd shouted it.

"Yes, well?"

"Well, of course, Mom. I'll be out in, say an hour? How's that?"

"Perfect. We can talk, there's so much to say to each other. Oh, David, we need to talk."

"Yes, I suppose we do."

"I'll be waiting for you. Oh, hurry, David."

"Soon. Love you." He hung up before she could respond.

Her heart hammered in her throat and her belly did a flip flop. She could do this, had to. Not ruin it all like she always did.

David was coming home.

Staggering to the closet, scrubbing at her wet hair with a towel, she pulled out a long, flowing hostess gown, stared at it a moment, dropped it to the floor, and rifled through the hangers until she found a blue pantsuit. Tossing it on the bed, she pawed through a drawer for bra and panties, slipped into them and sat on the edge of the mattress to pull on the slacks. Dizzy with excitement, she remained there a moment until her head stopped swimming, then slid her arms into the floral, long-sleeved blouse. A quick combing through her hair that would dry curly, she took a last look in the mirror, and turned.

One arm hit the bed table and toppled a bottle of pills. She picked it up, glanced at the label. Her friend, Prozac. Set it back down and found a pair of soft slippers. At the last minute, she slipped the vial into the pocket of her pants and went downstairs to start cooking.

Her family would be home for Sunday dinner. Despite the rain slashing across the deck, and the distant rumble of thunder, she felt as if the house overflowed with bright sunlight. She could do anything, be her old self, laugh, sing. All she had to do was try.

When Christi had called her the evening before and said that her father would be coming out with her, Becca had been sorely disappointed. She wanted the girl all to herself. The two together always managed to create a solid front opposing anything Becca might want. But she was afraid that if she refused to have Jon, Christi wouldn't come either. Now, with the news that David would be there as well, she was happy she hadn't said anything.

It would be wonderful having them all here again.

All, except for Jeremiah.

Standing at the refrigerator, staring in at the roast she'd taken from the freezer the night before, Becca surrendered to great sobs that racked her. With shaking fingers, she dug the bottle from her pocket, shook out a green and white capsule, and slipped it into her mouth, washed it down with water from the tap and grimaced at the taste. She leaned against the sink a moment taking deep breaths.

There, that was better. Everything would be all right. In just a few short minutes.

Then she could face David and Christi and Jon. Get through this day. And please God, not mess up.

When David walked up the driveway carrying a duffel over one shoulder, wearing disreputable slouchy pants and a thin jacket flapping open in the rain, Becca stood in the doorway, and hugged her quivering insides. He looked nothing like Jeremiah.

She bit her lip. "Look at you, darling. You're soaked. How did you get out here?"

"Hitched with Homer Atkins. He was on his way back from church, recognized me. Besides, they wouldn't let a bum like me through the gate, now would they?"

Moving into the shelter of the portico, he dropped the duffel and took her in his arms. He'd added another inch or two to his height, but still wasn't as tall as Jeremiah when he....

Stop, this instant.

David still wore his hair shaggy, like he might have cut it himself. She had to stand on her toes to embrace him. It felt good, having his arms around her after more than a year apart. She'd lost both her sons that fateful winter's night, and to have this one back strengthened her need to avenge the loss of the other. How her soul ached for them both. She would not do this today. She would be grateful for what she had. Stop this whining. Enjoy her family. She kissed his stubbly cheek and raked her fingers through his long, wet hair.

David laughed. "Yeah, I know. I need a haircut and shave. Figured it'd be easier to shave here than in some cruddy airport or restaurant bathroom. As for the hair, get used to it."

He was almost joking, but the remark carried a cutting edge that dared her to get bossy like a parent. Since high school David had challenged both her and Jon to boss him around. Unlike Jeremiah, he'd been a difficult teenager and, at twenty-two, it didn't look like much had changed.

Patting him on the shoulder, she said, "Once it's dry, I'm sure it'll look fine. Besides, you remind me of my Dad. Come on inside. It's chilly and you need to change. Your room is just as you left it."

Inside the door, with it closed against the storm, David dragged in a deep breath. "Smells good in here. Roast?"

She nodded, touched him again to reassure herself he was truly there. "Your favorite. Besides, it's easy to prepare. I'm not much of a cook lately."

"You look tired."

"How kind of you. I look like hell and you know it. Old, beat up...." She broke off and shrugged. "Go upstairs. Take a shower, get settled, and I'll put some potatoes and carrots in the roast. We'll talk when you come down."

Halfway up the winding staircase, he turned. "When will Dad and Christi be here?"

"Just in time to eat and leave," she said, then realized how bitchy that sounded and added, "Probably around two or so. I said we'd eat then. We all need to talk about something important to do with Jeremiah—"

The sound of David's feet clomping on the stairs interrupted her, and she looked up to see him disappearing along the second floor balcony. Fleeing the echo of her own words, and clenching her fists until her nails bit the palms, she hurried to the kitchen to finish preparing the meal.

Not supposed to bring that up. Don't talk about Jeremiah or that hateful Lucas Pell.

How badly she just wanted to push a button somewhere and become a good mother again. And while she was at it, a good wife. If only she could find that button.

Except for Raine, she was alone in this. Today she would not start a fight. She would keep everything light and pleasant, not even speak of Jeremiah. That had been a mistake, mentioning his name to David. Seeing his reaction only hardened her resolve to do this thing without their knowledge. Once it was over, they would see she'd been right all along about avenging her son's murder. Everyone would feel much better when the deed was done. Then they could go back to life the way it had been except no Jeremiah.

At the head of the table, Jon lifted a glass of red wine to his family. "Welcome home, David. Christi, we'll miss your pretty face while you're down under. Becca, the meal was delicious. To the family."

Everyone raised their glasses, and sipped. To keep from snorting in disgust at the toast, Becca downed all of her wine and managed a fake smile. To the family, indeed. All through the meal they'd chatted about inane things like David's adventures, Christi's hopes for the same, and Jon's tales of his business acumen, all intermingled with spurts of laughter, as if there weren't an empty chair at the table. A place setting not being used. A huge dark hole in their lives. A hole that could never be filled. Christi even went so far as to ask her, in all innocence, when she was going back to work at RainTree.

"I went in Saturday," she'd replied vaguely and tried out a smile.

"That's super, Mom," Christi said brightly.

Jon and David stared at her for a moment, then attacked their food with increased vigor.

Christi helped clear the table, chattering on about how good it was to see David. Wondering what he would be doing next, where he would go. Questioning what she would find in Australia when she arrived there. And all Becca could think of was getting her hands on Lucas Pell and wringing his neck for what he'd done to her family. Topped off by wine, the pill she'd taken left her light headed, and after they'd loaded the dishes into the dishwasher, she excused herself.

"I'll be right in," she told Christi, and headed for the downstairs bath to splash her face with water and make an attempt at looking presentable.

It was going to be a long afternoon, and one she must struggle through without blurting out her secret. She would destroy Lucas Pell without their help. Patting her face dry, she fumbled out another Prozac and swallowed it, then turned from the mirror without looking too closely and went to join her family.

Hunched against the light pole on the corner of South Street and Island Road, the name given Highway 125 for the mile or so that it passed through Chota, Lucas squinted into the rain. Dark clouds hung low, and from the highway he could barely make out the misty twinkling of lights along the shoreline. Traffic was light where Lake Drive cut off Island Road to the gated community with the stupid name of Rocky Cove. He studied the few oncoming vehicles. A new four-by-four, followed by a Dodge Ram pickup, left signals blinking, slowed at the intersection.

Without hesitating, Lucas sloshed through a puddle, crossed the road, and glanced in all directions. No one around, either on foot or in a car. As the Ram made its slow turn, he vaulted into the back and scrambled into the front corner behind the driver. Shivering, he hugged himself. The night was chilly for April and he wished for a coat. Might as well wish for that red Corvette. He wasn't getting either.

One thing he would get, though, was a face-off with the Krafts. They would listen to him, accept his apology for the accident, and he could get shut of this place. The job Spinner got him was a joke and so was that crappy room in the shittiest part of Chota. Soon as he finished here, he was heading for the interstate and hitching to Dallas. That was a town. A place where he could make good.

The Ram roared to life, its diesel engine throbbing as the driver accelerated across the highway and stopped at the huge black iron gates. Lucas kept his head down, arms locked around his knees to make himself nothing more than a dark shadow in case the guard paid any attention. His bet was he wouldn't do more than glance from his shack to check the guy's window sticker. What with the rain and all. Only place you could go now was into the gated community.

Lucas knew about the place because once he and Cappy and Saint had come all the way out here, intending to get a good look at the way those rich folks lived, only to find high fences and a closed gate. One glimpse of them and the guard had called for backup. A fancy black car come swooping up so fast, ole Cappy about pissed his pants. They'd run for the highway like the man hisself was on their heels.

Lucas drew a deep breath when the truck rolled through the gates without trouble. Just as he'd thought, the damned guard was too lazy to come out in the rain, just sat in there waving through the glass.

Scooting along the wet bed, Lucas waited until the truck swung a right around a thicket of bushes, then vaulted over the side and rolled into them. Asshole driver didn't even see him in the rearview. Just in case, he remained under the dripping shrubbery until the taillights went out of sight around another curve. One of those fancy yard lights sat on a pole at the corner of a drive that angled off to a ritzy-ditzy place. The house wasn't visible, so they couldn't see him either, and he hunched close to the light to look at the map he'd downloaded at the library to show him how to get to the Krafts'. Only good thing come out of what they liked to call his incarceration, was he'd learned to use a computer.

After checking out the name of the street he was on, Dune Lane, he moved along, careful to remain well out of sight whenever an occasional car came along. He wanted Bluff Drive, was only a few curly blocks from it. These rich folks liked to have lots of trees and bushes along the streets to make things look fancy. All it did was give him a place to hide.

Twice a security car crept through the gloomy afternoon, a few times cars carrying families passed by, tires swishing on the wet pavement. No one saw him crouched in the bushes. He walked a long time before he came to a fancy engraved wooden sign that read Bluff Drive. It wound off to his right, thick trees on either side that touched above the street, and cut off the worst of the rain. He felt as if he'd gone into a jungle.

"Guess they don't need street lights, ain't going to let no one in that could hurt 'em."

Up ahead was a mailbox and a paved drive that should lead to the Kraft house. On the box, only a number, but according to his map this was it. At about head height fancy lamps marked each side of the drive. The house, windows lit against the gloom, was barely visible through the trees. He hoped they didn't have a dog. If they did, it would be one of those yappy little things with a ribbon in its hair. He'd stomp the little shit if it so much as opened its mouth.

Standing hunched over in the rain, he carefully folded the map, slipped it into the pocket of his new jeans and walked across the wet grass. A row of shrubs promised a place to hide where he could take a look around. Two cars sat in the driveway and the double garage doors were closed, so no telling who all would be inside. Maybe they had company... a party, lots of people.

He grinned. Wouldn't that be fun? Busting up a party to demand forgiveness. Somehow, that didn't seem like a good idea, and he patted himself on the back for having some sense. If this was going to work, he'd have to be careful.

David fidgeted on the couch, gazed across the glass-topped table at his father, seated on a matching couch, looking ready to fight.

He sensed no matter what he said, it would be wrong. What had the old man asked? If he was going back to that godforsaken place and if so why? Yeah, that was it.

"I'm taking some time off, thought I'd hike the Ozark Highlands Trail, get some of the stench of poverty out of my system."

"You wanted to see poverty, you didn't have to go to Africa. Plenty of folks in this country need a helping hand, if you're so set on such a life." Jon uncrossed his legs, immediately re-crossed them.

David heaved a great sigh. "Could we talk about something else?"

"Like when you're going to grow up and take some responsibility?" Jon gazed over his son's shoulder at the darkened windows that reflected the luxurious room.

"I thought that's what I'd been doing. It's hard work over there, and you ought to see how much they appreciate the little we can—"

Jon held up a hand. "Don't get started on that third world country crap. Tell me, David. What do you get paid for all that 'hard work.'" He sneered the words.

"Is that all that matters? How much money we make?"

Jon leaned forward, pinned David with a hard stare. "It mattered when you wanted to go to USC. It mattered when you wanted to tour Europe for a year before you got a real job. It mattered—"

David sprang to his feet. "Okay, I get it, Dad. Same old thing. I know I owe you everything. I know I have disappointed you. I know I was a nerd who didn't play football and make you proud." He paused, took a deep breath. "I know I'm not Jeremiah."

Even as he hurled the final sentence into the room, his mother and sister came from the kitchen. To look at their faces, he might have brandished an ax over his father's head. Hot bile gushed into his throat, his eyes watered, and he turned and fled the room so they wouldn't see him cry. He slammed outside, realized he had no way to get out of there, and after pacing on the portico for a while, went back inside and upstairs to his room.

After David left the room, Becca covered her mouth to stifle a scream that had lurked in her throat since they sat down at the table to eat. Before turning toward Christi she searched Jon's face. It had gone white, lips tight, eyes flashing dangerously. Then he dragged his attention to her, and the expression crumpled. She thought he was going to cry, but the instant passed and with a flexing of his shoulders, he reset his features. Bland, non-caring, emotionless except for a slight upturning of one corner of his mouth. A mocking smile she'd seen before that said, this is your fault.

"I wasn't even in the room," she said in her own defense, and again studied her daughter and husband.

Christi put an arm around her, patted her shoulder. "It's all right, Mommy. He didn't mean anything. You know how David is. He and Daddy never could get along."

"Now, wait just a minute," Jon said.

"It's okay, Daddy. It really is. It's no one's fault. Really." Christi, ever the peacemaker, crossed the room to hug her father as well.

It wasn't okay, though. Resentment Becca couldn't hold back churned against this daughter who could turn even the cloudiest mood bright where her father was concerned. Angry words spilled out.

"It is not okay, Christi. David goes running around all over God knows where, you're getting ready to go to Australia, for God's sake, and your father, here," —she swung an arm in his direction— "can't even take the time to come home for his own son's anniversary." The last word hiccoughed out of her, driven by a blazing pain that shot from her middle to the top of her head.

"You mean for the anniversary of our son's death, don't you? Jesus Christ, Rebecca. How long are we going to celebrate that?"

"It is not a celebration. It's... it's...."

Jon raised an eyebrow. "Yes? It's what? Digging at the scabs for fear they might heal up if we don't? Isn't that what it is?"

"Please stop," Christi cried, and placed herself between her mother and father, who had stepped toward each other with each new remark, until they were only feet apart.

For an instant, they did stop, but Becca continued to stare at Jon with hatred.

"And you wonder why I'm going to Australia. Well, it's not Australia, it's you. The both of you. I can't be here anymore. I can't have you calling me to come see you, Mom." She swung to look at Jon. "And I can't have you calling to fix things for you so you don't have to deal with her and my brother's death. I loved him too. Damn you both to hell."

"Christi," Jon muttered. "Don't talk to us that way."

"How can you say such a thing?" Becca whispered. "My God, what if... if..."

Tears pouring down her cheeks, Christi threw her hands upward. "Well, at least the two of you agree on something. Little Christi is a bad girl. At least that should make worshiping Jeremiah a bit easier."

The words barely made it from her mouth as intelligible utterances. Becca watched in horror as her only daughter ran from the room sobbing. Stood frozen in place as the front door slammed, the car started, tires slipped on wet pavement.

"Well, I never thought she would—"

"Oh, shut up, Becca. Just shut up."

"Jon."

"I hope you're happy."

Raising her shoulders, Becca stared at him through tears. "What did I do?" She watched Jon leave the room. "Where are you going?"

He didn't reply, and the front door slammed again. Outside his car revved up and he too, was gone.

She crumpled to the thick, soft carpet and lay there for a long time, mind void of all thoughts save one. Punishing Lucas Pell for tearing her family apart. This was all his fault.

When the door of the Kraft house flew open the first time, Lucas fought the urge to scramble away into the darkness. Despite the thick

growth where he huddled, he felt frightened and exposed. So close to this family who held so much power over his life.

He knew they'd been fighting, he could hear the muted shouting beyond the lit window near where he crouched.

A young man came out, paced back and forth on the portico, muttering, then went back inside. It wasn't too long before a young woman rushed from the house, leaped into the small blue sports car, and peeled out of there. Before he could think too much about what might have happened, the door opened again, and this time a man exited, climbed in the Mercedes, and he too barrel-assed out of there.

He'd picked a bad time for a visit. It was for sure not a party. Lucas mulled over what he'd seen, tried to decide what to do. Damn, had he wasted his time, coming out here? He knew the Krafts had a son and a daughter besides the one who'd died, and figured what he'd witnessed was a family fight. Then daughter and father took off. That left the son and his mother still in the house. Damn. Maybe this wasn't the best time to approach the family.

In a panic Lucas whirled. He'd stood up after the Mercedes left and, with the porch light on, remained in full sight of anyone who might look this way, including the people still inside.

What if they caught him? Could they have him put back in jail? For trespassing or Peeping Tom stuff?

His heart ran like an overheated engine until he could barely breathe. What had he been thinking, coming out here on their turf? Catch them out somewhere, that would be best. Approach them one by one. Ask to talk. Make an appointment, like someone who lived in their world would do. Show he was civilized.

Yeah, that was it. He'd work it out.

He'd better get out of this place before he got his ass hauled off to jail.

Seven

Though David remained in the house, he did not come down for breakfast. Showered, made-up, hair done, dressed in a classy but dated azure blue pantsuit, Becca padded along the forest green carpeting in the hallway, stopped at his door, and listened. Silence. She lifted her hand to knock, hesitated, glanced toward the room of her youngest son. Her dead son.

Inside, everything the way he'd left it. She had only to close her eyes to see each detail. Favorite sweater over the back of a chair angled casually in front of his computer, worn Reeboks kicked into a corner along with his backpack, crammed with books and homework assignments that would never be finished. The bed made the way only a fifteen-year-old boy could make one. Spread tossed casually over sheets that hung askance. Clothes in the closet or folded in the four-drawer chest. On the walls he'd painted the brightest of blues when he was fourteen, hung posters of Shack and The Eagles, Jimi Hendrix and the Doors. Not very messy, her Jeremiah. All the same, he did leave things scattered about. She hadn't moved anything. Maybe she never could.

Without knowing how it came about she stood at the door, forehead resting against the panel, the knob cold under her damp palm.

No, please. The latch clicked. Drag in a breath, then another. Hadn't been in there in months, in an eternity. No. No. The door swung open. Go ahead, open it, check everything. Make sure… make sure of what?

Jeremiah always asked her not to mess around in his room, so she hadn't. Wouldn't. Still couldn't. Before any of his things came in view, she pulled the door back into the frame and let the latch re-fasten. The click sounded loud in the silence. Hunching her shoulders, she expelled a breath and turned away, dizzy with the effort of remaining upright.

Downstairs she sat at the breakfast table gazing out over the lake and drinking coffee. Beyond the windows the sun shone brightly, reflecting off the lake like Fourth of July sparklers. She hadn't been up this early in months—actually more than a year, and she couldn't remember the last time she'd put food in her stomach at this ungodly hour.

If you could call this food. This whole wheat toast with bits of what suspiciously resembled sawdust, a slippery spread that held no resemblance to butter, and something laughingly called jam that had neither real fruit or sugar in it. She definitely needed to go shopping. For food, for clothes. Let's face it, everything in this house could stand replacing. Maybe she'd call someone in to redecorate.

Her own body could stand a make-over as well. If it weren't for her hip bones and good elastic, the pants she wore would've drifted to the floor in a puddle. Looking in the mirror hadn't been an option in a long while, but this morning she'd studied her image in the full-length glass, posing in her gown, then fresh out of the shower in the buff, then when fully dressed. Found herself appalling. Hair that once gleamed in shades of gold and copper was a dull dishwater blonde, blue eyes that used to sparkle with anticipation looked like algae clotted pools, and a body once accustomed to walking, running, and bicycling, nothing but skin hung on bones.

Disgusted, she vowed that this day she would begin a new regimen. No more drinking. No pills. No lying around all day whining. She had to be strong if she was to face up to that little thug who'd killed Jeremiah.

Biting into the soggy toast, she spoke to her son as if he were in the room. "Don't you worry. He won't get away with what he did. I'm not going to let him tear this family to shreds and walk off as if it were nothing."

Memories of the previous afternoon's bitter arguments with her family, their stony leave-takings, only served to harden her resolve. If they weren't behind her in this thing, then so be it.

David appeared in the doorway, and without speaking went to the sideboard and helped himself to scrambled eggs, bacon, and toast she'd set there earlier.

"Good morning." She dropped the remainder of the bread onto her plate, finished the coffee, and rose. "I'm going into the shop for a while. Would you like to go along?"

"No, thanks, Mom. There's some guys I want to hang with before I go back. Maybe I'll see you this evening."

"Okay, have fun."

The silver Nissan Jon had bought her for Christmas a week before Jeremiah was killed awaited in silence in the garage. She probably hadn't driven it more than a dozen times, but it started at the touch of the key. Still smelled new inside.

Good. That's good. Everything needs to be new from this day forward. As if I've never seen it before, touched it, used it.

The leather seat squeaked beneath her shifting weight. How strange to sit behind the wheel. More strange to take her life in her own hands rather than handing it over to some mysterious fate she really didn't believe in anyway. The one she'd been quick to blame each time she popped more pills or poured another drink.

"Out, damn spot, begone," she shouted, backed into a curling turn and headed down the lane to the street.

Parking spots along the curb in front of RainTree were filled, so she cut down the alley to the back of the building where she and Raine had reserved spaces. A beat up brown panel van sat in hers.

"Well, what did I expect?" she asked aloud, and nosed in behind Raine's little red Maserati, a remnant of her marriage to What's His Name, her friend's official tag for the abusive husband whose real name she could not bring herself to utter.

The back door was still locked and she fumbled around on her key ring, not sure she could remember which was the proper key. Finally coming up with it, she let herself in.

A pretty blonde in flame red pants and a filmy purple top that revealed her belly button, sans gold ring, turned from a shelf with a squeal, scattering several packets of coffee on the floor.

"Oh, my word," Becca exclaimed.

"Who are you?" the girl asked, squatting to pick up the packages. "Are you supposed to be here? I thought I left the door locked."

"I'm Rebecca—Who are you?"

"Cherry. Oh, you must be Mrs. Kraft," the girl said over her question. "I'm so sorry I didn't recognize you. I should've known you the minute I laid eyes on you. Everyone talks about you and I guess I didn't think. We didn't know you were coming... that is, if we did, Raine didn't say anything. She'll be so happy to see you."

The way she babbled the sentences, Becca thought the girl could've gone on like that all day without taking a breath. One word running into another with no periods or commas. Blessedly, Raine's arrival cut her short.

"Becky. I'm so glad to see you. Why didn't you tell me you were coming?" She plowed past the girl, whose mouth still appeared on the verge of spouting more words, and put her arms around Becca.

The embrace touched her heart. Raine looked and smelled like a million dollars. Wearing her favorite Michael Kors Shimmering Fragrance. Dressed in peachskin pants and oxford style shirt in shades of coral, a trademark scarf in splashes of earth tones tied creatively at her throat, she could have been the wife of one of those successful businessmen who worked in Tulsa and visited on weekends. No one could ever guess she had escaped a drunken Cherokee father and a whore for a mother, only to marry a vicious man who tried to kill her. Left her neck scarred so those lovely scarves had become her trademark.

Becca returned the embrace with a special warmth for this best friend. "I would've called, but I wasn't sure I could do it until I actually parked out back."

"Oh, never mind. You're here. It's so good to see you. You look—"

"I look like hell."

Rubbing at her chin, Raine stepped back and eyed her up and down. "Well, now that you mention it, you could stand to eat a little more." She laughed.

The girl giggled, and soon Becca joined them. It may not have been much, this letting go a bit, but it was something and she welcomed it.

After officially introducing Becca to Cherry, Raine took her arm and led her further into the shop. "I want you to see what we've done. Oh, I know, I've kept you abreast of everything, but seeing is so much better than hearing about it, don't you think?"

Everything about the place made Raine happy. One day perhaps it would once again make her best friend happy too.

On impulse she turned and hugged Becca again. "I've missed you so much. You can't imagine how glad I am to have you here. Remember when we found this shabby place? How we scrubbed and plastered and cleaned."

Becca smiled, eyes gleaming with unshed tears. "And those dreadful old tables you found at flea markets. I didn't think they'd ever turn into these." She sighed. "I've missed this place so much, and being with you."

"Me too." She led Becca to a table. "Here, sit. I'll make you one of those new coffee blends."

Cherry hurried to them. "No, both of you sit. I'll do it."

Becca watched the girl sashay toward the counter.

"She does twist that lovely butt, doesn't she?" Raine said. "Don't look so pained. The customers love her. They do get a kick out of her shenanigans."

"Probably wish they were that young again." Becca said, hands fisted tightly together on the table top as if she were containing feelings that struggled to escape.

"I have to admit, that bare middle and belly button ring are a bit much."

"Sure are. I think if she shows any more skin, you ought to talk to her about it."

"My thoughts exactly," Raine replied. "But she's a good worker and so cute. So willing to do anything I ask of her."

"Well, good help is hard to find. I'd hang on to her, if I were you."

Both hands clasped over Becca's, Raine said, "We'll hang on to her."

Becca's haunted expression had calmed as they talked about the business. This was good for her, coming back like this. Maybe things would begin to be better for her. Raine could scarcely bear to think of the tragedy that had befallen her best friend. Jeremiah's death had changed her till she feared Becca would never be the same again.

Cherry carried over the tall cups of specially blended coffee known as Island Mocha Coconut, placed them gently so the peak of whipped cream held its shape.

"Can I bring you anything else? A chocolate éclair would be scrumptious with this yummy stuff."

"You know, I believe it would. Bring us two," Raine said with a laugh.

Becca shook her head, but didn't say no.

For a few moments they sipped at the delicious blend in silence.

"What are those?" Becca finally asked after indulging in several bites of the rich éclair.

Raine turned to look on the shelf behind the counter. "Oh, we had this idea to wrap some individual blends in bright cotton fabric and tie it with a ribbon. That way, customers can carry home some to try out. We included instructions on preparing it."

After they finished their treat, Raine pointed out the newest additions to the coffee shop—several ancient and slow-moving rattan fans she'd found at an auction and had installed from the high, sky-blue ceiling. A corner alcove that allowed a small group to gather with some privacy for special events. It resembled a cabana built of palm fronds, the entrance guarded by a torch with an electric flame.

"Oh, and there's the newest fountain. See, it's filled with koi and underwater lights to show off their lovely colors."

"Sort of a mixed decor, isn't it? Island cabanas, Japanese fish, South American motif?"

"You don't like it?"

Immediately, Becca backed off. "Yes, I do like it. You've done wonders. I'm very pleased. If it weren't for you, this place would've closed down months ago. I'm so sorry, Raine, for all the trouble I've put you through. I'm ready to carry my weight again."

"You're really back to stay? This isn't just a visit?"

"Yes, I'm back in the thick of things. And about time, don't you think?" The statement sounded forced, much too bright, but Raine let it go.

Becca tied an apron over her good clothes and immersed herself in the business of helping run the shop.

Tables emptied as patrons left to tend to their daily tasks. Becca was pleased to see that RainTree continued to attract a goodly amount of customers from the lakeshore communities of Monkey Island. Most were wives of successful professionals or young couples learning to spend their trust funds. Very few residents of the town of Chota patronized the upscale coffee house. Spending seven-fifty on a cup of specially blended coffees, spritzed and fizzed and served in delicate footed cups, did not appeal to the working population who lived there. A majority of them were Cherokee or mixed blood. They'd go to the diner over in Bernice for their coffee, complaining because it cost seventy-five cents.

After much discussion she and Raine had agreed on the hours, opening at nine in the morning and closing just before supper time Monday through Friday. Over the first few months, she and Raine had learned that these were the best hours to offer their product to their specialized clientele. Women who did not rise early, couples who spent two hours in their own private gym before coming to town, could not be expected to want service early in the morning, nor late in the evening, when they were entertaining or being entertained.

Soon after they began the business Jon had advised that they offer their special blends on a website to add to their income. They hired a very efficient widow to fill those orders from her home. The arrangement had worked out wonderfully and they shipped the unusual blends all over the USA to buyers eager to purchase exotic coffee blends from "Cherokee Country." They broke even on their investment at the end of their third year.

To celebrate Raine bought a small house on a tree-lined street in Chota. Making excuses that though she couldn't afford it, it was something she needed to do. But what they'd both needed more than a successful business was the companionship, the sense of something accomplished that was their own. Both were lonely, abandoned in one way or another.

And Jon, having done his part in helping them set up and manage their business, returned to what he did best. Running his company and the companies of others who weren't savvy enough to do so on their own. With Becca busy, he didn't ever have to come home if he didn't want to. Often he would stay for weeks at a time in their condo in Tulsa. And it had been a long time since he'd wanted to show up on Monkey Island. If she'd ever entertained the idea he might be having an affair, she pushed it aside to concentrate on RainTree and the children, who were growing so fast they didn't need her mothering them anymore. But she loved them.

Then Jeremiah died and the world spun to an end.

She wiped at the counter, yanking her thoughts away from bad memories to come back to where she was, what she was doing. Enough reminiscing. No thinking of Jeremiah. She'd promised herself.

Think instead of why you're here, in town, back in the action. Think of that bastard Lucas Pell and how to go about finding him.

The bell above the door tinkled and Becca looked up to see a tall lanky Indian blocking the opening. The local Cherokees had expressed a desire to be referred to as American Indians, rather than the white man's term of Native American, which they hated. This one was dressed casually in tight jeans and a black tee shirt, long hair pulled back in a ponytail. He certainly didn't look like the type to come near a coffee house. An impressive specimen, he could be a delivery man, could be here to repair something, but he carried nothing, no clipboard, no tools.

He closed the door behind him and scanned the room, which had begun to fill up for the late morning rush. His eyes lit on Becca and surprise colored his expression.

He made his way toward her. Then his eyes drifted beyond her to where Raine stood and he smiled.

"Well, hello," he said, obviously relieved.

What was going on here? Becca studied her friend, whose expression had brightened considerably with the arrival of the Cherokee.

He and Raine talked for a moment, then Raine guided him over to Becca. "Honey, this is Spinner, he's with the Department of Human Services over in Vinita. We met when I visited you at the hospital. He recognized you and wondered if you'd talk to him."

The room spun. Only one reason for this man to want to talk to her.

"If this has something to do with Lucas Pell, then I'm not interested," she said and stared at him.

"It would help if we could discuss this," he said in a voice she could imagine convinced people of almost anything.

"Help who? That little hellion who killed my son? Sorry, I'm not interested."

"Honey, it's okay." Raine took her arm, turned on Spinner. "You didn't tell me what you wanted. You'd better leave, now. You're upsetting her."

Becca backed off, took refuge behind the counter.

The man called Spinner turned his back to her, said to Raine, "Perhaps we could talk. I'll come back. Tomorrow?"

She jerked her hand from his, said too sharply, "No."

"I thought we—"

"No, we can't."

"Ma'am?" a shrill feminine voice behind her demanded.

"Yes?" Raine said, but didn't pull her gaze from Spinner's.

"May I have another latté?" the impatient woman said.

She turned to the customer. "Yes, of course." When she returned from refilling the woman's cup, Spinner had gone.

Curious, Becca studied her friend. Something was going on between those two, but Raine wasn't happy about it.

Eight

Lucas awoke from another restless, dream-spiked night in the lumpy bed, believing for a moment he was still at juvie. Till he got a good look at the grimy windows and the cruddy boatyard beyond.

Shit. Was he always gonna live this way? Spinner said it was up to him, but he'd long ago given up taking to heart what people told him. He sat up and thunked his feet onto a pile of discarded clothes from the day before. Gathering up shorts and jeans, he slipped into them, then headed for the bathroom poking both arms into the tee shirt. A few minutes later he came out rubbing a hand over his cropped hair. Yesterday's buzz cut made him feel light-headed.

Stomach rumbling, he pulled on a new pair of socks and the shoes Spinner had bought him, and walked the short distance to the garage, hurrying because mornings Hank brought in donuts and he was starving.

The previous night's trip to Rocky Cove had gotten him nowhere. Seemed the Kraft family had their own problems. Looked like they didn't even all live at the house.

Shit, if he had a house that nice, you think he'd kick up a fuss like those Kraft kids did? He'd just hunker in and take all he could get. Not even open his mouth to complain.

How the hell was he was going to approach them when they didn't all stay in one place? Maybe he'd have to be happy with the mama.

At Hank's garage, he hurried inside, grabbed a cup of coffee and two donuts, and wolfed them down gazing at the clock. He'd made it with a minute to spare. Couldn't say he wasn't keeping up his end of the bargain.

Hank was underneath a fifteen-year-old Chrysler, only his work boots showing. Lucas stood near his feet licking sticky frosting off his fingers.

"That you, Luke?"

"It's me."

"Well, your feet glued to the floor?"

"I don't reckon." He gazed around. What was he supposed to do?

"See that pickup in the next bay?"

Lucas leaned around the car and peered at an old red and white Ford that looked like it'd been driven through clay mud up to its windows. "Yeah."

"See what you can do about the muffler and tailpipe."

"Put on a new one?"

"Hell, no. John can't afford that. Patch 'em so the cops leave him alone."

Lucas scratched his head. "Patch 'em? Me?"

Hank rolled out from under the car and stared at him, one hand holding a greasy wrench. "You can do that, can't you?"

"You mean use baling wire and whatever?"

"Cut out the rust on the pipe, patch it. Hell, I don't know, use a damned Pepsi can. Whatever. Just get it tied up best you can. You can do that, can't you?"

"I guess."

"Hell." Hank slipped back under the Chrysler, still muttering. "Send me these worthless damned kids, expect me to pay 'em for standing around looking goofy."

Anger swelled in Lucas. He was supposed to be a gofer, supposed to help keep the place clean, not dick around with some blanket Indian's used-up truck.

The creeper shot out from under the Chrysler. "And put on them coveralls. I don't want Spinner in here giving me hell for letting you ruin your clothes."

"Yes, sir," Lucas said.

Goddamn, he wanted out of here. He wanted a shot of whiskey. He wanted to be someplace where no one could tell him what to do. No one could put him down. Where he could buy a six-pack and drink ever' damned one if he wanted to. Till he got past this business of saying he was sorry, he was stuck living in this town full of raggedy-ass Indians who, all they could do was watch them rich folks tool around in their fancy cars and live in their fancy houses and look down their noses at them. He was better than that, and he wasn't no Goddamn Indian either. He just had one watching over him, making him toe the line. Be damned if that'd stop him from doing what he desperately needed to.

Maybe it was a waste of his time trying to talk to them Krafts. He wormed into greasy coveralls. Maybe instead, he'd tell Spinner he wanted to take him up on his offer to get him situated in another town. Then he could just get on with what he was going to do.

"Whatever that is," he muttered, and scooted under the truck, scraping his back over the greasy concrete, seeing as Hank was using the only creeper in the whole damned place.

After leaving Raine, Spinner slumped in the Nova across the street from RainTree, arms crossed over the steering wheel. Needed to go by Hank's and see how Lucas was faring, but goddamn, that woman had thrown him a curve. And just as they were getting to the point of exploring each other's secret desires. He didn't like losing before he found out what winning might be like. It left him feeling like he'd anticipated a sunrise only to wake up to a cloudy morning. Hell, she could've given them a little more time before she bolted. He usually managed to keep from scaring a woman off, at least until they saw his tattoos.

Mind still wrapped around the mystifying woman, he reached for the key and cranked up the engine, but didn't put the car in gear.

Chota being a small town, she'd probably found out all about him. After all, he'd been here a few days. Word had a way of getting around. But he sure wished she'd given him a chance. Be damned if he'd apologize for who he was or what he'd done, but he could've softened the blow, if she'd only asked.

"Oh, what the hell," he muttered, shifting the stick and flooring the accelerator. Tires squealed and kicked up debris in his wake. She was too good for him anyway. You could see that by looking. But God almighty, she sure did give off an air of sexuality. He'd wanted her the minute he laid eyes on her. And she felt the same. He knew she did. So what the hell was going on? Probably just slumming. She had said he scared her, and who could blame her? Sliding the Nova to a stop outside Hank's, he shoved open the door, unfolded himself from the seat, and went inside. In the garage he helped himself to a cold Coke nested in ice in a box that was at least fifty years old, popped the tab, and drank half of it down.

A dull clanking sound came from under a muddy and ancient Ford pickup, and he walked over to it, the smell of old grease and tires thick in his nostrils.

"Hank, that you?" He leaned down to see a familiar pair of shoes. "Lucas, you under there? What you doing, boy?"

A loud clattering, followed by muttered curses, and the kid scooted out. "I can't do miracles. Lousy piece of shit," he said, got to his feet, and kicked the door. It made a screaking noise and sagged open.

"Well, I see you fixed that," Spinner said. "Guess old Hank gave you a promotion."

"Promotion? Promotion? I'd rather drink from a mud hole than work on something that's already used up. He told me to fix it 'cause it cain't be fixed." He hauled off and kicked the truck again, this time howling with pain and hopping about on one foot.

"And you're doing a mighty fine job of it, son. I can see that right away. Maybe if you'd kick the fender you could fix that dent."

Lucas hopped around, held his toe and grimaced. "I ain't your son. If I was, you'd probably beat the shit out of me. But I ain't, so leave me alone altogether. You and me can both be happy."

"You know, Lucas, half what you just said makes no sense at all."

"Well, what do you expect from a stupid, no account, ex-con, killer?"

"All right, boy. Simmer down. Let me buy you a Coke. Hank won't mind you take a break."

"Probably fire my ass, but that's okay. I'd just as soon he did. Yeah, I'll take that Coke. Yessir." Strutting away from the pickup, he went to the Coke box and lifted out a dripping can. "Now, I'm gonna sit me down on this here pile of tires and drink my Coke and wait for ole Hank to come in and fire me." He took a deep swig and sighed loudly.

Amusement mixing with compassion, Spinner finished his Coke and watched Lucas in silence, giving him a chance to cool off.

"Where is Hank?" he finally asked.

"Oh, he's out doing my job while I'm doing his. You know? He went to pick up some parts. I thought you said I'd be the gofer, but I don't think he trusts me to drive his truck."

"Oh, shit," Spinner said. "You need to get a driver's license."

Lucas eyed him suspiciously. "Why? So you can get it revoked before I even do anything?"

"You don't have a driver's license, do you?"

The Coke can became very interesting to Lucas, who finally muttered, "Reckon not. They took it away from me after, well, after the accident. But Hank wouldn't know that, would he?"

"Hell, yes. And so should I. I messed up. It never occurred to me."

"Some counselor you are." Lucas finished off his pop and tossed the can in a large trash receptacle in the corner.

"What are you doing Sunday?" Spinner asked.

"Why, you wanna get me another job so I gotta work seven days a week instead of five?"

"No. Thought you might like to go fishing with me."

"Fishing? Shit, I don't do no fishing. Besides, you don't got a boat."

"We can rent one. Go out on the lake, find a nice quiet cove, and drown some worms."

"Sounds like fun. Not." He angled a hard stare toward Spinner. "Can you make me go?"

"I guess I'm big enough to, but I'd rather you'd go because you want to have a good time. Have a desire to learn to enjoy living in this world."

"I don't know. If it means I got to fish, I might pick another world."

"You ever fished?"

"Why would I do that?"

"Tell you what. I'll pick us up a couple of poles and come get you early Sunday morning. We'll rent a boat and go for a spin. Hell, if you don't want to fish, at least you can get the stink blowed off you."

Lucas appeared to consider the notion, then his eyes brightened. "Can we go all around Monkey Island?"

"Sure, as long as we stay away from the private docks. What, curious about all those fancy digs?"

He stood, wiped his hands down the sides of his coveralls, angled a gaze over Spinner's shoulder. "Sure, whatever. Guess I'll go then. What time?"

Spinner left a few minutes later, slightly puzzled, but feeling better about his relationship with Lucas. Nothing like a day alone in a boat to earn some trust from the boy. But he wasn't kidding himself. It was going to take a lot more than a fishing trip to get this damaged young man to trust him. Getting beat on and worse most of his life by adults who were supposed to care for him hadn't exactly produced a normal boy, and he prayed it wasn't too late to pull Lucas back from the precipice. His kind of life too often created killing machines.

Outside, someone leaned on a horn, blasting through the quiet. Lucas grumbled, stuffed the pillow over his head, and tried to go back to sleep. Now someone was beating down his door and shouting.

"What the hell?" He sat up and stared around the dark room. "Shit, it's the middle of the night. Who is that? Shut the fuck up out there."

"Lucas, wake up. Time to go."

He couldn't rightly tell whose voice that was, but it had to be that damned Cherokee.

Hadn't slept good in a week, and first time he got some z's along come…. "Who is that? I've got a gun, you'd better go away." By this time he was wide awake, and the hammering hadn't stopped. "I'm warning you, you don't quit that I'm gonna shoot you."

"Lucas, you don't have a gun. Open the damned door before someone else shoots me."

Exactly who he thought was standing out there beating down his door. Spinner. That goddamned Indian. Only way to shut him up was to open the door, so he swung his feet to the floor and padded across the room.

"What the hell you doing here? It's the middle of the night."

"No, it's early morning and the fish're hungry. I've got a boat ready and we have to hurry so we can be there when the sun comes up and feed the little buggers."

"Why?" Lucas rubbed a hand over his face and through his hair. "Don't fish sleep like normal people?"

"Well, they like to eat early, and we want to be the ones feeding them."

"If I did have me a gun I'd shoot you right here."

"Get dressed and quit talking like a tough guy. Could get you in trouble."

"I ain't going nowhere in the dark of night. Man, you crazy as a maggot in hot ashes."

Spinner picked up the boy's discarded jeans and tossed them at him, then dug around till he found a shirt. "You going dressed or naked, your choice."

Grumbling some more, Lucas put on his clothes, flopped down on the bed, and lay back with an arm over his eyes.

"Shoes, socks," Spinner prompted.

"Oh, crap," Lucas groaned. "Just put me in jail and be done with it. I can't take this rehabilitation shit."

"Put your shoes on."

Doing as he was told, Lucas finished tying his shoes and followed Spinner out to the Nova. Might as well get this done and over with. The man would not leave him be. Until that moment he'd forgotten why he'd agreed to this trip in the first place, but as he climbed into the car, he remembered. Hoped he would know the Kraft place from the lake side of the island. The house was something fancy, and he had seen it in the daylight, so he hoped he could. The idea of going in from their private dock hadn't occurred to him.

'Course, Spinner wouldn't allow that today, but Lucas figured he could go back. Rent a boat hisself and go see the woman. The mama. Tell her he was sorry for what he'd done and get it over and done with. Surely she wouldn't be too pissed. If he'd been killed when he was a kid, the only thing that would've made his mama sad was losing the money he brought in. She would've had a party to celebrate being rid of the little rat-turd, her favorite name for her only child. An unwanted brat who had to make up for existing some way.

"You're suddenly awfully quiet," Spinner said, steering into a left turn at Lake Drive.

"That's 'cause I'm sleeping," Lucas muttered.

"I got us some worms."

"Oh, good."

"And some Cokes and sandwiches."

"Go good together, huh."

"The fella that rents the boats had fishing gear too."

"Oh, hey. We're all set. Gonna go out and murder us some innocent little fishies."

Spinner quit trying, and neither said anything while he drove down to the town docks, parked and opened the trunk to fetch everything.

"Give me a hand here," he said, and Lucas did so without comment.

The sky to the east glowed like polished silver, painting a gleaming path across the water. Lucas eyed the small aluminum boat and its smaller motor, then looked out across the huge expanse of water.

"Who told you that was a boat? Man, you been screwed." He watched

Spinner step into the craft, saw how it rocked when he loaded their stuff off the dock, and moved to the back. "I ain't getting in that thing."

"Don't be a baby. Just step in and sit there, in the middle."

"In the middle?" He set one foot down into the bottom, and the boat drifted away from the dock, leaving him splayed out, one foot on each.

Spinner laughed. "Get on in, don't stand there like a turkey wishbone."

Squenching up his mouth, Lucas threw himself forward, landed with a thud on both knees in the bottom. The boat rocked violently. Still laughing, Spinner untied the line holding them to the dock, dropped the motor down and pulled its cord, while Lucas scrambled to get himself onto the seat.

"You said we could go around Monkey Island," Lucas reminded him, hanging on until his knuckles whitened.

"We will. There's some coves around there'll be good for fishing."

The water's surface lay still in the windless morning, but with the sunrise the damned Oklahoma wind would start blowing. Bad enough being out there on a calm day with nothing solid under him, but he never had learned to swim, and if they turned over he couldn't imagine the Cherokee wasting time saving his bony white ass.

"Beautiful, isn't it?" Spinner asked.

"I guess."

"Turn loose, boy. Enjoy yourself."

"Why?"

"Why? I reckon because it makes you feel good."

"Don't need to feel good."

"Everyone needs to feel good."

"Not me."

Spinner swung the boat into a long arc, following the shoreline of the island. "There's some beautiful homes along here. Sort of makes you wonder what sort of people live like that, don't it?"

"I know what sort." Lucas studied the houses hanging out over the water. Each had a dock, some with boats tied up, others with those garage kind of things out over the water that probably held yachts and stuff. He tried to place where the houses were in relation to the roads he'd followed. He'd begun to think he wouldn't know the Kraft place from all those others when they rounded a spit of land and he saw it. Just as he'd remembered. A pale blue house with dark blue trim around towering windows on the first and second floors. A deck hung over the water and steps led down to the dock and a boathouse.

He watched it slide out of sight when Spinner steered into a cove and cut the engine. Though they glided into a sheltered darkness, streaks of yellow and pink and gold flared along the horizon. The sun would be up soon.

"Look," Spinner said in a hushed tone.

Where he pointed, trees hung out over the water and a long-necked white bird stood in the shadows, still as a statue. Suddenly he darted his head beneath the surface and came up with a fish in his mouth. Lucas found himself staring in awe, a knot in his throat. What was that all about?

Embarrassed for Spinner to see his reaction, he turned away.

They baited up and fished in silence, getting nibbles from minnows until they tired of feeding them. After a while, they moved on around the island and Spinner finally caught a couple of bass, which he threw back in. Lucas didn't care whether he caught anything or not, and would sit for a long while after knowing that something had chewed off all his worms, gleaning an unexpected satisfaction from feeding the fish. Besides he plain didn't get a kick out of sliding those slimy worms onto a hook. First you killed the worms so you could kill the poor fish. What kind of sense did that make?

"Let's eat those sandwiches," Spinner finally said, much to Lucas's relief. His belly had been rumbling for a while, but he'd be damned if he'd say anything.

After they finished, Spinner started the motor. "Might as well go back. Fish ain't going to bite till evening. Sorry you didn't catch anything."

"Don't matter," Lucas said, watching the coastline for sight of the Kraft house.

The wind had kicked up considerably, and the boat rose and fell, slapping the water in loud smacks. Lucas's belly heaved, threatened to hurl his lunch. The hum of the motor sputtered once, twice, then stopped, plunging them into silence.

"What's wrong? What happened? We going to sink?" Lucas gripped the sides of the boat buffeted by the wind. Blamed thing was doing its best to toss him in the water.

"Take it easy." Spinner cranked at the motor a few times with no luck, then pulled a couple of oars from the bottom. "We got these." He poked one at Lucas.

"What do you want me to do with that? Maybe club some poor innocent fish to death?"

"Row, like this." Spinner chuckled, dipped an oar into the water, and pulled. The boat moved forward in a curve.

"Uh-huh." Lucas dipped his in the water and pulled awkwardly. The boat went back the opposite direction.

"Turn around, put it in on the other side and start rowing. We'll make for that dock yonder. See if we can get some help. It's a long way back to the dock at Chota, rowing against the wind."

Lucas started to protest, then saw Spinner was talking about the Krafts' dock. Couldn't be better if he'd planned it. He wasn't used to things going his way, and wondered why they were this time. Maybe Spinner knew.

One glance over his shoulder at the Indian told him that couldn't be. No sense in questioning, just row, fool, he told himself, and dipped the oar deep.

After eating breakfast out on the deck, Becca sat for a while, eyeing the lake and boats moving about. A few skiers braved the cold water. Other larger cruisers carried people with places to go. Families spending their Sunday together. An urge hit her to go on board *Dream Kraft*, maybe clean her up a bit. No one had used her for a long time. She supposed Jon had seen to her maintenance over the long months since that last summer they had spent as a family together. Christi loved the boat, as did Jeremiah, and both could pilot her, so they were out on it a lot that summer before everything flew apart. Most times without Jon, but once in a while he'd come out for the weekend.

Hurrying inside, she went upstairs to change clothes and came back down feeling odd in an old pair of gray sweats and white sneakers. Everything she did lately felt odd, almost as if she had awakened to a different life. That wasn't the case, though. She'd simply retreated to another world and then returned to her own. On a trial basis, and only to accomplish one thing. Once that was done, where would she go? The answer to that frightened her.

A gust of wind caught at her hair and twisted a few locks loose from the clasp at the nape of her neck.

Jon used to tug strands of her hair loose and arrange them around her face before kissing her. "There, makes that beautiful face all the prettier, like it's framed," he'd say, running his tongue over her lips, smacking and growling and burying his face in her neck.

She shuddered and rubbed at her throat. Goose bumps rippled over her flesh. In his day Jon had been a magnificent lover. Eager, gentle, inventive, and thoughtful. Hand on the railing, she started down the steps and tried to forget what she could never have again. Her husband. Her son. Her family.

The dock heaved under her feet and she spread them apart, remembering what it was like to be aboard the boat and how, when they came home from a day or two on the lake, the firm ground heaved underfoot until she could scarcely walk straight. And the kids would stagger around hooting and hollering and falling into the grass all the way to the house.

Something like drugs made her feel now. She stopped and stared out across the lake. Funny, she couldn't remember taking any pills the past few days. Maybe she hadn't.

A tear escaped the corner of her eye and she swiped at it angrily.

"Yo," someone shouted from out on the water.

She shielded her eyes against the morning sun and saw two men approaching in a small jon boat. With the glare of the sun, she couldn't make out their faces, but waved anyway, then went to tie up the line they tossed to her.

"Can I help you?"

The one in the back rose. She'd seen him somewhere before, but where? Then the younger one came scrabbling out of the boat on hands and knees, crawling onto the dock with the awkwardness of someone who'd never been on the water before. And when he stood up and looked her straight in the eye, she felt as if she'd been shot.

Hands clenched over her mouth, she retreated a few steps. "Oh, God. Oh, God." That face.

The Indian hopped onto the dock, glanced from her to the boy, and then back again.

"What? What's wrong? We broke down. Don't be afraid. I just need to maybe borrow some tools to see if I can fix that motor, that's all."

He stared at her, eyes going wide in recognition. He held out a hand. "Mrs. Kraft, it's okay. Hell, I'm sorry, I didn't realize "

Stricken, Becca pointed a shaking finger at the boy. "Lucas Pell. You're Lucas Pell. You murdered my son."

The sound of her screech rent the air like a sword slashing flesh.

Nine

Lucas staggered backward on the dock and stared at the woman, whose face had gone wild and ugly. Coupled with the unearthly shout, her pointing finger scared the bejesus out of him. His mother used to do that just before she hauled off and hit him with whatever was convenient. Scream in his face and point that finger, then bam or whop or slug him with anything from a beer bottle to the iron. Whatever was handy.

The recollection sent him scrambling, one arm over his face. He bumped into Spinner, who took a firm hold on him.

"Easy, Lucas. Take it easy."

His breath came in frantic gasps. What had he been thinking? He should've jumped off the boat when he saw where they were headed. Drowned himself. Who could tell someone they were sorry when that someone went nuts?

"Get that killer out of here." The crazy bitch screamed and her features grew even uglier. Monster scary ugly. He was afraid she might spit fire and burn him up.

"Ma'am," Spinner said softly, not easing his grip on Lucas's arm one little bit.

Probably a good thing, too. If he had've turned him loose, Lucas might've jumped into the lake and been done with it.

And then Spinner started talking in that soft way of his that almost sounded like singing. "Ma'am. I'm sorry you're upset. Believe me, this was an accident, our coming here. I didn't even realize you lived out here. I'm Spinner Grayfeather. We met at RainTree. I work for DHS. Believe me—"

"Then you know what that little monster did. Get him out of here before I call the police and have you both jailed for trespassing. This is a private dock. You can't just come here like this. You can't." She began to sputter and fly apart.

Horrified, Lucas could not speak, feared his breathing would stop. Right there. He wasn't the monster, she was, with spit coming from her mouth, her hands like claws and her hair standing out in the wind.

"Do you know what he did?" she screamed, and lunged as if to tear his eyes out, or worse.

"Lucas, get back in the boat. Now," Spinner said. "And stay there."

Backpedaling, Lucas didn't take his eyes off her until he made a flying leap into the bobbing, swaying boat. Draped over the center seat, his heart pounded so hard he could hardly breathe and tiny pinpoints of light darted around in the darkness of his vision. Still she screamed and screamed and screamed. Plenty of people he'd been around all his life were mean. They did terrible things without much emotion. Like his mama and that fool she married. But he'd never experienced such intense hate. This was the woman he'd hoped would forgive him. There wasn't much chance of that. Spinner tried to reason with her but it was no go. She'd go after him next.

"Get out, get out, and take that little killer with you," she yelled. "You're just lucky I don't have a gun."

Behind him, Spinner heard Lucas sobbing. Finally exhausted, the woman staggered backward to the steps and sat down hard, legs splayed and head drooped between them. Her long blonde hair had come loose and hung on either side of her face.

The way she collapsed, Spinner figured he might have to carry her up those steps to her house. Nope. Better not even think of that. She wouldn't let him near her. To prove it, she raised her head and opened her mouth to let out another shriek. He hated like hell to leave her in this condition, but saw no other choice. It was clear when someone was completely out of control and could not be reasoned with. Trying to do so could do more harm than good. Best thing to do was remove the object of her hatred.

He had no idea whether she lived out here alone or with someone, but he recalled that Raine had said they were good friends. Odd he hadn't put this one together with the family of the dead boy, Jeremiah Kraft. Screwed up again, Spinner. He ought to be fixing cars off somewhere in the desert, where he wouldn't do any harm instead of pretending to be someone he wasn't. Hell, truth be told, he carried the same stigma the boy did.

As soon as he took Lucas back—and he saw no choice but to row all the way—he'd call Raine and explain what had happened. Perhaps she'd want to check on her friend and make sure she was okay.

Untying the line, he jumped in the boat and made his way past Lucas, who had managed to crawl onto the seat where he slumped, head in hands. One more try with the motor before giving up. He knelt on the stern seat and yanked on the starter rope. The damned motor coughed, caught, and came to life.

"Son of a bitch." Spinner silently thanked the spirits. You'd almost think this was supposed to happen, but he didn't believe in that shit. He did believe these goddamned two-cycle motors were stubborn, cantankerous, and impossible to predict.

Reversing away from the dock, he steered for Chota. If the damned thing quit again, he'd sink the damned boat and swim back dragging Lucas by his shirt tail.

The sun, high overhead, beat down relentlessly until his sweat-dampened clothes stuck to him. Summer was coming fast. You could feel it in the wind that, at midday, did not cool things off. Spinner liked it though, the hot weather. He liked sweating and working in the sun and taking long showers at the end of a hard day with his muscles all aching and his gut craving food and a cold beer, and his groin going all crawly for a woman. So what the hell was he doing in this job, anyway? He ought to be in the oil fields or building a bridge. Hell, even digging ditches. At least then he wouldn't hold these fragile kids' future in his hands.

The boy kept his face turned away from Spinner, as if ashamed he had broken down. Boys like this. That was what the hell he was doing in this job. Boys who, without guidance and a lot of tender loving care, were lost. Irrevocably lost.

He lay a hand on Lucas's back, and sensed beneath the sweat-soaked shirt and trembling flesh a dreadful despair. A hopelessness that the boy kept hidden under a layer of toughness, until someone knocked a chink in that armor. Rebecca Kraft had done just that.

Lucas jerked away from his touch, still refused to look at him. After a while, he said with false bravado, "Boy, that old bitch sure did fly off the handle, didn't she? I thought I was gonna have to hit her upside the head."

Spinner kept his counsel. Anything he said would only make matters worse. Later, they'd talk about what had happened and why. And try to reason out these urges Lucas had to hit people. It was only natural, considering his past, but dammit, Spinner didn't want the kid to wind up like his abusive old man, who was finally knifed in prison, or like his mother, a drunken whore who was murdered by a man she lived with. When she was found, Lucas was lying beside her covered in blood. Spinner always suspected the twelve-year-old kid was trying to protect her in some misguided way, in spite of the hell she'd put him through. That had touched Spinner in a way he hadn't thought possible, and he had to make something happen to prevent the boy heading down the same road as his parents.

It was hard, feeling such a responsibility for these kids. He wondered how Gano Burke had dealt with such guilt trips and self-doubt. Too bad he didn't get to ask him. But in those days, Spinner was Burke's Lucas Pell, and he wouldn't have thought to ask such a question, being hell-bent on his own destruction, as well as that of anybody else who came too close.

They made it back to Chota without further incidents, and he drove Lucas to his room, again eyeing the dilapidated building with distaste. What a dump, and only a step up from living in the street. It was all he could find for what money was available, but he hated the kid living in a place like this. It did little for his self-esteem.

Without speaking, Lucas heaved on the Nova's door handle, but it stuck. "Why don't you get a good car?" he asked.

Spinner reached across and hit the side panel with the palm of his hand. "Now try it. And there's nothing wrong with this car."

"Not if you jacked it up and drove another'n under it."

Spinner put a hand on Lucas's shoulder before he could climb out. "Don't take what she said to heart. She's grieving the loss of her boy."

"Uh-huh."

"She loved him, Lucas. It's hard to lose someone you love."

The boy's head whirled, his eyes flashed on Spinner. "You don't gotta tell me that. You think I ain't never lost anyone I loved?"

A lump formed in Spinner's throat. "Sorry, no. 'Course, I know you have. I'm just saying, don't let it get you down."

"Ain't no down to get to, man. I'm there already."

"Feeling sorry for yourself's not the way to go, and you know that."

"I ain't feeling sorry, I just know the truth. Why do you care, anyway? You do what you're paid to do, that's all."

Because Lucas remained in the seat instead of jumping out of the car, Spinner felt a ray of hope that he might be getting through to the kid. He squeezed his shoulder.

"I do care, Lucas. And not 'cause I'm paid to. That's too simple."

"Yeah, well, you let me know when you can do something besides getting me a nowhere job and a crappy room."

The anger was back in place, a shield against the caring Spinner offered. "You'll have to do that for yourself. Just remember, I'm here when you need me."

Lucas crawled out of the car and shuffled to the door painted with graffiti. He didn't say goodbye or look back. Spinner gunned the Nova's engine and drove off.

Long after the sound of the boat motor faded, Rebecca remained slumped on the steps above the dock, trembling with fury and unable to move. How dare those men come here? That dirty little piece of crap and his overseer, thinking they could—trying to…. It escaped her why they'd come. If the boy wanted her forgiveness, he could forget it. If she'd had a gun she'd have shot him, right there. And who would've blamed her?

"Mom?"

The disembodied voice broke into her thoughts and she started, raised her head, listened.

"Mom, you okay?"

Feet plodded down the steps, a hand touched her back. "What is it? What's wrong? Did you fall?"

"Jeremiah?"

The hand pulled away, then dropped back and patted her. "No. It's David. I came looking for you and saw you down here. I was afraid you'd fallen. What's going on?"

Ever since that awful argument last Sunday, she hadn't seen much of her son. Each day RainTree had kept her blessedly occupied. He'd come and gone quietly, remaining in his room when he was home, and she'd almost forgotten he was on the place.

Sighing, she rose and shoved her hair back from her face. "I just had a visit from that dreadful Lucas Pell person. Would you believe he and his counselor, that big Cherokee who, by the way, is also making eyes at Raine, came right up to our dock? Pretended their motor was broken or something. I don't know what they wanted."

A sob rose from her throat and she covered her mouth. "I sent them packing. Told them not to come back." The words muffled, stuttered.

David put an arm around her shoulders. "It's okay, Mom. Let's go back to the house. You need to lie down."

"It is not okay, David. It never will be okay."

"I know, Mom. I know." A familiar resignation colored his tone.

He held an arm around her shoulders until they reached the top of the wooden steps, then walked with her across the lawn to the house, neither of them saying anything.

But she could sense his withdrawal. No one in her family wanted to be around her, and she couldn't say she blamed them. But couldn't they see what they were doing? Going on with their lives as if Jeremiah had never existed?

Couldn't they see they were negating the value of his life?

Once inside, David went to the fridge. "I'm hungry. Want to have some lunch? I'm buying." He turned and grinned, dimples popping into his cheeks.

For an instant she saw him as a bright-eyed toddler, hair in dark ringlets around his perfect face. So long ago. So long. Her heart gave a sigh. How did it all get away so fast?

Crossing the kitchen, she cupped his cheek. "Ah, David. It's so good to have you home. I'm so sorry about all this." She shrugged and tried out a smile. "I'd love to join you for lunch. What are we having?"

"I thought grilled salmon with lemon sauce. Crackers and caviar. Or maybe you'd settle for ham and cheese sandwiches and Cokes? Do we have any Doritos and salsa?"

He rummaged about in the fridge, bringing out cold cuts, lettuce, tomatoes, and a jar of dill pickles, all in one armload. Becca fetched a bag of Doritos from the cabinet and took two Cokes from the fridge.

"Mayo, mustard?" David asked formally after depositing the food on the breakfast table near the tall windows that looked out over the lake.

"Yes, please. Who bought all this stuff?"

He bowed formally. "The larder was a bit bare. There's some rye bread too, if you'd like."

Touched, she nodded.

By the time they had the table ready, she had stopped shaking. They sat across from each other where both could look out the windows.

"Have you talked to Christi?" she asked.

David slathered mustard on a slice of bread and layered thin slices of ham on top. Without looking up from building his sandwich, he said, "I went to see her Thursday before she left."

Becca swallowed hard. "She left already?"

He glanced up, surprise on his features. "She promised she'd call you."

Fiddling with a slice of cheddar cheese, Becca stared out across the lake. "Well, she didn't."

David eyed a smear of mustard on his finger, then licked it off and piled cheese on top of the ham. "I think she was pretty busy. You know. Packing and all."

"Yes, I'm sure that's it." Becca took a bite of the cheese and gazed at the two slices of bread she'd laid on her plate. "She'll enjoy Australia. I'm sure." She cleared her throat, tried not to cry.

She'd made such a mess out of everything, and now she didn't know how to get back to where she'd started. Truly, there was no getting back, because Jeremiah's death had left a gap that couldn't be spanned. And it wasn't her fault so much as that of Lucas Pell. She needed to tell the slimy little bastard that. Make him understand what he'd done to her. To her family.

"David?"

He mashed a slice of bread down hard on top of his sandwich and took a bite. "Hmmm?" he asked, chewing and watching her.

"I'd like… I mean, what would you think about taking me to see that boy, that Lucas Pell?"

"Mom, please don't do this."

"I only want to explain to him what he did to us. He thinks it was nothing, what he did. That he can just walk away from all this without punishment, and that isn't right."

David swallowed, studied her. "No, Mom. It isn't right. Nothing about this is right. Let it go, now. It's time you let it go. Jeremiah is dead and that's terrible. It broke our hearts to lose him, but we can't let it ruin our lives."

"But it has," she cried, standing so abruptly she knocked over her Coke. "It has ruined our lives, and I think his killer should know that."

David rescued the can and laid a wad of napkins in the puddle before it could flow onto the floor. "And then what, Mom?"

She cocked her head. "I don't understand."

"If I go with you. Take you to tell this boy that he ruined our lives, then what? Will you stop this—this insanity? You're wrecking our lives."

His accusation hit her like a slap across the mouth. How could he think for one minute she was responsible for causing destruction when it was that evil boy's fault? But she couldn't say that to this son, because he had stricken her mute.

Speechless, she hunched forward and leaned both elbows on the table. "I will go see him on my own. I will tell him what he has done to us, force him to see how he destroyed our lives. Then, David, I will come home and be the good mother you think I should be. I will never mention your brother's name in this house again. Will that satisfy all of you? Your father included?"

David slammed the remainder of his sandwich down on the table. "I have no idea what will satisfy Dad or you, for that matter. And I'm not going to hang around to find out. Never a day goes by when we're together that we don't have this same argument. This fight over who has been hurt the most by Jeremiah's death. It's like a goddamned contest. Well, you win, Mother. You win. You were hurt more than any of the rest of us. You do what you want. I'm out of here."

Dear God. She was on the verge of losing this son now, too. How much she loved him. She didn't want him to go, wanted to grab his arm, haul him back. Apologize for hurting him, for chasing him away.

Instead, she stood in horrified silence, watched him storm from the room, listened to his feet pounding on the stairs and the slam of his door, a sharp crack like the breaking of her heart.

Christi was gone, David leaving, and Jon showing no inclination to be with her. All had abandoned her, and she was left to finish this alone. Exactly what she would do. She would not crawl back in a bottle or shake open another vial of pills. She would go find Lucas Pell and put an end to this suffering, once and for all.

That Indian friend of Raine's knew where that little killer was and he was going to tell her.

Because he was worried about Rebecca Kraft, Spinner couldn't wait till Monday to talk to Raine at the coffee shop. He called her at home as soon as he left Lucas, all the while wondering if he wasn't simply using this as an excuse to talk to her again.

Well, so what if he was? The phone kept ringing. She picked up just as he was about to decide she wasn't home.

"It's Spinner," he said.

"Oh, is it?"

The tone not half bad. Almost as if she was glad to hear from him.

"Tell you why I called."

"Okay."

Still cold. He went on. "Something happened this morning. Something with your friend, Rebecca, and I thought maybe someone ought to check on her."

"What in the world are you talking about? Is she all right? Where did you see her?"

"It's a long story, but—"

"I've got time."

"Maybe I could come over. Tell you in person."

A long pause, and he held his breath.

"I don't think that's such a good idea. Tell me about Becca."

He did then, leaving out as much as he thought she didn't need to know. He really wasn't sure how much she knew about Lucas's involvement in the Kraft boy's death.

"And when we left, she looked wiped out. I tried to help her, but she was having none of it. I swear, Raine, we didn't go there on purpose. It just happened. All I wanted was to take the kid fishing. Neither of us realized it was the Krafts' place. The damn motor quit and—"

"Heck of a coincidence, though. You have to admit that." The friendly voice iced around the edges.

Before he could object, she went on. "Okay, Spinner, I'm not sure I buy that it was a coincidence, but I do know Becca and how she's been since Jeremiah was killed. If she ever recovers I'll be surprised. I'll give her a call, or maybe just run out and see her. I wasn't doing anything but reading anyway."

"Raine?" he said quickly, before she could hang up.

She didn't answer, but didn't disconnect either.

"I miss you."

"Get used to it."

Damn, this one was tough. "Yeah, but I had all these plans, you know? I miss doing the stuff with you I had all figured out in my head. That's all I'm saying."

"You know, Spinner, I'm not so sure it's in your head you miss me. And I know all about your ideas for what we might do."

"What makes you think so?"

"What I think is I'm not interested, so you might as well put your, uh, thoughts away."

"Okay, but you don't know what you're missing. See you around, pretty lady." He hung up before he did indeed wade into the quagmire.

Clearly Raine wasn't about to let him get to know her, and he was truly sorry about that. On thinking about it, though, it was probably for the best. He sensed the beautiful woman could break his heart, given the chance. And he knew beyond a shadow of a doubt he'd break hers.

Ten

Raine circled through the driveway at Becca's behind a taxi carrying a passenger. She tried to see who was inside, but couldn't. Becca wouldn't take a cab, so it had to be a visitor leaving. She climbed out of her car and went to the door, sandals crunching on the stone pathway. The distant hum of a boat out on the lake barely disturbed the quiet of the Sunday afternoon.

Noisy activity probably wasn't allowed with all the restrictions of the gated community. No lawn mowing, no dog barking, no music drifting in the wind that danced through the manicured yards, no laughter of children at play.

"I'd never get used to this," Raine muttered, thinking of her house, deliberately chosen for the neighborhood that included children and pets, because she enjoyed the sounds of life being lived to the fullest. Her cat Charlie appreciated it too, and spent hours curled in the second-floor bay window gazing down on the yards filled with joyful children. The dead silence of Becca's neighborhood would drive both her and Charlie batty.

She thumbed the doorbell several times and waited. Twin hanging baskets of pink, white, and red rose geraniums exuded a musky aroma into the warm afternoon air. Those were new, and a good sign. Ever since Jeremiah's death, Becca had let all her carefully tended plants dry up and die. It was good to see her getting back to normal.

Just as she touched the button again, the door swung open and her friend peered out. Eyes swollen, hair looking as if she'd been caught in a whirlwind, she didn't look much like she'd left the old, grieving woman behind.

"Oh, thank Heavens you came," she cried and threw her arms around Raine. "I tried calling, but the machine picked up."

"What happened? Come on, let's go inside and sit down. You look like you're about to collapse."

Seated next to her on a living room couch, Becca allowed the happenings of the entire sordid afternoon to pour forth, some words indistinguishable when she couldn't help but sob.

"And then David got angry with me and he stormed out. I don't think I can take much more of this."

"Stay there, honey," Raine said, patting her friend's shoulder and rising. "I'll get you something to drink and a washcloth so you can clean up."

Becca drew a deep breath. "I don't want a drink. I mean, I do desperately want a drink, but water will be fine. Thank you so much."

Well, that was a good sign, anyway. Raine hurried to the kitchen for a bottle of water and stopped in the small bath to wet a washcloth.

She watched her friend scrub at her face like she might be trying to remove all her features.

"I know I look a mess." At last Becca put the cloth aside, opened the bottle of water, and took a long swallow. "I'm so damned mad I could spit nails. Mostly at myself. I swore I wouldn't break down like this anymore, but it was all too much. That damned Indian." She smiled wryly. "Imagine him bringing that little son of a bitch out here and sneaking up on me like that. I should've had them both thrown in jail."

No sense saying anything. Raine simply waited for the tirade to end.

"And then for David to take their side."

"He took their side? Surely not."

Becca wiped her nose with the cloth. "I suppose not really, he just told me that he couldn't take what I was doing to myself and the family any longer. He just left, I'm surprised you didn't run into him."

"I saw the cab as—"

"Can you imagine, blaming me for grieving over Jeremiah's death. I can't understand him, or Jon or Christi. What's wrong with them? Or is it me? Am I crazy?"

Raine again patted her shoulder. "No, of course not. You're a mother who's lost her son. You have a right to grieve." She couldn't bear to tell her friend to shape up, get on with it. Never having had children, she couldn't possibly know what Becca was going through, but she did know how devastated she'd been when the man she loved turned on her. Killed the tiny being they'd made together before it had a chance at life. The pain dug much deeper than her physical scars, and it had taken her a long time to recover. In truth, if it weren't for Becca she wouldn't have done so. So how could she do any less than support this devastated woman who had done so much for her?

Still, sixteen months now since the accident. It seemed she should be adjusting to spending the remainder of her life without Jeremiah. If she wasn't careful, she'd live it without any of her family.

Becca sat up straight and cleared her throat. "So, I've made a decision, and I need you to help me."

"What is it? Of course I'll help you."

"I want you to take me to see that counselor, that Spinner fellow, make him tell me where this Lucas Pell is so I can confront him."

"Oh, honey, I'm not sure that's such a good idea."

"Maybe not, but I intend to do it. Will you help me or not?"

Raine studied her friend, the determination in the set of her jaw, the harsh expression in her eyes. Perhaps she ought to take her to Spinner. She remembered thinking earlier that he might be able to help her since he was a counselor, but had never seriously entertained the idea past that random thought. He was, after all, a children's advocate or the like. Probably didn't care to deal with loopy adults.

"Well?" Becca demanded.

"Okay, I'll take you to see Spinner. I don't know about the rest. I don't think I could look at that monster without tearing his eyes out myself. Why don't we let Spinner decide, okay?"

"Spinner is a strange name. He's Cherokee, isn't he?"

"Yes."

"Is Lucas… is that boy Cherokee?"

"I don't think so. This isn't a cultural thing."

"What isn't? Murdering someone?"

"Honey, you know he didn't murder Jeremiah. The courts said so."

"He made a choice to drink and drive. He had to know how dangerous that was. Of course, he murdered my son. What do the courts know, anyway, but the letter of the law? There's more to morality and the way we live than following the law, you know. Some things go beyond blind justice and the so-called law."

Raine only nodded. She couldn't bring herself to argue with Becca on this particular subject. "So, when do you want to see Spinner?"

"Now, today. Do you know where he is?"

"No. But perhaps I can find out."

"Well, call him, or whatever it is you can do. I'll fix my hair and face and we'll go. I want to get this over with. I know I'll feel much better."

Raine wasn't so sure she would, but couldn't deny Becca this if it would set her life to rights.

The Wig Wam Motel where Spinner was staying wasn't in Chota itself, but up where Highway 85A cut west to Bernice. Not a Super 8 or Motel 6, and certainly not an Embassy Suites, the twelve-unit motel, a survivor of the fifties, which was run by the third generation of a family who had built it, and remained true to the style of days long past.

Raine parked next to Spinner's Nova, the only vehicle there on a late Sunday afternoon, and turned off the ignition. All the way over, she'd hoped he wouldn't be home, but there sat his car and she was stuck. His call earlier today had set off her silent alarms, and she wasn't anxious to be around him so soon. He was a dangerous man, and she was dangerous when around him. When it came to men like him, all her senses went off kilter, ignoring the warnings that rippled through her.

"What a dreadful place," Becca said.

"It has its charms. It's just old and outdated."

"Hmmm, I suppose. We lived in a Volkswagen bus when I was a kid, but we drove past places like this, and me, just a kid, begging to stop and stay. Enjoy the shower and soft beds. Motor Courts they called them then."

Becca had shared some of her childhood memories with Raine. That she'd been a child of flower children or hippies, or whatever they were called in those days. That she grew up on the move with little if any schooling. That she remedied that herself when she ran away, worked two jobs, studied in night school for her GED, then went on to work her way through Oklahoma State University where she met Jonathan. The two of them built his business from the ground up while she worked as an executive secretary until they could get on their feet.

She and Jonathan had achieved their dreams of a successful business and yet they had nothing else, their life empty and unhappy. How sad.

Raine wished she could conjure up a genie and make things right for Becca once again. Instead, she had to do all she could. Yet this could go wrong in so many ways.

"Well," she said, coming out of her reverie. "Looks like he's home. You're sure this is what you want to do?"

Becca nodded, eyes large with trepidation.

"Okay. Let's go in."

Becca grabbed her arm. "Raine?"

"What?"

"Thank you very much. No matter how this turns out, you're doing the right thing helping me. I can't not do this. Do you understand?"

Though she really didn't, Raine nodded. "Come on. He's really a nice guy. I'm sure he can help you."

"The only way he can help me is to take me to see Lucas Pell." She spat the name as if it were filth caught in her mouth.

Raine didn't say any more. What was there to say? She might set her heels, kick and scream that she couldn't go in there with him. In that small room that was nothing but a bedroom with only this half-crazed friend as a buffer between them. But she didn't. Composing herself, she took Becca by the arm and waited beside her at the door for their knock to be answered.

Spinner had been sleeping, the book he was reading open on his bare chest. It took him a moment to realize the tapping wasn't in a dream. Barefooted and shirtless, tatoos bared, he went to the door.

"Who is it?" he said through the panel.

"It's me, Raine."

"Oh, shit," he muttered and looked around for his shirt. It was piled outside the bathroom door where he'd left it when he showered earlier. At least he was wearing clean jeans. He snatched up the shirt he'd worn fishing and dropped it over his head.

"Spinner? This is important."

"Coming, coming. Hang on a minute." Fingering his long hair back away from his face, he swung open the door and finished rolling the shirt down in time to hide the snake coiled on his chest. His insides lurched at the sight of her, standing there in the late afternoon sunlight, dark hair like a shiny cap above her pixie features.

She wore sky blue pants that belled around her ankles and a white blouse topped by a scarf splashed in blues and knotted at one shoulder. Her toes peeked from multi-colored sandals. He lifted his gaze from her feet to look into eyes that danced with green fire, and read the same sexual message he found every time he encountered her.

"Hello." She licked her lips and stared at him.

Gaze fastened on the movement of her tongue that darted back inside her mouth, he replied, then spotted the other woman, who might as well have been invisible up to this point. It took him a moment, but he recognized her. Her stoic presence startled him into silence, and everyone stood there as if suspended in a time warp.

"Spinner, this is Rebecca Kraft. I believe you've met. Could we come in?"

"Mrs. Kraft. Of course." He backed up, let them in the cluttered room. Clearing some books and files out of a chair, he offered it to Mrs. Kraft, then smoothed the bed and sat. "Sorry there's not another chair. Won't you join me on the bed?"

He smiled his best smile at Raine and watched her face flare crimson. But she gathered her resources quickly and sat primly on the edge of the mattress leaving a wide space between them.

If the other woman hadn't been there, he would've known what to do next. He'd rehearsed it often enough. But in this situation, he simply waited for his visitors to lead him. He had no idea what this Kraft woman could possibly want other than to bash him on the head. He sure hoped she wouldn't have another screaming fit.

For a long while she did absolutely nothing but stare beyond him at the far wall. Then clasping her hands in her lap so tightly her knuckles whitened, she said, "Mr. Grayfeather."

"Spinner, please."

Nodding, she gulped and began again stuttering her way through the words. "Spinner. I, you know that boy, that, uh, Lucas Pell? I want to, I wonder if you would take me to see him."

"Why?" Indeed, why. She been face to face with him earlier.

"Why? I want to see him, that's all."

"What about? You saw him this morning. Things didn't go real well."

She waved that off, as if it were of no consequence. "Because I was surprised, that's all. And, well, a bit frightened. You have to admit, you are, well, a bit frightening. And I was alone, and—"

Time to rescue her, so he interrupted. "Okay, I'll give you that, though I don't think of myself as frightening."

"Well, you should," she said sternly. "I mean, to women alone."

"Is that right?" He switched his gaze to Raine, as if asking her.

She smiled tremulously at him, nodded her head ever so slightly.

"Well, I admit I'm surprised by your request."

"Mr.—uh, Spinner. Are you going to take me to meet this Pell person or are we going to play games with each other?"

"I'm afraid I'd need to know why you want to meet him, considering your reaction this morning." He held up a hand. "I know you were scared, but beyond that, you accused the boy of murder. Don't you think that might've scared him just a little? You have to under—"

"What I understand is that he killed my son. I don't want to hear his sob story, I just want to confront him, let him know how he's destroyed my family. I do have that right, don't I? They do it in court all the time, and he needs to know what he did. Take responsibility."

"Oh, Mrs. Kraft, he knows what he did, all right. He has nightmares about it nearly every night."

"Good. He should. May they continue for the rest of his life."

Rocked by the heated rage, spoken like a curse, Spinner studied his toes a moment, tucked them under the bed. "How long do you think he should be made to suffer for an accident?"

"How long do you think my family will suffer for that so-called accident?"

Stress crackled her voice, but she kept control, and he had to admire her for that. "Until you forgive him, and yourself, I suppose you'll continue to suffer, Mrs. Kraft."

"Forgive him? Forgive him?" What little control she'd managed burst like a balloon pricked with a pin. "I will never forgive him. He took my Jeremiah's life, his hopes, his dreams, his future, and mine. Ours. How the hell am I supposed to forgive him for that?"

This was getting them nowhere. He rose. "Mrs. Kraft, I'm terribly sorry for your loss and for your pain, but I can't let you subject Lucas to any more than he has already suffered. He has begged me to let him apologize to you, ask for your forgiveness so he can build a new life. He grew up being treated like an animal, beaten, abused in ways you can't even imagine, and I'm trying to save his life. He doesn't need your idea of justice. I'm truly sorry, but he is my main concern here and I have to protect him. I am so sorry."

She stood, facing him as if she weren't a head shorter. Grit she did have. "And what will you do when he murders someone else? Pat him on the hand and say it's okay, you've been mistreated all your life, so it's okay? Dear God, what's wrong with this world?"

She staggered to the door, wrenched it open, and stumbled outside.

Raine took a weary breath and stood.

"In a way, she's right," Spinner said. "I'm so sorry, Raine. I want to help your friend, I truly do. But I have to protect Lucas. If you knew him, you'd realize that what I told her was the truth. If I can keep him from crawling back into a bottle or getting on drugs, he has a chance. I have to see that he gets it, or we'll have lost two young men to this tragedy. If only your friend could see that."

Raine touched his arm, sending a tingle through him. "She won't. She can't. Not yet. Maybe never. I had hoped maybe you'd let her see this boy, then she'd realize that nothing she does to him will change things or make them different. All she can do is cause more hurt, but I can't tell her that. She's my best friend, and she helped me when no one else would or could. I owe her."

Spinner took her hand in both his, its warmth rushing through him. "If you really owe her, make her see how much harm she can do to both herself and Lucas. She'll never get out of this hell she's in if she doesn't forgive him. And she's carrying a lot of guilt herself. Mothers always believe they should have protected their children, and when something like this happens, they naturally blame themselves for not having done their job. Even though she won't admit it, that's classic and she has to get past it."

From outside, Becca shouted at Raine to come on.

"I have to go. It was good to see you again. I wish—"

"Yeah, so do I. So do I. Take care. Take care of both of you."

Before he could guess what she was up to, she stood on her toes and kissed him on the side of his mouth. The touch of her lips built a fire in his gut. When he tried to keep her close, she pulled back.

"Thank you. Thank you for trying."

She was gone, leaving a faint fragrance of roses in the room, and he stood there for a long time inhaling it, wishing for something he couldn't have and grieving its loss.

Monday morning early, Becca parked her Nissan on the side of the highway in sight of the Wig Wam Motel. When Spinner came out and climbed into his Nova, she let him have a head start and followed him. Sooner or later he would contact Lucas Pell, and when he did she'd be there. She would not give up until she had done this thing. Perhaps then she could have some peace.

Eleven

Lucas kept the width of the shabby room between himself and the big Indian, who was pissed, his eyes flashing fire. "He told me to clean up the stinking bathroom. I didn't hire on to be no janitor. He didn't have to fire me."

"Goddamn it, Lucas. What did you think would happen when you trashed Hank's garage?"

"I didn't hit him."

"One for your side," Spinner said.

"Well, he didn't need to hit me."

"I told you not to buck him, Lucas. He'd clean your plow. He comes from the same place you and I do."

"You said... you told me hitting don't solve anything. So why is it okay for him to hit me?"

Spinner sighed and stared at the floor. "It isn't okay, Lucas, and I'm sorry it happened. You pushed him too far. I'm sure he's sorry he hit you."

"But not sorry he fired me?"

Spinner's chuckle wasn't pleasant. "Probably not."

"I told you this wouldn't work."

"I'm glad you didn't hit him, but dammit why did you tear up his place?" Spinner moved forward, spread his arms. "He'll never take on anyone else who needs a break."

Keeping out of his reach, Lucas darted nervously toward the window and its lousy view of the weed infested boatyard. "Why do I care about that?"

"Because we need to care about things like that, Lucas. If you don't care for anyone or anything but yourself, you'll always be…."

"Taking care of myself, that's what."

"I was going to say, you'll always be unhappy. You got to look outside yourself if you want to heal. Care for someone."

"I ain't got nothing needs healing. I don't want to care for no one. That don't get you nothing but hurt. I just care for me, take care of me best I can and hammer on anyone who tries to hammer on me. I only didn't hit him 'cause of you. Maybe next time I will."

Spinner batted his eyes, as if Lucas had hit him. He cleared his throat. "I appreciate that, I really do, but dammit, I can't help you if you won't let me."

"Then don't. I can take care of myself."

"Yeah. So far you're doing a fine job of it."

"Get out of here. Leave me alone. Don't do me no favors. Don't get me no jobs or buy me no more clothes. Don't pay for this lousy place no more, 'cause I ain't staying."

"You leave, they'll pick you up doing something you shouldn't be doing. You'll be in jail with the big boys this time. And I won't be able to help you then."

"Go away," Lucas said, fists clenched against his thighs. He ached to pound on something and didn't want it to be Spinner. Reaching for control was new to him and he shuddered with the effort.

"Okay, I'll leave so you can cool down. But do me one favor. Stay here a while. The rent's paid till the end of the month. Just stay that long so we can try to work our way through this. If we don't get all this stuff settled by then, I'll leave you be. I promise. Just stay here till the end of the month."

Lucas didn't answer 'cause he didn't want to make such a promise, but he knew he would stay because he really had no place else to go. Not yet, anyway.

Becca sat in her car half a block away from the apartment Spinner had entered. The east end of Lake Drive was the worst part of town. Abandoned warehouses and old rundown buildings that had been turned into rooms to rent. The boy lived in what looked like it had once been a garage. A dreadful place.

"What could he be doing in there so long?" The habit of talking to herself when nervous had returned with her need to remain sober long enough to face this boy. This had to be Lucas Pell's apartment, but if it wasn't she'd know soon enough because she was going in there as soon as Spinner left.

He was probably telling the kid to get out of town before the crazy lady attacked him. Despite their differences, she had been impressed with Spinner. Physically he gave the impression of being tough and mean and not too literate when he was exactly the opposite. She found him well-spoken, considerate in view of the circumstances, and touchingly concerned for Lucas. She admired his loyalty to the boy, even though it went against her assessments of his worth.

Worst of all, though, it forced her to rethink her own conclusions. Even so, she wasn't about to back down in her desire to repay Lucas, though she could never hurt him the way he had hurt her.

Spinner exploded out the door, leaped in his car and left, looking none too happy. For a long while she couldn't move, but continued to sit there staring at the door that was badly in need of a paint job.

What would she say to Lucas? How would he react? Perhaps she shouldn't have come alone, but could think of no one she wanted to be a witness to what might happen. Not even her best friend Raine. At that moment, she needed Jon's support so badly her heart ached. There was a time when he was at her side whenever she needed him. She tried to think when that ended, when she began to reach for his hand, and find him gone. Long before Jeremiah's death.

Her throat closed and tears surfaced, but she wiped them away angrily. Enough of this. Think. Think of something else. She would not lose control this time.

The good times, think of that. After she married Jon in 1980 they lived in Tulsa, in a small house built in the fifties. One of those efficiencies thrown up by the thousands to handle the growing families of a post-war America. Imagine today's young families settling for a house with one bath, two bedrooms, a crowded living room, and a kitchen the size of her closet. No, today they needed a house far too large for them, too fancy. Yet she and Jon were ecstatic when they bought the house though it was thirty years old. It was all they could afford and neither of them wanted to waste money renting.

Within a couple of years the consulting business took off. Teaching someone how to do something turned out to be lucrative and the company grew so fast that when David was born three years later she was able to quit working with Jon and stay home. Soon after that Jon had begun to spend more time at the office. But still they remained a family, doing things together. Maybe she only missed him because they no longer worked together. Now that she looked back on it, that move to the lake house had ended their closeness. She and the baby in their new home from early spring to late fall, then spending the holidays and inclement winter weather in their upscale condo in Tulsa. Jon was rarely home, but enough so that she conceived Christi. She'd always felt he thought that another baby would keep her occupied and off his back. Christi was only thirteen months younger than David.

Appearing satisfied that he'd done his husbandly duties, Jon remained in town through several weekends without seeing his family. Time between visits lengthened from a month to six weeks to two months. Her accusations that he might be having an affair fueled bitter arguments, but had little effect on his behavior. It was the business, always the business, he insisted. After one such episode they had a dreadful row that ended with some rough lovemaking and nine months later, there was Jeremiah. Their unplanned baby, conceived in anger, soon became the most dear to her heart. A secret she guarded closely for fear of hurting David and Christi.

When was the last time Jon had stood beside her, supported her decisions? All of that aside, her head spun with the anticipation of facing Lucas. Heaving a sigh, she turned to gaze at the door behind which he waited. The killer of her son. She couldn't take her hands from the steering wheel. Her brain whirled and she gasped for air. Maybe she shouldn't do this. God, her chest hurt. Her head pounded. The beat of her heart clogged her throat.

Oh, Jon, dammit, why couldn't you help me do this?

A car cruised by slowly, two faces turned in her direction, one shouted something she couldn't understand. This was no place to be alone. Relieved, she watched the dilapidated vehicle move away. Enough stalling.

She had to do this herself, and that was that. She was weary of lying around whimpering and suffering, popping pills and guzzling booze.

Grabbing up her purse from the console, she opened the door and stepped out. She'd dressed carefully but casually, in gray pants, a shell pink blouse, and sensible gray Hush Puppies. She wore no jewelry save her watch and wedding ring. Nothing in her purse but a driver's license and a woman's usual junk.

If he hit her on the head, there wouldn't be much for him to steal. If she had to run away, the comfortable low-heeled shoes would serve her well.

What nonsense. He wasn't going to rob or kill her.

She tapped on the door. Waited, clutching her handbag tightly in front of her. A shield, a weapon.

No reply. He wasn't home. Somehow he'd left and she didn't notice. She'd go. Come back later.

No, that wouldn't do.

Again she rapped at the door with her bare knuckles, this time with more force.

"Yeah? What? You forget part of your lecture?"

The door swung open before the question ended, and she and Lucas Pell stood face to face. Him looking surprised? Frightened? Annoyed? She really couldn't tell, had no idea how she appeared to him either.

Sweat beaded above his lip. His buzzed hair stuck straight out from his head. He was scarcely taller than her, with a slender build that had only just begun to layer on muscles. If he was shaving, it wasn't often. He still had the skin of a boy. New jeans hung on his hips. He was shirtless and shoeless. His ribs stood out as if he didn't eat well. Scars of several varieties marked his skin, and she turned her eyes away to keep from staring.

"What do you want?" he finally asked, blocking her entry.

Not quite sure how to answer that, she simply asked, "Could I come in?" The earlier nervousness fled and she felt a deadly calm settle over her, the first in a long while.

Shrugging, he stepped back and motioned her inside, slammed the door with too much force.

"You sure you wanta be in here with me?" He looked around the dump, had the good sense to be embarrassed by it, but meant more by his question than that.

"I'm not afraid of you, if that's what you mean." Her eyes strayed back to the scars.

He picked up a tee shirt from the bed, pulled it on. "You called me a killer. You wanta be around a killer?"

"I had to come."

He stared past her out the dingy window. "I been looking for you, you know."

Startled, she studied him. "Why?"

"I tried to tell you yesterday, you wouldn't listen."

"So you did come there on purpose."

He shook his head. "No. Well, in a way. Spinner, he didn't know nothing about it." He nibbled at the end of his thumb. Creases in his hands were stained black. "I— I wanted to tell you I was sorry, ask you to— to forgive me."

The statement rocked her and she shuddered. Couldn't speak.

"If you won't, then you won't. But I done what I needed to do. For the program. You go now. Go away and leave me be."

Tears stood in his eyes and he ignored them, glaring at her with what she thought might be a practiced, tough-guy look.

"You killed my child. My baby."

"I didn't do it on purpose," he shouted and wiped his runny nose with the back of one hand. "And he wasn't no baby, either. I read in the papers. We was almost the same age."

"You ruined my life, my family's life, and that's all you can say? You didn't do it on purpose?"

"Well, I didn't. I'm sorry. I can't do no more than say that."

"Oh, yes. Yes, you can."

"What then? Tell me."

"You can suffer more. I can make you suffer more."

"No," he shouted. "No, you can't make me suffer more than I done. You git out of here now. If you can't forgive me, then I don't want you here. Git out, and don't come back."

Unable to control her emotions, Becca shouted, "You'll rot in hell for what you did. Rot in hell." Nausea boiled in her stomach. She had never been so angry or out of control in her life. If she'd had a gun she would've shot him, right then and there. That knowledge scared her so badly she couldn't think or speak.

He cast a wild gaze around the room, doubled his fists as if to hit her, then spread his fingers wide. Leaped for a chair and threw it against the wall.

She jerked when it splintered with a loud crash.

Clearly, he'd wanted to hit her, but stifled the urge. Instead, he strode to the door, threw it open, and glared at her, tears running freely.

As she ran toward the car, he yelled at her, "Goddamn you. Goddamn you to hell."

"He already has," she muttered, but not loud enough for him to hear, for she couldn't find the strength. It was all she could do to wrench the car door open and fall into the seat.

After several deep breaths, she dug in her purse for her keys, tears blinding her. She sat there a long time before regaining some semblance of composure, then drove off.

Through tear-drenched eyes Lucas watched the fancy car move out of sight. That couldn't have gone any worse, unless he'd killed her. Obviously, the old woman hated his guts. And when you got right down to it, he wasn't sure he blamed her. Her Jeremiah was surely worth more to this world than he and his scabby hide would ever be. Rich boy. Probably would've grown up to be a doctor healing people, or a businessman or somebody important. What would Lucas ever be? No more than he was right now. And eventually, even less.

He hadn't hit her, though, and he felt a certain pride in that. But throwing the chair. Spinner would've been disappointed. How hard the man had worked with him, sent him to classes to learn to stifle his anger, what they called channel it so he didn't explode and lash out. Even admitted that he himself had gone through much the same situation when his wife OD'd on heroin and died. Been so mad at the world already, and then that happened, and he went crazy for a while.

Lucas remembered how he'd felt when Spinner told him that. Like he was trusting him with a deep dark secret from his past life. Admitting how he'd lost it. That took some guts, too.

Maybe he ought to try again with this lady. After all, he didn't have nothing else to do, seeing as how Hank had fired him. Sitting on the bed, staring at his toes, he had an idea that might make everything right. Both with Hank and with this Mrs. Kraft.

Spinner drove straight from Lucas's place to RainTree. By the time he parked across the street, he'd cooled off considerably. Teaching him to control his temper had been one of Gano Burke's successes when he took over counseling a young man so angry he was fixing to kill someone.

Spinner knew that to be true. Gano kept him literally from committing murder, he was so freaked out. All he could think of was choking the life out of the drug dealer who had traded heroin for sex with Marty after Spinner refused to connect for her one more time.

Gano made him see that the reason for his desire to kill stemmed from guilt as much as anger at the dealer. He blamed himself and couldn't deal with it.

But that was a long time ago, and though it had taught him a valuable lesson, he didn't like to dwell on those dark times. What he wanted more than anything at this moment was to go inside that coffee shop, sit down at a table, and watch Raine approach him in that languid way she had. Talk to her, touch her, be with her, until the world righted itself once more. She had a way of soothing his spirit with a mere look, a gentle smile. Despite his own self-doubts, and no matter what she said, he had to try again with her or he'd never forgive himself.

Inside the coffee shop, several tables were filled with chattering, well-dressed women, and he made his way to a single-serve table against the wall. Nearby, water danced from a fountain over rocks and floral arrangements that gave off a sweet scent that mingled with the aromatic blended coffees. The young, garishly dressed waitress spotted him and started over.

Disappointed that Raine wasn't around, he waved Cherry away and started to get up. When he turned, he almost bumped into Raine emerging from behind the elaborate jungle display.

She was wearing something frothy at her throat that reminded him of spun candy, and a brilliant pink outfit that barely succeeded in disguising her shape. Painted toenails peeked from matching pink high heeled sandals that brought her expressive eyes even with his mouth.

Dear God in heaven.

He took her elbow and she let him, glancing up so her sleek cap of black hair shifted like liquid silk.

"You," she said.

"Me," he replied.

"Mmmm."

"Indeed."

The corners of her full, pink tinged mouth turned up ever so slightly, and her eyes sparkled. His heart did a crazy flip-flop, like he was some smitten teenager.

"Glad to see me?"

"How like you to ask."

"I need to know." Something clutched at his insides, waiting for that look to turn to ice or melt in acquiescence.

"How about, are you glad to see me?"

Glancing all about him, then back at her, he raised his hands in supplication. "I'm here, aren't I? And I don't even like almond latté matte, or whatever it is."

The smile turned to laughter. "You're impossible. Can't I teach you anything?"

"Only if you try harder."

A flush worked up from her throat to flame her cheeks, and he touched one with his thumb, folding his fingers along her jaw line. "I like it when you do that."

She clutched his wrist, but didn't pull his hand away. "And I like it when you do that."

An intense sexual reaction crawled through his groin, and public or no, he wanted it satisfied. If they didn't get the hell out of here soon, he was going to embarrass her customers.

"Down, boy," she whispered, leaning close.

"Yeah, well, tell it to" —he glanced down— "him."

"Tonight. My place. Meanwhile, take a cold shower." She danced away from him, agile as a damned cat, and didn't even look back when she raised a hand, butt swaying ever so slightly.

"Tonight? Jesus," he whispered, and walked stiffly among the tables, twisting this way and that to conceal his condition.

At least she had said yes to them getting together. He tried not to anticipate what might happen when they did, for she could be tricky and stand-offish. He wished he knew why she was having a problem with the two of them. Couldn't believe it was because of their unequal status. But he was, after all, not well off or polished. And of course, there was the biggie. He was a Cherokee Indian. Bigoted or not, she had to consider the consequences of such a liaison between them.

So, suppose they fell in love, got married, had little half-breed kids? Did she want to handle that? Did she want to bring kids into the world who had to handle that? Even though it was the twenty-first century, there was a certain stigmata against such things. Especially among the elite, where she came from.

He grinned with wicked intent. Maybe he could be her token Indian.

These thoughts carried him across the street to the Nova. He adjusted his jeans before climbing in. Leaving her presence hadn't cooled his ardor one bit, and he drove all the way to Hank's Garage in a state of extreme discomfort.

Firmly relegating her image to the back of his mind, Spinner went inside to talk Hank into rehiring Lucas if he would come clean up the mess he'd made earlier that morning. That would only leave Lucas to convince, but it was worth a try.

David held the phone to his ear a bit longer, listening to it ring on the other end. "Come on, Dad. Answer. I know you're there or the machine wouldn't be turned off."

As if in reply to his muttered plea, Jon picked up, sounding half asleep. Oh, shit. He hadn't even checked the time.

"Do you know what time it is?"

"Dad, I'm sorry. I really need to talk to you."

"David. Where are you?"

"I'm at the pay phone below your window."

"Well, come on up, then. I'll make some coffee."

David hung up and crossed the street, stepping inside when the buzzer went off at the security station. The guard glanced at David and nodded. "Go on up. Your Dad's waiting."

Flipping the man a mock salute, David headed for the elevator that would deposit him at his father's floor. The expensive condos sported elevators keyed individually for each living unit. Each could only be accessed by a password or through security. David grew up living here or on Monkey Island, yet he never used the password to go up. It felt somehow as if he were encroaching on Jon's privacy. Especially now that his mother never came in at all, even in the winter.

The elevator bell ponged softly and he stepped into a foyer decorated with fake plants that looked so real one had to touch them. Soft lights illuminated tasteful paintings hung against the wine and cream wall paper. Moving across thick burgundy carpeting, he tapped on the large double oak doors and they swung open immediately. His father greeted him somewhat muzzily, dressed in a blue patterned robe and black slippers, tufts of his silvering hair sticking out comically.

Jon hugged David, then led him down the hallway to the gleaming kitchen. Easy to see no one cooked here anymore. They did make coffee though, the aroma filling the air accompanied by the gurgling sound of water flowing.

Jon had already placed mugs on the stone counter top.

"Still drink it black?"

"Yes. Too hard to find cream and sugar in the jungle."

Jon poured the coffee, handed David his. "Let's go in the library where it's comfortable."

And indeed it was, looking much as David remembered it from his childhood. Large leather couches and chairs grouped in the center and surrounded completely by bookshelves from floor to ceiling. A lamp burned on a round table and each chair had its own reading light suspended from a beamed ceiling. David settled in what had once been his favorite reading niche and Jon sat beside him, a table between them.

Blowing at his coffee, Jon studied his son. "How are things going? You still like traipsing around Africa?"

"It's not Africa, but yes."

Jon waved his hand and sipped at the hot brew. "No matter. What's up?"

Faintly, David wished it did matter to his father, but no use in that. It wasn't going to happen. "I didn't come to talk about me. I'm worried about Mom."

Jon made a rude noise. "Who isn't?"

"I know, but this is different. Worse, somehow."

"Worse than drinking herself into a stupor and popping pills till we have to drag her into the hospital every few weeks and have her stomach pumped?"

"Maybe." David didn't want to argue, or even discuss his mother's problems with his father. Certainly didn't want to point out that his father was never around to drag his mother anywhere. There was no sense in engaging in a litany of blame leveling and self-righteous indignation.

"Dad. You know that Lucas Pell guy? Well, he showed up in a boat at the private dock. Mom was down there and I guess she nearly had a coronary."

"Jesus Christ. Did she call the police?"

"No. It wasn't like that, I don't think."

"Wasn't like what? He comes to our home, to the home of the parents of the boy he killed. Tell me, David, what was it like?"

"Well, I guess he was out fishing with his counselor and their boat quit."

"Your mother bought that?"

"No, actually she didn't. I guess she came unglued. Tried to scratch the kid's eyes out or something. Then got scared and when I found her they were gone and she was sitting at the bottom of the steps, totally out of it. I thought I was going to have to take her to the doctor."

"Well, that would've been something new, wouldn't it?"

David set his mug on the table, regarded his father with disbelief. "Don't you care for her at all anymore? Or did you just never love her?" He hated how his voice shook, but couldn't seem to help it.

Jon's eyes flared, then softened. "I've always loved Becca. If I didn't, I'd've been long gone. You should know that. Hell, why do you think I don't divorce her?"

"I don't know, Dad. Why don't you tell me why you keep torturing yourself and her?"

Jon cleared his throat and David was surprised to see tears gleaming in his eyes. "Dammit," he muttered. "Why is this any of your business?"

"Because I love you both and I can't stand to see what's happening."

"Well, since you're gone most of the time, I guess you don't have to see it, do you?"

"You're one to talk." David leaped to his feet. "You're gone from her, too, so you don't have to see what's going on. Why don't you act like a man and take care of your family, your wife? You've run away just like I have, but it's not my place to take care of her, it's yours."

He could not face Jon's expression of feigned innocence another minute. As always, he wasn't getting anywhere.

"I shouldn't have come," he said. Ignoring his father's voice calling his name, David ran down the long hallway and pushed his way out the door and into the elevator, standing open in readiness for his retreat.

He was inside a taxi and on his way to the bus station before he stopped shaking.

Twelve

Spinner found Hank's garage looking like it'd been hit by a tornado. Fan belts, tools, plastic jugs of oil and transmission fluid lay scattered all over the place. In the middle of the chaos sat an old black Thunderbird. Hank's well used work shoes stuck out from under it. The man spent most of his life lying on his back under leaky cars. Spinner tapped the bottom of one of the soles with his own boot toe. "Hey, buddy. You in those shoes?"

"Nope. They empty. I'm down at the Pud Nut tipping back a few." The man didn't sound too happy, and Spinner didn't blame him.

"I'm sure sorry about this mess."

"Yeah, well," Hank grumbled, but didn't slide out. "Little bastard," he added and thunked something under there hard. Probably wished it was Lucas's head. "Gonna have to hire someone to clean it up. I got three rust buckets coming in today."

"I suppose that means you won't consider taking him back."

"Why would you think that? Hell, I like working with these head cases of yours."

Spinner grinned, sidled over to the Coke box, lifted out a dripping can, popped the top, and downed a few swallows.

Hank slid out to his waist. "Why? The kid say he's sorry?"

"Come to think of it, no. He didn't. But I think he ought to have to clean up after himself, and the only way we can get that done is for you to rehire him."

"Guess he couldn't come clean it up cause he should, huh?"

"In an ideal world, sure. Better if you rehire him. Show him that some effort on his part can bring about rewards."

"Oh, hell, yes. More, please. Wouldn't want these little head cases to think they should do something 'cause it's the right thing to do." Hank rolled the creeper farther out and glared up at Spinner, waiting for the inevitable comeback.

Spinner obliged. "Take a kid like him, he'll throw that right back in your face. Nobody's ever done the right thing by him, so why should he even consider it? Baby steps, man, baby steps. He cleans it up, keeps his job. You've done the right thing and so has he."

Hank jerked a rag from his pocket and wiped at his greasy hands. "Shit. All right. But you tell that dickhead he's gonna do what I tell him to. Explain that I'm the employer, he's the employee. He don't seem to grasp the concept." He paused, scratched his ear with a greasy finger, leaving a black smudge. "I shouldn't a hit the little creep, but he got way on the wrong side of me. You know how it is. Besides I just popped him easy like. No bleeding. I should a knocked him across the garage, the way he was mouthing off."

"No, you shouldn't have," Spinner said. "You gonna tell him?"

"Tell him what?"

"You're sorry."

"Sorry for what, that I didn't hit him harder?" Hank wiped at his hands some more as if that were all that mattered to him. "It won't happen again. Bring him on back here."

"Thanks, I owe you one," Spinner said.

"One, hell, you owe me closer to a hundred, and one of these days I'm gonna collect."

"I'll have him here in the morning." Spinner headed for his car, muttering under his breath. Now all he had to do was convince Lucas.

Damn, he had to hold on to this kid. Had to. He couldn't bear the idea of him slipping away. Ending up in some alley with a needle hanging out of his arm, or a knife between his ribs. The kid was yelling for help in the only way he knew how, and someone had to respond before it was too late.

He parked in front of Lucas's place, leaped from the Nova, and pounded on the door. No answer. Sidling to the window, he peered through the murky glass.

Lucas lay flat on his back on the rumpled bed, one arm over his eyes. If he was sleeping, he sure slept heavy. Spinner moved back to the door, hammered louder using his fist.

"Go away," came a strangled cry from inside.

Backing up, he kicked the flimsy door just below the knob. It flew open, bounced off the wall.

Lucas didn't budge from the bed, nor lift his head.

Quickly, Spinner went to him, sat and inspected his arms. No fresh needle marks. He sniffed the air, glanced around, saw no empty bottles nor smelled booze.

"What's wrong with you?"

"Go away."

Lifting Lucas's arm, he saw his eyes were swollen, his face wet with tears.

"What happened?"

"Nothing. Leave me be. Go away." He scooted across the bed, sat on the other side, back to Spinner.

"You think saying that enough times will make it happen? I'm not going away. Not till you tell me what happened. This isn't over getting fired, is it?"

Leaping up, pacing the floor in bare feet, Lucas railed. "Shit, no. I didn't want that nowhere job anyways. It was her. She come here. That bitch, and said I would rot in hell for what I did. I tried to tell her, tried to explain, but she wasn't listening."

Lucas fixed his watery gaze on Spinner, doing his level best to look tough through it all. Voice crackly as old newspaper, he asked, "Do you believe in hell?"

The kid's question struck him mute. How the hell had Rebecca Kraft found Lucas? And having done that, why her need to lash out at a boy no older than her son would be? Once, long ago, when he'd been so damn young, he'd lost a brother and in doing so lost all sense of reason as well, lashing out at those who would help him. This woman had to be in her forties. You'd think she'd have learned something. Maybe losing a child drove all rational thought from a parent's mind. He didn't pretend to understand half of what he knew about the human psyche, but she clearly needed help for her own sake, never mind Lucas. She was mired down in the anger stage of grieving and couldn't seem to work her way out of it.

As to whether Spinner believed in hell or not, hell, yes, he did. And it was right here, as far as this boy and all those like him were concerned. But he chose to avoid answering the question.

"Well, you have to realize she's lost her son and give her some slack."

Lucas didn't reply to that, surprising Spinner. Before he could think it over and ask that painful question again, Spinner told him about going to see Hank.

"And he agreed you could come back to work first thing in the morning, if you'd clean up the mess you made on your own time."

"He wants me to clean it up and not even pay me for doing it?"

"Lucas," Spinner warned. "Don't start with me. I'm not in the mood."

"And I'm not in the mood to work in that dirty garage." He paused, watched Spinner. "What'll happen if I don't go back over there?"

Outside a horn honked. Spinner glanced through the window at a girl in short shorts walking toward a car full of boys. He ground his teeth. "You know what, Lucas? I think I'll let you answer that. Mull it over. Try to figure out where you're gonna be a year from now, hell, six months from now, if you don't have a job or a place to live."

He dragged his attention from the girl's sexy little backside and back into the depressing room. "You want to live this way the rest of your life, fine with me. I got other things to do besides try to help someone don't want to be helped."

"I work in a place like Hank's, then I reckon this is the way I'll live. Ain't nothing ever gonna get any better for me. Nothing."

"I'll help you, Lucas. You keep the job, we'll get you enrolled in a tech school. You can work at the garage while you learn a trade. Help yourself. You don't have to be a punk all your life."

Lucas rocked on his feet, maintaining the cocky, street-wise pose. "Oh, yeah. I can be like you, huh? Driving a beat up old Nova, living somewhere not much better than this, working a job that don't pay as good in a year as I could make in a week selling dope. That what you got in mind for me?"

"Lucas, listen to me. Hear what I'm telling you. You go out there and sell dope you'll be dead in a year or two, three tops. All money is good for is buying you a place to live, three squares, some clothes, a life you can be proud of. You can do that without selling dope on the streets. What good is a new car and flashy clothes and a fancy place to live if you're dead?"

Spinner felt used up, helpless. If he couldn't turn this kid around, he might as well toss it in. Get himself a job at Hank's and forget all about trying to save the world one kid at a time. Burke used to always say that, and he'd bought into it. He himself had been tough to turn around, and Burke never gave up, though sometimes Spinner couldn't figure out why.

"Everybody dies. Not just dope dealers," Lucas said, his jaw jutting stubbornly.

The mantra of the young, who had no idea how fast life could pass them by, and how easily everything could go wrong if they lost their concentration for one minute. Spinner blew air between his lips and lifted his shoulders.

"Okay. You're right and I'm wrong. I've been wasting my breath and my time. You go ahead, throw your life away in the gutter. Prove your parents were right all along. You're not worth saving."

Hunching his shoulders, Spinner stomped out the door and slammed it behind him. It bounced open, but he didn't look back. With an aching heart, he climbed in the Nova, started it up, and drove off. He couldn't bear it if he lost this one, but he'd played his last card. It was up to Lucas now. He'd call Hank in the morning and see if the kid showed up. Meanwhile, he was going to go to the motel, take a shower, then go downtown and buy a dozen roses and a bottle of good wine.

He had a date with a beautiful woman. Maybe she could take away the pain—for a while, at least.

Jon hiked his feet onto his desk and stared out the window at the

Tulsa skyline. If Celie came in and saw his shoes on the expensive desk, she'd have a fit. But he had more to worry about than her scoldings, which were never really serious.

What was serious at the moment was his wife and her ongoing problems. If she had half the responsibilities he had, she might buck up and come out of this state. Sometimes he wished one of her attempts at suicide would be successful, so the family could find some peace.

"Ah, Christ," he said, and picked up the telephone. "Celie, would you get me my wife?"

Until he talked to her, he wouldn't be able to forget his son's visit of the previous night. David was rarely that distraught, and this latest scheme of Becca's was just about the last straw. She'd get herself hurt if she wasn't careful. As if she hadn't practically self-destructed already.

"Jon?" came Celie's pert voice. "No one answers out at the lake. Should I try the condo?"

"No, she never comes to town anymore. Do I have any appointments this afternoon?"

"A couple. Jerry McGraw has a two o'clock and a new client, Madge Jefferson, is supposed to be here at three thirty."

"Would you reschedule them for later this week? I have to be out of the office the rest of the day."

"Sir?" Celie piped. "Out of the office? First of the week? Call the first responders. I need reviving."

"Don't get smart." He kept his tone light.

She laughed. One thing he could always do was make Celie laugh, except for the night he and she…. He threw that thought away before he grew lost in memories of the touch of her, her pale freckled skin, and the joyous, guilt-ridden release they'd both experienced.

"Where can I reach you?"

"You can't. I'm turning off my phone. No emergencies."

"Now I know I'm calling 9-1-1."

"This is important."

She hesitated an instant. "Is she all right?"

"Who knows? Just hold down the fort. You can do that, can't you?"

"Of course. I'm well trained in evasive tactics. Can I go home at five?"

"Sure."

"My cat will faint." She clicked off.

Jon remained where he was for another minute or so. How smart was it to confront Rebecca about her latest insanity? Impossible any longer to remember how it had been for them when they first met and fell in love. The past year and a half and the endless trips to the hospital where he'd find her drained, pale, and disheveled after yet another suicide attempt drowned any effort to bring back those lovely days.

She claimed they were all accidents, the overdoses. Sure, if it could be called accidental that she drank booze all day then swallowed a handful of pills.

He'd loved her once, long ago. He really had. Now their life was just a series of desperate games played at the expense of the family. The only thing left for him was divorce, but he hadn't the courage to resort to that. Suppose he did, and she succeeded in killing herself, then what? How would he ever explain it to the kids? How would he ever forgive himself?

Sighing, he dropped his feet to the floor, grabbed his briefcase, and left the office.

A line of clouds the color of cold ashes hung to the southwest, thunderheads boiled into the blue sky. They blotted out the afternoon sun. For early May it was too hot and still.

For Oklahoma, these were perfect conditions for tornadoes—especially the big kind. They'd been spared anything deadly so far this spring, but the season wasn't over by a long shot. He hoped he didn't have to drive back in stormy weather.

An hour and a half later, he steered up the lane to the house. Rain splattered on the windshield. He keyed the remote to open the garage doors. Becca's Nissan was in one bay and he parked the Mercedes next to it.

Wonder why she didn't answer the phone? Probably sprawled out in bed drunk to the world.

Prepared for the worst, he switched off the garage light before going inside the house. The sound of his footsteps echoed through the immaculate kitchen, then faded when he stepped onto the carpet in the dining room and on into the empty living room. A few lamps burned in the shadowy corners, their glow driving away the rapidly approaching darkness of the storm. Across the entryway and up the sweeping staircase. The fucking place was too big, way too big. What had they been thinking? And why the hell was he tiptoeing like a thief in his own house? If she was passed out on the bed, he'd turn and leave her to it.

At the door to her room, he paused, put his ear to the panel and listened. Easing the knob he stepped into the room.

Lightning flashed, slashing through the room to reveal his wife sitting at her dressing table, long hair loose and hanging down her bare back. A lamp burned to one side, highlighting the reflection of her breasts and flat belly in the mirror. At forty-eight she still had a good body, though she'd grown a bit too thin in the past year or so.

Mesmerized, Jon watched her raise both arms and finger a strand of hair away from her face. He'd seen her do that hundreds of times, but the gesture caused him to catch his breath in awe. How long had it been since they'd made love except in frustration? Heat flowed into his groin, stirred a buried passion to life.

Jesus. Twenty-seven years since they'd met on campus, and at that very moment he wanted her as much as he had that first night they'd made love. They couldn't keep their hands off each other. Had rolled and tumbled and rutted like animals in his dorm room at OSU. The memory increased his passion, hardened his desire. Unable to stop himself, he breathed her name and moved closer.

She froze, caught his image in the mirror, let out a startled ooh, reached for a dressing gown draped over the stool on which she sat.

"What are you doing here?" She slipped her arms in the filmy sleeves before rising and facing him.

The cold inquiry didn't dampen his spirits one bit, though it should have. How well he knew that tone. Scornful and designed to cut him down, letting him know he did not belong here. Knowing he couldn't have her only made him want her more. It must have been the electric energy sizzling in the air. As if to belie that notion, lightning flashed and thunder shook the window panes.

Her eyes went wide and she flinched, fisted the robe up under her chin. How she feared thunderstorms. How quickly he could make her come when she was within the grip of that fear.

"Becca," he said, hating the tone of his own voice. Cajoling, pleading for what? Mercy, judgment, pity? "I was worried about you. I called and no one answered. The machine didn't pick up. I wish you'd leave it on when you're not going to answer the phone."

"What day is it, Jon?" she asked, still cold as ice.

"What day? Monday. Why?"

"And you actually left the office early. Aren't you afraid the business will collapse without your presence?"

Patience. He had to be patient. "I told you, I was worried about you."

"Why now, all of a sudden?" She stepped away from the dresser, tying the robe tightly at her waist.

He didn't know the answer to that. "I guess I wanted to see you, that's all. I miss you, Becca."

"I've missed you for a very long time, Jon, but it did me no good. So guess what?"

"What?"

"I don't give a damn. Now, why don't you just leave? Go back to town. You might miss something important."

"David is worried about you."

"So that's it," she said with a sneer. "It wasn't your concern at all, but David's that brought you out here. I should've known you couldn't spare me a thought." A flash of lightning hardened her features into a fearful mask and she uttered a small oh.

"We're both worried that you'll get in trouble trying to approach this Lucas Pell. He's violent, Becca. A street punk who won't hesitate to do you harm. You must stay away from him."

"Do you ever tire of trying to mold me to your specifications, Jon? First you want to tell me how to grieve, now you're trying to tell me how to react to them releasing the man who killed our son. Don't you care in the least, Jon? He's out there on the street, free as a bird while our son, our dear, sweet Jeremiah, is buried...." She sank to the floor, sobbing.

Instead of following his inclination to escape this unpleasant situation, Jon moved toward her, knelt beside her. Lightning split the sky, thunder boomed so loud the floor shook, and the lamp went out, plunging the room into inky blackness.

At the same moment he touched her shoulder. She cried out and wrapped her arms around his neck. He scooped her off the floor, shocked at how light she was. Temporarily disoriented, he stood there holding her trembling body, inhaling the familiar heather scent in her hair, her breath fresh with mint.

His mouth found hers, his tongue exploring the satin smoothness of her seeking lips that opened eagerly to his.

They'd always ended up making love during storms, her crying out with each climax as if fear spurred her into intense multiple orgasms. Perhaps she was remembering that now, for she pressed her breasts against him, spread her fingers into his hair, pulled him closer, made eager little sounds deep in her throat.

Where was the damn bed? He staggered through the darkness, bumped into a wall, turned and went the other way. A flash through the window revealed what he searched for. She tore at the buttons on his shirt. He bumped into the mattress and went to his knees, not turning her loose.

Outside the storm raged, wind blew tree branches against the windows, feeding her fervor. If he took his hands away from her to get out of his clothes, she would panic. So he let her peel off his jacket and shirt and go to work on his belt buckle while he pulled the robe off her shoulders and untied it.

His eager mouth found her cool flesh, the mound of her breasts, the nipples sweetly familiar. Her grappling to peel his pants down drove him blind with desire. Must've done the same for her. She scooted down beneath him, locked her legs around his waist, and met his mad driving thrust. Locked together as if in battle, driven by the howling wind and tumultuous thunder, their cries challenged the storm's ferocity.

Her moist heat took him in, welcomed him as if he'd never been away. Sweat-drenched and nearly wild with desire, he pounded her against the mattress, over and over, sure he would never have enough of the sheer madness. At last she shuddered, tightened around him, screamed as thunder continued to attack from beyond the walls. Emptying inside her, he reeled into near unconsciousness. The hurried, savage act left him spent, panting, awed, while she continued to writhe about as if she weren't finished yet.

Becca often liked to prolong the ride, so he hung on while she did, crying and shouting, "He's dead, damn you, he's dead, damn you."

She continued rocking viciously as if she might never stop, moaning the litany until he managed to untangle himself from her and roll away to sit on the edge of the bed, head in both hands. Drained of emotions. Listening to her sob.

Thirteen

Spinner hadn't gone out of sight before Lucas wrapped his extra jeans around his shorts, socks, and tee shirt, tucked the bundle under his arm, and boogied out of there. The battered door refused to shut and he left it ajar. To hell with it. Wasn't nothing valuable inside, anyway. To hell with Spinner and Hank and that bitch who wouldn't let him apologize. What kind of person won't accept someone saying they're sorry for what they done? His leaving oughta make them all happy.

They told him in group that saying he was sorry was a way to break free of the ghost of that kid, yet she wouldn't let him do it. Who did she think she was, anyway? Well, it was too late now. She would burn in hell before she'd hear an *I'm sorry* from him again.

He trudged up the highway, staying out of sight when he passed by Hank's Garage. He'd never get a ride till he got out on 85A. When he finally did, he started west toward Bernice and I-44, thumb stuck out. He was outta here. Head on over to Tulsa where he knew the streets. Get connected and get on with it.

Thunder rolled in the distance and he eyed the dark clouds. If someone didn't pick him up soon he was gonna get mighty wet. A dusty old Oldsmobile went rolling by, its taillights flicked on, and it pulled over to the side. He watched for a minute to see if they were joking with him, then ran to catch up with his ride.

Inside were two black dudes and a couple of white girls with an OD of body piercings and wearing hardly nothing. Once he would have thought they were ho's, but all girls wore skimpy clothes today, and plenty of them wore rings in their ears, eyebrows, noses, and belly buttons. Some even in their tits.

"We going to Tulsa. You wanta, hop in the back, dude." The driver leaned down and peered out at him. "You can have a space next to Lila. She hot enough for two."

Lucas gazed at the girl who smiled, sucked her finger, and then curled it at him in invitation. The boy next to her rubbed his hand over her bare belly and she giggled. Lucas's gut clenched with dread, but he climbed in the cluttered backseat. He'd worry about her later. Needed this ride, sure didn't need or want what she offered. Time they got to Tulsa he'd forget all about that Cherokee and his offer of a job and a better life.

Wrapped up in the girl, who had her hands all over him while the other guy stuffed his fingers under her top, Lucas didn't notice that they didn't turn onto I-44 but instead crossed over and pulled into a Mini Mart in Vinita.

The giggly girl had him hot and hard as a damned crowbar before the two guys bailed out of the car covering their faces with masks of some kind.

"What you doing?" he yelled, the words stifled by a groan when she unzipped his jeans and stuck her hand inside. How he hated the idea of sex, but his prick always betrayed him. Just let some little cutie mess with him and the damn thing came alive. She had him spronging all over the place by the time the two black dudes came running out of the store, leaped in the car, and sped off, tires squealing. He pushed at the top of her head, but she hung in there, sucking him damn near blind. Through ears that rang, he heard them talking. Words that bounced in and out of his brain like a damned basketball.

"Holy shit… guy's face… poked my piece in his belly?"

The girl really got down to her task. About to explode, Lucas tried to make out their faces with little luck. One of the dudes laughed, stared across Lila's hunched back. Lucas panted and sweated and writhed. Let out a holler and released in her mouth with such force he shouted, "Holy fucking shit," despite himself. The girl didn't flinch, kept gnawing on him.

"Like that, do you?" the dude asked Lucas, "She do too. She downright rav'nous." He roared with laughter. "Better watch out, she eat you up and spit out the bone."

"Geez, look at it rain," the driver said.

The sound of a siren froze everyone. Red and blue lights flashed in the rainy night, a siren wailed. Lucas pushed the girl roughly aside and stuffed himself back in his pants.

"Floor it, man. Floor it," the passenger dude shouted.

"Too late," the driver yelled, and slammed on the brakes.

Raising his head, Lucas peered out the window. His gut clutched. Cop cars everywhere. In front, coming up from the sides, behind them. Where the fuck did they all come from? Patrol units started spewing out cops with their guns drawn, all shouting at once till you couldn't understand anything.

The doors popped open while he tried to finish zipping his pants and he tumbled from the car with the brave foursome, hands high, screaming for them not to shoot. The girl on the ground on her hands and knees, grinning wolfishly.

"On your faces, do it now!"

Rain poured past his wrists, up his elbows, and to his shoulders. Without waiting to see what the others would do, Lucas took a bite out of the pavement.

A knee crunched into his back, his cheek ground into a gravely puddle. He was in it now, up to his eyeballs. No one would listen to him saying he didn't do nothing. Worse, he was eighteen. No more hiding in juvie. Like Spinner said, time to play with the big boys now.

"Stupid punks," said the officer hauling him to his feet. "Robbing a place just up the road from the sheriff's office."

Everyone laughed. Lucas shrugged and squinted his eyes against the rain. Not like this wasn't bound to happen. Sooner or later.

Spinner raced through the downpour to Raine's front door. He must've been quite a sight when she opened up, wearing a filmy robe, to find a soaking wet Indian holding a bunch of watery red roses and a bottle of wine.

"Well, look at this. A drowning man at my door." She laughed and stood back. "Come on in here. I'll take those and get you a towel."

"I'll drip all over the floor," he said, remaining just inside on a colorful throw rug definitely not intended for mud and rain.

Holding the roses, she ran a hand up the front of his wet tee shirt and wiped rainwater from his cheek. Her touch flamed the desire that had ridden with him all day, and he circled her waist, dragged her close, and kissed her. The bouquet fell to the mud-spattered rug, scattering a few loose petals. He managed to hold on to the wine while she slipped her hands under the shirt front and peeled it over his head. She froze, gazed at the snake coiled up his chest. With a smile, she rolled her tongue along the viper's body and trailed it slowly to his left nipple. Shudders rippled through him and he outgrew his jeans.

"Hold on to this just a second," he said, giving her the bottle and working his arms out of the shirt. The front of her robe clung to her naked body.

"I got you wet." He cupped a hand over one of her breasts. She was a perfect handful.

"You're early. I'm not dressed." Fingers worked at his zipper, slid it and the waistband of his jockeys down to release his erection so it poked her in the belly. A funny little sound came from her throat.

His wasn't so funny, more deep down like he was worshiping. Holy shit. He'd been struck by lightning. He had a good hold on her breast, massaged the nipple between thumb and forefinger. She'd surely back off, like she always did when he got too close. But instead she moaned, and circled her fingers around his ramrod stiff hard-on.

"Tell me you won't hurt me."

"I won't hurt you." He enclosed her in his arms, took a few quick steps forward, propelling them into a living room with a thick, charcoal gray carpet.

"Promise?"

"I promise." At that moment he would've promised her anything. He wanted out of his clothes, wanted her out of hers. Desperately wanted inside her, her all around him. He hadn't wanted anything so much in a long time. His vision grew blurry as they stripped each other, hands and mouths groping for a taste of bare flesh. Unable, either of them, to wait until all their clothing had been discarded before tasting, nibbling, licking.

She smelled of everything fresh and clean, of sunshine and rain, of spring grass and apple blossoms, of a woman in heated passion. He couldn't find enough places to kiss her, to touch her, to rub against her. She gave herself over to him. The touch of her hands, the suckling of her exquisite lips, the wildness of her thrashing limbs. Wordless sounds of feral arousal grew to a crescendo until, with cries of anguished pleasure, he came along with her. And came and came and came, never leaving her behind until nothing was left but drumming hearts and mouths gasping for air.

He had passed beyond life, struggled to return to look upon her again. To know the joy of holding her. Found himself sprawled on the carpet, legs and arms tangled with hers, rain and sweat slick between them. Caught up inside her, he refused to move and lose the connection. Wisps of her sweet breath tickled his skin. One of his hands cupped her buttock, the other her thigh, his fingers lying in the moist heat where they had come together.

Neither of them spoke for a long while. Outside the storm moved on, leaving behind a stillness broken by errant rays of sunlight that trickled through the half-open blinds like liquid gold.

She stirred, moved away from him, leaving him reaching as if for something lost.

"Look at you," she said, amusement tingeing her voice.

He opened his eyes reluctantly. Hadn't wanted to. Liked the darkness and reliving the past few minutes, or hours. Which, he didn't know.

She knelt beside him, trailed a fingertip around his belly button, touched the face of the blue dragon on his thigh. "Barely got your britches off." Leaning forward, she kissed him lightly on the mouth. "That was fine." Her lips, so close to his, gave off the essence of her being, and he took a deep breath. Tasted her, sensed her, smelled her.

Wanted her again. But this time slow and easy as a still pond on a windless day. Taking forever. Never stopping. What was going on? She was a woman, sure. A beautiful woman. But this gut-wrenching need was something new. And it had a hell of a lot more to do with capturing a spirit than with lust. He would not be without her. Had not truly existed before her. Odd sensation.

Arching a brow, she leaned over him, one hand on either side of his shoulder. Perhaps she wondered why he had as yet said nothing. "It was fine, wasn't it?".

He chuckled, traced around her face with the tips of his fingers. "So fine that if you don't take your body away this instant, we'll make it super fine, and then super super and then—"

"Hush, now. Hush," she whispered into his mouth, lips on his. "Another time. Wow, I've never made love with a man with tatoos. I especially like the snake. Do you have any more?"

He nodded, rolled sideways so she could see his left buttock. "Ooh! That's gorgeous. What is it?"

"Art," he said seriously, crinkled his face. "I'm a walking masterpiece. The man who did it wouldn't tell me what it was either. Said true art doesn't have to be explained."

She leaned forward to inspect the work, breasts brushing his flaccid penis. "Did it hurt?"

"Yep, but I was brave."

"Why don't you have any where they show?" She kissed the work of art.

He could barely reply to her question. "I like to surprise my women."

She laughed, punched him playfully. "If you want to pull up your pants and put your shirt back on, I think you promised me a night out. I could certainly use one." She rolled off him and sat on the rug, legs crossed.

Rising to lean on his elbows, he eyed her throat, reached out and traced a jagged scar running from her clavicle up toward her jawbone. "What happened?" The question would scarcely come out, for it was clearly a near death wound.

She spread a palm over it. "Not now. It's too ugly to talk about."

Shock sent hot anger through him. Had someone done that to her? The same someone who made her so frightened of her own emotions?

One hand cupped her cheek. "Nothing about you is ugly."

She scooted backward. "My night out? You promised."

Forcing a grin, he stared at her bare breasts. "You going like that?"

"Thought I might. What do you think?"

"I think you could start a riot, is what I think." Fumbling around for his pants, he discovered they were still wet from the rain. "Can't wear these. Guess we'll have to stay here." He leered, lunged forward, and grabbed at her.

She scrambled away. "I'll put them in the dryer. Your shirt too."

"What am I supposed to wear while I wait?"

"Oh, I don't know. I rather like you naked. You look so savage."

Kicking out of his boots, he peeled off the pants and handed them to her. "I am savage, naked or dressed."

She stood and walked hastily and dignified from the room, bare bottom swaying. Gave him barely enough time to contemplate what had happened and come to absolutely no conclusion before she returned with a terry cloth robe which he put on. It struck him above the knees, and he felt quite ridiculous. She needn't think he'd forgotten about the scar, though. One way or another he'd get the story out of her. He was, after all, a talented shrink.

While she dressed he found wine glasses and poured them each a drink. A few minutes later she returned wearing a filmy electric blue, low cut dress with points along the bottom that barely covered her knees. At her throat, a shimmering scarf cascaded down her bare back. On her feet, matching silver sandals with high heels and open toes that revealed silvery painted nails. He was rapidly developing a toe fetish.

"You look good enough to eat," he said, smoothing the slick cap of gleaming dark hair.

She laughed and shook her head.

"Sorry, did I muss it up? I can't keep my hands off you."

Suddenly she turned serious, her eyes deep pools darkened to midnight hues. "Spinner, is this real?"

"God, I hope so."

"No, I mean it. I'm frightened of—of getting too close and getting hurt. Are we just playing here, or are we starting something real?"

"This is about as real as it gets. What about you? Are you playing?"

Slowly, she shook her head. Then a breathtaking smile lit her face. "I can't believe I'm discussing this with a man in a knee-length terry cloth robe and artwork on his butt."

Then her arms were around him, her cheek against his chest, and he held her, prayed she wouldn't ask again if he was playing. He'd loved one woman. True it was love so blind it denied the impossibility of their relationship. Her a junkie, him a wise ass Indian filled with fury and a rage he couldn't curb. But when he'd lost her that had been the end of love, as far as he was concerned.

Now look here what he had offered to him, all wrapped up in his arms and asking him to be serious and not hurt her. He'd hurt her all right. Of that he was sure. But not yet, not right away, and it wouldn't be physical. He'd never hit her, would kill anyone who did.

Becca cried out in her sleep, opened her eyes, and tried to see beyond the darkness of her bedroom, remembering the storm and Jon being there. A dream, surely.

"Jon," she whispered.

Under her patting hand his pillow was smooth and cold and empty. Yes, definitely a dream. He would never make love with her that way. Never again. Between her legs, an ache matched the one in her heart.

"Mom?"

She sat up, fought the darkness with flailing hands. "No, no. Don't do that."

"Mom, it's me. Jeremiah."

"I know," she moaned, covering her mouth, her eyes. "You're gone, gone. You're dead. You can't be here. You can't."

His face floated before her, the way he'd looked when she went to the morgue to find him laid out on a cold slab. Jon told her not to go, said he would, but she had to see. Her baby couldn't be dead and she would prove it.

Even then she came away not believing. For a while. Then when she did accept his death her world caved in for good.

"I have to stop this. I have to. Go away, Jeremiah. You have to stop coming. I can't keep losing you over and over again."

"I can't, not yet. Not yet. Help me, please."

"Oh, Jeremiah, I love you, but I don't know how to help you." Hands cupped over her mouth muffled her cry, and then he was gone.

She opened her eyes, this time fully awake, the nightmare vanished.

Footsteps echoed down the hallway, someone rapped on her door, and she turned to see him, backlit by a bright glow. Not dead, her Jeremiah. That was all a dream, and this real.

"Mom, I'm going to drive over and see Amy. I'll be back in an hour or so. Okay?"

"Okay. Be careful, it's raining."

"I will. You be all right?"

"I'm fine. Just fine."

"Dad didn't call?"

"No, but he's busy. He'll be here Saturday for sure."

"I'll see him then."

"Jeremiah?"

He turned back, his face bright, expectant, eyes sparkling. A happy boy, always a happy boy.

"I love you."

"Love you, too."

"Don't go. No, don't," she screamed, but he'd already left. Why hadn't she stopped him? Protected him? It was happening all over again, and it would be branded into her heart forever, the pain excruciating and everlasting. The policeman at the door, strobing lights reflected against the icy trees, the world going upside down. Becoming a place where reality and nightmares exchanged places with regularity.

Hugging herself, she listened to the rain against the window.

The following morning, Spinner left Raine with a great deal of reluctance. Last night's rain had washed the sky to a ceramic blue, polished tree leaves shiny as new. Walking across the immaculate patch of green lawn that fronted her house, he turned over and over the differences between them. Her with money and an innate sense of class, him— well, yes. Him. A Cherokee with little sense of direction, no idea of class, and maybe five-hundred bucks in his checking account at any given time. He didn't even have a decent place to live, and up to this point hadn't much cared.

Didn't make any difference, though. This couldn't last. No way in hell could it last. Hell, he didn't even want it to.

But Jesus. Wasn't she something else?

Back at Hank's Garage, he found more pressing matters to worry about. The kid hadn't shown up for work. Leaving a steaming Hank, he climbed in the Nova, disappointment replacing his euphoria. What had happened to Lucas? If he didn't find him in a reasonable length of time, his work here would be over. He'd go to Vinita and pick up files on some other mistreated juvies. Dammit. He'd wanted this one to make it.

The kid wouldn't have bolted had it not been for Rebecca Kraft's visit—though he couldn't say that with absolute certainty. Still, Lucas was mighty upset about it.

The Kraft woman might be at RainTree this morning. Maybe he could talk to her, find out if Lucas had made reference to leaving or where he might be going. A good excuse to see Raine again, but he didn't allow that idea to hang around too long.

Good thing too. She wasn't there. Inside he found a morning rush putting both Cherry and Rebecca Kraft to the test. He took an out-of-the-way table, and prepared to wait until the crowd thinned.

"Well, hey, there," Cherry piped when she made it around to him. "Good to see you. Raine isn't here yet. What'll you have?"

"A plain black coffee, none of that foam or goo. It isn't Raine I wanted to see. Well, that is, I do, but I came to talk to Mrs. Kraft. No hurry, though. I'll wait."

"It'll be a wait." Cherry wiggled her fingers at him as she sashayed away, swinging her long blonde hair.

The delay gave him time to study Rebecca Kraft. Impeccably dressed in a navy blue pantsuit and white blouse, her streaked hair caught into a neat twist at the back of her head, she was a handsome woman. Yet her expression was one of extreme weariness. Cheeks sunken, dark circles under her eyes, lips that never quite smiled, all spoke of the grief she still carried. In spite of that, she wove her way through the crowded tables, making it look easy to take care of several groups at one time.

Since he had obviously chosen a table in Cherry's section, she didn't spot him right away. He finished his coffee and leaned back to study the unusual decor. Many of the patrons drifted away over the next thirty minutes or so, and still he sat, watching koi lazily swimming in a nearby pool.

"You wanted to see me?"

He looked up to see Rebecca standing above him, anger furrowing her brow and tightening her mouth. Rising, he indicated the chair opposite him.

"Could you join me for a moment, please?"

She warred with that for a beat, then shrugged and sat on the edge of the chair, prepared to flee if need be.

For a moment, he couldn't think how to begin. Why hadn't he rehearsed what he was going to say?

"Well? If it's about that Lucas Pell boy you can save your breath. I told him and I'll tell you, apologizing won't get him anywhere with me."

Catching her darting gaze, he asked, "What would?"

"Absolutely nothing. He killed my son. Do you honestly expect me to forgive him for that?"

"It was a tragic accident. Lucas isn't the boy he was then. Surely you could give him a chance."

"What chance did Jeremiah have?"

"I'm sorry. None. Of course, he had none. But neither did Lucas. Did you know that his mother and father fed him liquor from the time he could walk? And do you know why?"

"No, and I don't care to." Her expressive eyes said different.

Spinner studied her for a long moment, until her sorrowful gaze shifted. "So they could sell him for sex to men and women and he wouldn't fight back." He never took his gaze from her face.

"Oh, dear *God.*" She looked as if she'd been struck. Laced long fingers together on the table till her knuckles turned white.

"And that's only scratching the surface. I shouldn't be telling you this, but I have to break through that wall you've put up. All he lives for is to have you forgive him. Nothing else means anything to him."

"I don't think I can help you or him, Mr. Spinner."

He ignored her misuse of his name. "Could you at least tell me if he said anything when you went to see him? Anything about where he might be going?"

"No, nothing. He told you I came?"

"Oh, yes, he did. Then he disappeared. I need to find him. Mrs. Kraft, you could help me save this boy if you would. I know you're filled with hate for him. But what would Jeremiah think?"

She rose to her feet, leaned forward and pounded on the table with her fist. "Don't you dare. Don't you dare presume to bring my son's memory into this. You don't have any idea what he was like. How sweet and gentle a boy he was. And to think someone like Lucas Pell is alive and he's dead."

The few customers remaining in the shop stared in mute silence, and she stopped, hand over her mouth, tears pouring.

Spinner stood. "I'm so sorry to have upset you. I'm so afraid of what will happen to Lucas. He needs a break, just one. I thought you could give it to him. I was wrong. I won't bother you again. You know, there are people who could help you work your way through this, if you'd let them."

When she didn't reply but stared at him, eyes like crackling ice, he rose and left the shop. He didn't turn to see if she was watching him, but he hoped like hell she was.

Fourteen

An overweight, puffing deputy dragged Lucas downstairs from the jail for his arraignment in the Craig County Courthouse in Vinita the next morning. Chains hooked his wrists to his waist, another around his ankles.

Must've thought he would run or attack someone. And they were right. Given the chance, he would. Lucas hobbled down the hallway and sat where they put him, a knot in his stomach the size of a baseball.

On the long bench outside a lighted courtroom, the two black dudes who'd picked him up on the highway slouched in their own chains.

"You better tell 'em the truth," Lucas yelled at them. "You know I ain't got nothing to do with this, you motherfuckers. Just hitching me a ride."

The deputy cuffed him on the arm. "Shut up, scumbag."

One of the dudes flipped him a birdie, neither looked at him. There was no sign of the girls who'd been with them.

When it came his turn to go before the judge, he shuffled into the courtroom and met his lawyer, a harried young man who looked like that nerdy kid on those old reruns of Happy Days they watched in juvie, except he had rimless glasses that kept sliding down on his nose. He scarcely spared Lucas a glance, concentrated instead on the charges. Didn't even introduce himself.

"I didn't do it," Lucas told him.

The man lifted a finger, shook his head, and continued to scan the police report.

Fidgeting, Lucas let him finish, peering at the clock between the two windows. Craned his neck to look behind him at the sparsely occupied seats, looking like church pews. Didn't see Spinner, but wasn't surprised. The man was done with him.

He leaned toward the public defender, whispered, "I was hitching, they picked me up. I didn't know they was gonna rob the store." Terrified down to his very bones, Lucas did something he'd never done in his life. Instead of demanding he begged. "Could you call Spinner Grayfeather? He's over in Chota. Please let him know where I am."

The man didn't look up, like he never even heard him.

The bailiff called his name. His gut clenched tight as his fists and he resisted hurling right there. He wanted to kick someone, pound something, rip someone to shreds with his teeth. All such stupid crap he almost laughed.

The PD led him forward past a rail that separated the pews from the judge's domain. Chains rattled and clinked around his ankles. While the charges were read the judge, a fuzzy-haired old man with a gravelly voice and the jowls of a bulldog glared at him as if he'd already been found guilty.

Armed robbery? Shit, what was that? He didn't see no gun, sure didn't have one. His heart froze, sank like a stone into the pit of his stomach.

The PD touched his arm. "Not guilty."

"Bail?"

Lucas tilted his head back, stared at the ceiling tiles. There were some missing and covered over with plastic.

A man behind him spoke. "Your honor, the defendant was picked up with two other boys, one of them had a weapon. They were fleeing the scene of an armed robbery."

"Your honor," the PD said in the same flat voice. "He has no money, he can't make bail."

"Then he can sit it out in a jail cell," his honor growled. "Bail is set at twenty-five thousands dollars. Trial." He glanced at the desk nearby, behind which sat a tall, black, bald-headed dude. "Two weeks, your honor. June second."

"What about the other two?"

"Coming up next your honor."

"I want 'em all three tried at once. Save the court's time."

"Your honor," Lucas' PD said. "This boy has nothing to do with them. He doesn't even know them. They picked him up on the highway. I ask that he be tried separately."

"He ought to watch out who he rides with." The old fart slammed the gavel down. "Next."

As a deputy led Lucas away he heard charges being read against the two black dudes that had drug him into all this trouble. Four counts of armed robbery. Shit, they'd done this before and not been caught. He was going away for a long time. Even he knew better than to use a gun. Rage against the injustice overpowered his common sense, and he strained to get loose from the deputy, rattling the chains that bound him. The deputy cuffed him on the head, and deep inside a dark hole opened up and he tumbled head over heels into its great, black mouth.

After Spinner left, Rebecca sat in the back room of RainTree trying to pull herself together. How could she have made such a fool of herself in public? Yelling at him as if he'd been somehow responsible for Jeremiah's death. True, she resented his helping that Lucas filth, but it was his job.

She couldn't go on like this, but could see no way to put an end to it. Other people appeared to recover from losing a child, why couldn't she? Spinner had said something about places she could go to get help. Maybe she ought to try one of them. It was difficult to imagine existing this way for the remainder of her life, and clearly she could not commit suicide and put an end to it. She would not do that to David and Christi. She had put them through enough already.

Maybe Spinner could tell her who to see. Half the people she knew were seeing shrinks. It was quite the chic thing to do. Why should she be any different?

With the decision came a strange sort of calm, as if at last she might climb out of the morass into which she'd sunk over the past sixteen months. Drying her eyes, she rose and went to help Cherry.

While she dumped ingredients into the latté machine Raine came in.

"Good morning, everyone. Sorry I'm late. Did you have any trouble keeping up?"

Becca darted a warning look at Cherry. All she needed was the girl blabbing about her outburst. The pretty blonde seemed oblivious to her fears and greeted Raine with a wave.

"You're sure happy this morning," Becca said to her friend. "And no, we didn't have a bit of trouble. Did we Cherry? Besides, you deserve a day off now and again. In fact, you deserve a few months off."

Raine grinned. "And I might just be asking for them, too."

Cherry stopped rinsing cups and saucers, Becca paused, and both stared at Raine.

"What happened?"

"Oh, well. I guess it won't hurt to tell you guys. I think I'm in love."

"Lorraine Gregory. You are not," Becca said.

"It's that hunky Cherokee, isn't it?" Cherry asked.

Raine raised her shoulders and smiled, the dimples popping into her reddening cheeks.

"No, Raine. Surely not. He's, well he's...."

"He's well what?" Brow arched, she pinned Becca with a questioning stare. "An Indian?"

Becca felt a flush crawling over her cheeks. "I wasn't going to say that exactly. You don't know him, that's all. Don't forget what happened—"

Raine cut her off with a sharp stare. "What he is, is a gentle man like I haven't met in a long time, if ever. He's honest and—"

It was Becca's turn to arch a brow. "And what? He works for the county, a glorified social worker with no home or anything. And he's far from gentle. You of all people—"

Raine's eyes flashed a second warning, her voice sharpened. "Why, Becca. I didn't know you were such a snob."

"Snobbery has nothing to do with it. You have nothing in common. Nothing at all."

Raine whirled round and round like a child at a party. "Oh, yes, we do, my friend. Yes, we do."

"Lorraine. You've slept with him."

"So to speak, but we didn't sleep much."

"Sex, no matter how fantastic, is not really having something in common. The entire human race has that in common."

Cherry giggled and went back to rinsing, clattering the china until Becca scolded her.

"Child, be careful. Those are very delicate."

For a long moment all three women stared at each other, then burst out laughing, with Becca the last to join in.

That relieved the tension, but Becca wasn't sure they had much to laugh about. The shop remained busy enough the rest of the day, preventing her and Raine from discussing Spinner, but she was certainly going to try to talk some sense into her friend. It was one thing to have a little fun, quite another to get serious over someone like Spinner. A man she barely knew. With her first husband in jail for trying to kill her, Raine certainly ought to know better.

Spinner drove around town, aimlessly searching for Lucas. When his cell phone beeped he pulled over and stopped, found the thing under some junk on the passenger seat. Half the time he forgot to carry it with him, the other half he forgot how to use it. He'd probably be better off with smoke signals, just like his boss had said more than once when he failed to reach him.

"Yeah?"

"Spinner Grayfeather?"

"That's me."

"This is Walt Whitman, over in Vinita."

"No kidding? I thought you were dead." Spinner couldn't resist the quip, even knowing the poor fella had probably heard all the jokes about his famous name.

The voice didn't change in tone one bit. "I'm a public defender, not an author. Nor am I dead. I've got one of yours in jail over here. Promised him I'd call, though I doubt you can help him out."

"Oh, shit. Not Lucas Pell."

"The very same."

Damn. Spinner let a breath whoosh out, disappointment riding him down. "What'd he do?"

"Armed robbery."

Head leaned back, Spinner took several deep breaths. Dammit to hell. What was the kid thinking?

"He says he didn't do it. Says he was hitching, that they picked him up, and next thing he knew they were robbing a store while he was getting—uh, well worked over in the backseat by, as it turns out, a juvie, who is as we speak in custody as well. That's statutory rape, but I don't think it's an issue here, considering her record."

"Ah, Christ. You know what, Whitman? I believe him. About the robbery, I mean. You know why?"

"I'd be interested," Whitman replied.

"Because Lucas doesn't have enough imagination to make up a story like that. And wild as he can get, he's never used a gun."

"I can't take that to his trial, but we did plead not guilty. The judge has decreed all three will be tried together on June 2. If you could help with the boy's defense in any way, I'd be grateful, and I'm sure he would too."

"He has a long juvenile record, but of course that's sealed. Was he drunk or high on anything?"

"No, he tested clean."

"Thank God for small favors. He just turned eighteen and I thought I had him on a leash, trying to help him get straightened out. This tears it. God I hate losing some of 'em, you know?"

"How well I do. Look, I gotta go. Let me give you my cell number and if you can come up with something to help get this kid off, that'd be great. My record's not so good, and well, I guess I believe him too, much as I've heard 'I didn't do nothing.' Keep in touch."

"Will do, and Whitman?"

"Yeah?"

"Sorry about the joke."

The man actually chuckled. "Forget it, I'm used to it. Had the name all my life. Besides, yours isn't any great shakes. Though you might keep in mind I didn't joke about it."

Spinner laughed. "Doesn't pay to insult a Cherokee. Could get you scalped." He thanked a chuckling Whitman and hung up.

Now what? The kid had no record of ever using a weapon, unless it'd be whatever he picked up if someone came at him. Rocks, garbage can lids, boards, bottles, yes. Guns or knives, no.

He needed an investigator to go over there and talk to some witnesses at the store, see if he could find someone who could put Lucas in the car when the robbery went down. And then he needed someone to vouch for the boy. Someone with class, clout, and the desire to honestly help him out of this jam.

First he called Vinita and put Ned Keeler on the job. Keeler also did freelance investigative work for insurance companies when he wasn't dragging in fugitives who'd jumped bond. He agreed to get right on it. Then Spinner sat holding the phone and staring out the window. A young mother pushed a stroller down the sidewalk, ponytail swinging to and fro. Across the street some kids gave their in-line skates a workout in a parking lot. A beautiful, normal day in Oklahoma.

At length, he punched in some numbers and when the phone was picked up by that spritely Cherry, asked to speak to Rebecca Kraft. This was a long shot, but if she agreed it would be good for both her and Lucas. If he could talk her into it.

Amazed, Becca listened to Spinner's request. "You want me to testify for him? How could you think I would even consider such a thing?"

"Because what you need right now is to do something positive for yourself, your son, and this boy."

"And he's charged with armed robbery?"

"Yes, but it looks like he probably had nothing to do with it except to be in the wrong place. He didn't even know these kids. He was running away, they picked him up on the highway and next thing he knew they were holding up a convenience store."

Becca held the receiver out from her ear and stared at it as if she could penetrate the wires and reach this man.

"And I'm supposed to care about his problems?"

"Mrs. Kraft. Your earlier actions could well be the reason Lucas split."

"Blaming someone else for his misbehavior again, Mr. Spinner?"

"Just Spinner, ma'am. And no, I didn't intend to say that. Your son would be this boy's age today. If this whole thing were reversed, wouldn't you want someone to give him a hand? Just a little boost? Imagine Jeremiah in such a fix."

"My boy is dead. I can't imagine a worse fix."

He didn't reply for a minute, but she could hear him take a deep breath. "For Lucas, there are worse things that can happen to him if he's convicted. Before it's over, he'll wish he were dead. Can't you have some compassion? He's a child, a badly abused, alcoholic child. He deserves one little break, seeing as how he's never had one."

Silent tears flowed down Becca's cheeks as she stared across the peaceful coffee shop. "How can you ask this of me?"

"Because you're the only one who can possibly care enough to do something for him."

"I hate him. Don't you understand that?"

"Mrs. Kraft. I don't think you actually hate him. What he did, yes, but not the boy. You're more charitable than that. And even if it were true, hate or love are caring. Sometimes they can't be separated."

"I'm not having any trouble separating the two." Damn him, why didn't he leave her alone? Her stomach rolled over and she thought she might vomit at the idea of actually helping this boy.

"Help him, please. You won't have to deal with him at all. Just agree to testify at his trial. Ask the judge to give him another chance. It will mean a lot coming from you. The PD is going for a hearing before a judge if he can get Lucas separated from the other two who actually committed the robbery. He doesn't think Lucas will come across well in front of a jury."

"No kidding." She wiped her nose with a tissue and gazed at Raine, who had stopped serving to study her.

"Rebecca, you don't have to take him to raise, just help him. And help yourself."

Becca fought for control, then cleared her throat and stood straight. Maybe him calling her by her Christian name swayed her, she really didn't know. All she did know was that she could understand why Raine was attracted to this man. He had the magic power of persuasion. He never raised his musical voice, nor did he seem to be begging. And he appeared to genuinely care for this boy who could mean nothing to him but a case.

"All right. All right, I'll try. Just tell me where and when."

"Thank you. You won't regret this, I promise. I'll let you know in plenty of time, and I'll be glad to drive you over."

"I can drive myself, thank you. Just get the information to me, and then I don't want to see this boy again. You hear me? I want him to leave Monkey Island so I never have to look at him, ever again. Do you understand?"

"Perfectly."

"And Spinner, Mr. Grayfeather?"

"Yes?"

"You better not hurt Raine or you'll have me to deal with."

For a moment he appeared to have been struck speechless, then he replied meekly, "Yes, ma'am."

She hung up, wondering how she had been talked into this. She would be in for more grief before it was finished. Too late she remembered that she had been going to ask him for his advice concerning her own mental health. She wasn't about to call him back.

She returned to work, determined to tell no one about this latest plan. She had heard enough criticism about her decisions concerning Lucas Pell.

Three days later a bulky envelope arrived in the mail. Carrying it and a pair of shears to slit the fibrous paper, Becca poured herself a glass of iced tea and went out on the deck to study the handwriting. There was no return address. The May heat was tempered by a light breeze off the lake. It would soon be Memorial Day, signaling a full-fledged invasion of tourists. The lake would teem with all manner of water craft. She didn't mind, really. Their privacy was seldom invaded, and she enjoyed watching people at play. Or had not all that long ago.

For a few years after they bought the house, she and Jon took David and Christi on boating excursions when he came home on weekends. She remembered well how they had christened their first trip by anchoring in a cove and making love on deck after the kids were asleep in the cabin. The boat rolled gently beneath their bodies while water slapped the hull in a rhythmic serenade. Lapping water underlined his eloquence of speech like exquisite, comely, angelic. No man had ever uttered such words to her.

Such a tender touch, fingers kneading her back, warm moist lips nibbling her breasts, long, lithe body moving to cover her in slow motion until her desire for him grew frantic. God how he knew the art of lovemaking. Whispering those delicate words one at a time while he prepared her. All the while his tongue circled one nipple then the other, explored prickly flesh along her ribs, around her belly button, up and down her inner thighs, prolonging their joining until she gasped with a fiery need that erupted from the very center of her soul.

He could go on for long, enjoyable hours, bringing her and himself to the brink only to drag them back time after time to find something more intriguing to add to their lovemaking. The act of merely brushing his fingertips over her throat set her on fire, for she never knew what was coming next. Full of surprises, this man she had thought she would love forever. Even after she bore him the children, he worshiped her body, and she never expected that to change.

Growing up, the kids had spent summers waterskiing and boating and swimming. And then Jeremiah came along, and a change took place. At first so subtle she could never put her finger on it. Jon was absent more and more of the time tending to the needs of their growing business until it became his mistress, she his neglected wife. They had all learned to get along without him in spirit. But not in body. At times she ached so badly that she secretly bought a dildo to handle the harshest of the desires. It wasn't the same, but it had to do.

How she missed those days when the house was filled with childish gaiety and more love than it could hold. Now only ghosts dwelled in the empty rooms. And she could find nothing similar to that rubbery penis to take the place of all she had lost.

Perhaps it was time she too abandoned this place. She played with the envelope that had arrived in the mail, ignoring its significance. Had she and Jon really made love the other night, or had she dreamed it? When she awoke there was no sign he'd been there save the creamy wetness between her legs and the languid serenity that came after exceptional sex. And later she'd come to think she'd imagined even that. It had been so long since they'd come together with such passion that it had to have been a fantasy created by her drug dulled mind.

The next day she called the office, just to listen to the sound of his voice, to determine the truth. But he was in a meeting and couldn't be disturbed. Even when he knew it was her calling he wouldn't come to the phone. Told Celie to tell her he'd call her back, but he hadn't. So much for her daydreams.

Becca pulled herself out of the reverie and, taking another sip of lemony tea, cut the envelope open with the shears. Inside, she found a plastic folder, secured with a string wrapped around a small button and a handwritten note.

Mrs. Kraft,

This is something I would not ordinarily do, but I think you should have this information, and in order to save Lucas Pell, I'll break a few rules. Please understand that this is privileged and should go no further.

It was signed with a huge looping *S* followed by a scribbled line that was unreadable.

"Break a few rules, indeed." She had a feeling that damned Cherokee would break them all to get what he wanted, and probably had on more than one occasion. If he ever lied to Raine or hurt her with his deceitful ways, she'd brain him. And that he could be well assured of.

Inside, she found what she expected. Lucas Pell's juvenile record going back to when he was taken from his parents. Spinner had told her some of it—how his mother and father had used him as a sex toy for all their acquaintances, which consisted mostly of alcoholics, drug addicts, and perverts. Keeping the boy drunk, and later stoned, had made an alcoholic and an addict of him by the time he was ten years old.

A wonder he'd survived. If only he hadn't, he wouldn't have been around to kill her Jeremiah.

Still, she felt a stirring of compassion. The boy's memories must be horrendous. After going through several foster homes in which he acted out with violence at home, in school, and on the street, he was put in juvenile detention at the age of thirteen.

He fared no better there. Fighting constantly, he managed to smuggle in drugs on several occasions, and attacked a guard who had to beat him nearly senseless to stop his rampage. Those were only a few of the infractions.

Becca shuddered as she read them. By the time Lucas had broken out of detention, stolen a car, gotten drunk, and killed Jeremiah, he had turned sixteen and spiraled completely out of control. Damaged beyond redemption. Or so everyone but Spinner thought.

Unable to read more, she put down the file.

Jeremiah was fifteen that winter's night. A good boy, raised in a good home. Well, not so good as far as togetherness, but not much different from the families of his peers whose fathers were too busy to spare them much time. He'd grown to be the kind of kid everyone liked, boys, girls, teachers, other kids' parents.

How terrible that such an extraordinary boy could be destroyed by a defective like Lucas Pell. How tragic for them both.

Becca wiped her eyes and realized she was crying for Lucas as much as for herself, her family, her beautiful Jeremiah. That she could cry for him surprised her. She might never be able to forgive him, but she should do this one thing for him. Maybe for herself as well.

Yet, what if he got out on the street and committed another crime? Killed another mother's son? Oh, hell. That hadn't occurred to her until this very moment. She couldn't take that chance. She had to talk to Spinner. Explain it had all been a mistake. What had she been thinking? Turn her son's killer loose on society? Never.

Fifteen

Sunday afternoon, Becca decided to take a chance Spinner would be at the motel, and drove over. She had to return the records he'd sent her and explain that she'd had a change of heart about testifying for Lucas Pell. After lying awake all night debating with herself, she realized she couldn't be even remotely responsible for what the boy might do if he went free. Best if they put him in jail where he could do no more harm.

Spinner looked at the world through glasses tinted by his own experiences, and could not possibly see it through her eyes. He thought everyone deserved a second chance, and she wasn't so sure. Especially when that chance might cause them to do something even worse.

When she pulled into the motel parking, Raine's red sports car was parked beside Spinner's disreputable rattletrap. Pulling up beside it, she shut off the engine and drummed her fingers on the steering wheel. Now what? Intrude or go away?

The idea of carrying the dreadful packet filled with the horrors of Lucas Pell's short life back home with her was unthinkable. She would knock. They were free not to answer. If he didn't come to the door, she'd toss it in his car with a note and be done with it.

But he did answer her knock, wearing no shoes or shirt. For a frantic moment she couldn't take her eyes off the red and gold serpent coiled on his chest. He caught her staring and grinned in such a way she felt the impact of sensuality that attracted Raine to this man.

Embarrassed, she moved her eyes elsewhere. Behind him the bed covers were in disarray. The intimacy suggested by his attire and the condition of the bed embarrassed her further, and she didn't know where to look next.

Raine sat at a small table near the back window wearing a too-large tee shirt and nothing else, shapely legs crossed, one bare foot swinging. A red and white cardboard bucket of take-out chicken sat before her. Raine had never looked so radiant and un-put-together. And the Cherokee beamed as if he'd been at a big bowl of cream.

"Come in, Mrs. Kraft. Join us. It's Kentucky Fried, greasy and lip smacking."

"Becca," Raine said. "Come on in." No shame marred her features. On the contrary, she appeared quite pleased with herself.

For a long moment Becca couldn't speak. This was just too utterly confusing, considering Raine's opinion of men.

Because the two of them acted like they'd won the lottery, she had to say something, and finally managed to sputter, "Hello, Raine, Mr. Spinner."

"It's Spinner Grayfeather, but please don't call me Mr. Grayfeather. That'd be too much." He flashed that grin again, but aimed it at Raine.

Swallowing harshly, she tried not to watch while Raine and Spinner gazed at each other in adoration.

"Yes, well… ummm, you could call me Becca, if you wish."

Raine laughed.

Spinner echoed her. "Becca. Will do." He glanced at the packet under her arm.

Without discussing it, she tossed it on the bed, blurted what she'd come to say so she could escape all this sickening admiration.

"I'm sorry to interrupt. I won't stay but a moment. I couldn't do this on the telephone. I came to tell you that I've changed my mind. I'm sorry, but I can't take a chance that boy will get out on my say-so and do something like he did to my Jeremiah. We're better off with him in jail."

The words wiped all pleasure from his face. "Mrs.— I mean, Becca. Lucas isn't like that anymore, I assure you. He doesn't belong in jail."

She raised her shoulders. "Perhaps he doesn't, but I can't be responsible for getting him out. You'll have to do that yourself."

"So you'd rather be responsible for what happens to him in that place. You have no idea what goes on in there. He needs a chance."

"No, nor do I want to know. They're vicious, violent criminals, as is he. I wouldn't be surprised at all what goes on in there. Dreadful things, I'm sure, that I am not responsible for. As for a chance, I thought that's what the law gave him, after he killed my son. Three years in detention, and look what he did when he got out. Robbed a store with a gun."

"He didn't do that, Becca. I promise you, he didn't."

"You can't know that. You have no way of knowing it." Becca glanced at her friend. "Help me out here, Raine. You know what I've been through, what my family's been through."

"Spinner, perhaps... I mean, I don't know exactly what's going on here, but Becca is in no shape to confront this boy, much less help him. I take it he's in jail."

"She'll never be in shape to confront her own life if she doesn't stop hiding from it," Spinner said. "I'm sorry, but it's the truth." He tossed that at Becca.

"How would you know?" she snapped. "You don't know anything about me."

"I know you can't forgive yourself for what happened, any more than you can forgive Lucas. Until you do that, you'll live in hell. Believe me, I do know that.

"This boy, this child, who has been mistreated in the worst ways possible since he was born, needs someone to believe in him. Someone to let him know he matters. Can't you see that?"

"I guess I can't." Tears burned her eyes. "Believe me, I'm not heartless. I would do this if I could. I just can't." She hit herself in the chest with a fist. "Inside here, my heart is cold as stone. My life is empty."

Raine crossed the room and put an arm around her. "Honey, please." She glanced at Spinner. "Leave her alone. Can't you see how she's suffering? She's the victim here, not your precious Lucas."

His eyes slitted. "And you, Raine, are an enabler. Don't you see you're just making it harder for her to recover?"

Becca pushed her way free of Raine's embrace. "Stop it, both of you. Stop it. I'm a grown woman, perfectly sane. Don't talk about me as if I'm in a coma."

"I'm sorry, but I thought you had two more children and a husband. I don't understand how you can say your life is empty."

"If I had a dozen children, losing one would still leave a black hole."

"I don't deny that, not for a minute would I suggest such a thing. But a hole is not the same as an empty life. You can recover from this. You'll never get over it entirely. You'll never forget your son. But you need to honor his memory, make his life worth something, not darken it with despair and suffering. He must have been happy, he must have made you and those around him happy. What happens to that if you don't stop this? Must you always think of Jeremiah in darkness, rather than in light?"

"Somebody help me," she sobbed. Blinded by tears, she staggered to the door, wrenched it open and fled, their voices reaching out to her to come back. To wait. To listen.

She would listen to no more. How dare he tell her how to grieve for her own child? First her family turned against her, now this stranger pretended to know what she was going through.

Fumbling for the car door handle, she threw herself inside, searched her handbag for the keys, throwing pens and sunglasses, tissue and wallet out on the seat. Finally, in desperation, dumping the contents out and pawing through everything to come up with the car keys. Sobs constricted her chest, filled her throat until she could hardly swallow, but she finally punched the key home, turned the ignition.

Vaguely, she heard someone pounding on the glass, flicked the lock button so they couldn't get in, and without looking to see who it was or if they were in the way, reversed with a squeal of tires and fishtailed out onto the highway.

"Leave me alone, leave me alone. I don't want this. I can't stand this." Hands clutching the wheel, she stomped the accelerator, sent the Nissan hurtling along the narrow highway.

Blinded by tears, she vaguely saw a car approaching on her right. Moving, moving, moving.

Oh, shit! It wasn't going to stop.

With a scream that hammered at her eardrums, she stood on the brake, felt the car hunker, tires grabbing at the pavement while it hurtled ever closer to the other car, now in the middle of the intersection.

Through the driver's side window a woman's face, frozen in a rictus of fear, stared at her. As the Nissan's antilock brakes controlled the stop, she saw with horror a child peering out the back.

"Oh, God. Oh, dear God. No."

She could do nothing but hang on to the wheel and press the brake, like a bystander without any power over the situation. Later, she couldn't quite remember what happened next, she only knew that the other car sped out of the way and she slid to a stop in its very tracks. Head on the steering wheel, she gasped for air. Her stomach turned over and she gagged. Pawing at the lock button, she shoved the door open and vomited in the street.

Long after her stomach emptied, she continued to dry heave, unable to stop.

"Ma'am, you all right?" A young man stood there, visibly unsure what to do, but willing nevertheless.

Waving a hand, she tried to reply… to speak even the one word that would send this helpful person on his way.

"Perhaps you could move your car over to the shoulder," he said. "You're blocking the road. Could I help you? Are you ill?"

At last she was able to sit up, fumble in the seat for a tissue to wipe her mouth, and reply. "No, I'm fine, thank you. I will. I'll move my car. Thank you so very much."

All perception, all thought dimmed by a dense fog, she tried to form some sort of action. But her hands would not function. All they seemed able to do was clench the wheel. Cars honked behind her and the man went away. The other car, the one she'd almost hit, was nowhere to be seen. They'd driven on as if they hadn't almost died here moments earlier.

What if she'd hit that car broadside? Killed that mother and her child? What if…?

Steering the idling car to the shoulder of the highway, she let it roll to a stop, fumbled blindly with the ignition, and shut off the engine, then clutched trembling hands over her mouth. She sat there for a long while before she stopped shaking enough to drive home.

"We shouldn't have let her go in that condition," Raine said when Spinner joined her in the parking lot.

"I don't think we could've stopped her. She'll be all right."

"You don't know that!"

His hand on her arm tightened. "No, you're right, I don't. Let's go inside. We make quite a sight standing out here less than fully clothed."

My God, had she really done this? Taken part in a wild night in a motel with a man she barely knew? Now stood in the parking lot of a sleazy motel wearing his tee shirt that barely covered her butt, while her best friend fled in agony.

"You know what? I need to get dressed and go find Becca. See if I can help her."

Limping through the scattered gravel on bare feet he guided her back into the room. "You're not helping her, you know."

"I'm her best friend."

He trailed knuckles over her clenched jaw. "I know you are. And a better friend she couldn't ask for. You care deeply for what's happening to her. But you're allowing her to continue wallowing in self-pity. Giving her your permission."

"That's nonsense. In the first place, she doesn't need my permission. In the second, I have some compassion for what she's going through. Grieving the loss of a child is hardly wallowing in self-pity. She helped me when I... when my marriage came apart. I can do no less for her."

"You recovered. How did you do that? Did she help you recover, or help you continue to be defeated by what had happened?"

" She—we—I—*damn* you."

"Yes, damn me," he said and took her in his arms, holding her close.

"Someday you need to tell me all about this marriage and the man who hurt you so badly. But right now, you need to help your good friend. Encourage her to forgive Lucas, even if she doesn't appear for him in court. For her own sake she needs to forgive him, believe me. And she needs to forgive herself and probably that husband of hers as well."

She leaned back and gazed up at him. "You told her to forgive herself. I don't understand that. She has nothing to be forgiven for."

"Probably not, but that doesn't stop her thinking she does. Anytime a parent loses a child, they eventually get around to blaming themselves and their partner. If only they'd been there. If only they'd told them not to go out. If only they'd taught them better, or not bought them the car, or maybe they should've kept them locked in their room till they were thirty. When a loved one dies, there's always something we can blame ourselves for."

The somber tone of his voice told her he spoke from experience, and she realized how little she really knew about his past. As he knew nothing about hers. But did she want to know more? Or might it be better if she ended this affair? She'd vowed never to trust another man, certainly never to get close to one again. Now, here she was spending nights with him, wearing his tee shirt just like Meg Ryan in some romantic movie. What came next? She certainly did not know. Because she still had serious doubts about their future, she refrained from asking him about his personal life.

"I suppose you're right. Yet, it's hard for me to tell Becca she's wrong. I can't bear to see her hurt any more, and that bastard of a husband of hers is no help."

Spinner sat on the edge of the bed and pulled on his socks. "Does he abuse her?"

"Oh, no. nothing like that. He's just not been at her side, helping her through this like he should."

"Not unusual. A lot of marriages fall apart over the death of a child. People grieve differently, and often don't understand even those they're closest to. Are they separated, divorcing?"

"Not exactly." She gathered her scattered clothing from the floor. "I'm always hearing that about marriages failing over the death of a child. No one ever says if those marriages were strong before. Maybe they were just failing all along, and this final tragedy ended any try at reconciling. He quit coming around long before Jeremiah was killed. He stays in Tulsa where his business is, and she stays out on Monkey Island. For a while after the accident, I hoped they were getting it together, but then he took off again. Said he was tired of her drinking and taking pills. All he does is work. They hardly see each other, and now her kids have gone off to do their own thing. She's so alone. I can't, I won't abandon her."

She skinned his tee shirt off and handed it to him.

Spinner grabbed her hand and pulled her down beside him, cupping her bare breasts in both hands. "You sure look scrumptious naked. Feel good, too."

"Spinner, where are we going with this?" she asked, not pushing him away in spite of her serious mood.

"Well." He leaned down to kiss her belly button. "Here, and here," he continued, nibbling his way lower. "And then on down here."

She moaned and lay back, opening herself to him, completely forgetting her desire to discuss their liaison and where it was taking them. She forgot, as well, her best friend and her distraught flight a few minutes earlier.

As he moved over her, she released the snap on his jeans and ran her hands inside to peel them down. Her head swam as if she were an old fashioned heroine ready to swoon. Seemed she could not get enough of his often frantic, sometimes languid lovemaking. If that was a sign of something, she wasn't sure what.

Mind whirling with what had almost happened, Becca ached to hear Jon's voice. Wasn't sure why. Perhaps she should fight the urge, but her hands would not obey. On this Sunday afternoon she had no idea where to find him, but she snatched up the phone. They were so out of touch, so lost to each other, she had no idea what he did when he wasn't working. She called his cell phone first, got the message that he was not available. She clicked off without saying anything. Next, the condo in Tulsa, again got a machine and disconnected. Speed dialed the office. Same story, disconnected again. She would not leave some wild rambling message that would tell Jon she was out of control once more.

Where could he be? Though she'd once accused him of having an affair, she couldn't in her wildest imaginings fathom him having even a casual relationship with another woman. He didn't have time for her, so how could he find time for something like that? Still, she was no fool, and knew that many men like Jon, with his personality, often had not one, but several affairs. It was in their nature to conquer, not only in the business world, but in their private lives. He'd been unable to stop her downward spiral, so he might have gone elsewhere.

All right. She'd start over. Be rational. At each of his numbers, she collected herself and left as calm a message as she could manage.

"Hi, Jon. It's Becca. Could you give me a call when you get this? I have something important I want… need to discuss with you. Thanks."

There, that sounded perfectly sane and sober, didn't it? If only she could listen to it play back to make sure. Too bad she didn't have his mistress's telephone number.

God, she could be so pathetic. Already decided he was having an affair and pretending the possibility only just now occurred to her.

Idiot!

Going to the kitchen, she dug around in the fridge, found some eggs and cheese, and tossed together a quick, no frills omelet, which she ate out on the deck while watching the sun set across the lake. Still starving, she went to the freezer and dragged out one of Christi's Sara Lee cheesecakes. Cutting herself a large slice, she went back outside and let it sit on the table until it thawed enough to eat.

Every bite was nirvana. Food hadn't tasted this good in a long while, and she wondered if it was because she had so narrowly escaped killing someone today. If she had died it would have been of little consequence, but she had avoided killing a mother and child. Once she recovered from the terror of the near miss, she could celebrate that.

What would she have done had it turned out differently? Would she have been at fault? Of course, no doubt. She'd acted foolishly, speeding down a narrow highway while bawling her eyes out and not paying attention. But what about the woman's family? Would they have forgiven her? And if not, would she have been able to mend her life?

Grateful to have escaped such a fate, she licked the last of the cheesecake off her fork and watched the sun disappear in a flare of yellow, gold, and orange that painted the lake in exquisite hues. The sky turned from blue to lavender to an ashen gray and darkness settled around her shoulders like a shroud.

Still she didn't move. Behind her the empty house echoed the rowdy ghost laughter of children. When she turned to look, all was dark and silent. She was alone.

Sixteen

Locked behind bars, Lucas seldom slept. And when he did he dreamed hideous dreams in which the ghost of Jeremiah Kraft stalked him through endless dark hallways that smelled of death. Nights when he didn't sleep were worse. The dead boy watched him from the corner of his cell. Because he was awake, Jeremiah must be real. Lucas screamed out a lot, both waking and sleeping, and the guard threatened to send him to the loony bin or hang him by his heels out the fourth-floor window. The other prisoners promised worse if he didn't shut the fuck up.

Good place for him. Where he belonged. The loony bin.

When the guard didn't carry out his threat, the prisoners did. On the second day, four of them caught him in the shower and beat him until he couldn't get up. Then they stuck a bar of soap in his mouth and promised to put it elsewhere the next time.

"You know, up your ass," one of them said, and they all snickered.

They were just getting started on his punishment, and what might happen next terrified him.

On the third day his PD, Walt Whitman, came, looking out of place in his suit and tie and nerdy haircut that attempted to hide his bald spot.

"What happened to your face?"

Determined to tough it out, Lucas touched his bruised cheek. "Nothing. I fell in the shower."

"I'll just bet you did. Try to stay out of trouble."

Lucas wanted to throw something at him, but he ground his teeth and sat very still, fists gripped in his lap till they ached.

"We're trying to find a witness who can put you in the car during the robbery. That won't get you off, but it will help. If we could find someone who saw them pick you up on the highway, that would be better. Exactly where were you hitching?"

Lucas glared. "You doin' this? With all the work you got?"

"Well, not exactly. Your friend Spinner Grayfeather has someone working on it. He sure wants you out of here in a bad way."

"Not any badder than I do." Spinner? His friend? Not so's you'd notice it.

"Then you need to think. Where were you?"

"Needing to get far away as I could from Chota and that rich bitch. Walking up Highway one twenty-five just past where eighty-five-A cuts over to Bernice."

"Going west, yes?"

"Who knows? I was gonna head toward the interstate."

"West, then. And they came up on you from behind, means they probably come over from Missouri. One of the boys is from Neosho, so that figures. Was there a house or business or anyone around where they stopped for you?"

"I can't think if there was. Why don't you go out there and look?"

"You could make it easier."

"But I can't, don't you understand? I don't remember nothing but that girl and she...." He crossed his arms over his chest and glowered.

"This isn't about what you and her did."

"It's about I didn't have no gun, about I didn't do no robbery, about me going to prison for not doing nothing cause they didn't punish me enough for killing that Kraft kid."

Whitman's brown eyes widened. "Is that what you think?"

"It's the truth. Ask his mom. That bitch." Lucas clamped his lips shut. He wasn't saying anymore.

"That kind of language isn't going to help."

"Tell me what is, I'll do it."

"Behave yourself."

"Yeah, sure. That'll work."

Whitman left after a while and Lucas went back to lockup. Where he belonged. Where he'd always be. Until they killed him, or until the ghost of Jeremiah Kraft drove him crazy and he did it to himself.

Jon returned Becca's call late Sunday night. She was in bed staring at the pages of a J.D. Robb novel she couldn't even remember the title of.

"How are you?" he asked, sounding cool and distant.

"Actually, I'm doing better. Thank you for returning my call."

God, could they get any more formal? For a frantic moment, she couldn't remember why she'd called him and didn't know what to say.

"Well, that's good to hear. And you're welcome."

"I do appreciate it."

"Becca," he said, voice impatient.

"Excuse me. Wouldn't want to waste your valuable time on incidentals."

"If you called to argue, I'm hanging up." His tone more controlled now, as if this were exactly what he expected and he knew how to handle it.

"No. No, I didn't. Have you heard from Christi or David?"

"A postcard from David, nothing from Christi."

"Oh, where is he?"

"Somewhere in Arkansas. Said he'll be out of touch while he hikes through the mountains. That's all he wrote."

Disappointed that David hadn't written her, she paused a moment, then launched into the reason she'd called Jon.

"I wanted to tell you something. A decision I've made. The Pell boy has been arrested in Vinita, and I'm going over there to testify for him." The words fell out of her mouth in an uncontrolled jumble. She hadn't known for sure until she uttered them that she had made such a decision.

Silence. The line hummed. Had they been cut off?

"Jon?"

"I'm here. Struck speechless, but here. Why in the hell would you want to do that?"

"I'm not sure. I think it's because I really need to... need to—"

"Need *what*, for Christ's sake?"

"I guess I need to forgive him."

"Jesus."

"Jon?"

"What?" He shouted, control deserting him. "Then why don't you just tell God you forgive the little bastard and forget it. How can you even think of facing this boy in public?"

She gnawed at her thumb. "Because it's what I have to do."

"Who's been filling your head with this nonsense? Next thing you'll be spouting some ridiculous, meaningless psychobabble about closure and getting on with your life and putting this behind you. What exactly does that crap mean? No one knows, not even those who coined the idiotic phrases."

"It means absolutely nothing. It's just the way people talk. We know there's never closure to such a thing as this. What happens is, we might learn to exist despite everything. To think about Jeremiah with love and be grateful we had him. I think I'm beginning to understand. Spinner said I should remember Jeremiah, not in darkness but in light. And I can't stop thinking of that. I have to do this, Jon. I wish you would support me in it. Go over to Vinita with me. But if you won't, that isn't going to stop me."

When he didn't reply right away, she said in a small voice, "I thought this was what you wanted me to do, Jon. Get past the grieving."

His exasperated sigh reached through the lines to grapple with her resolve. "Oh, hell, Becca. I didn't mean for you to…. So this is all his idea? That figures. Well, nothing I can say will stop you doing what you've set your mind to. But I have to tell you this is the worst idea you've ever had."

"Maybe. Jon, you're the one who told me to learn to deal with Jeremiah's death. This is the way I've chosen to do that. No more drinking or popping pills. You should be happy."

"About that I am. About this, I definitely am not. Think, Becca. Why is this boy back in jail? What has he done this time? What good will it do for you to testify for him? I don't understand. When I said move on I meant forget about him. Erase him from your mind."

"Oh, Jon, I know you don't understand. But how can we tell someone how to handle something like this? I'm not you. I'm not even sure I understand myself." She took a deep breath. "I'm tired now and I'm going to hang up and go to sleep. His trial is set for June second. I'm going to be there. It would be good if you could come too. I'll talk to you some more later.

"Oh, and by the way. It would be very considerate if you'd let me know the next time you hear from either of our kids. Good night, Jon."

She hung up on his sputtering objections, turned off the telephone and light, and closed her eyes. It was a long time before she fell asleep.

When she awoke the next morning, she was pleased to recall no bad dreams from the night before. Could peace of mind come with one simple decision? Somehow, she rather doubted it. This was a brief respite, that's all.

Jon called several times in the next two weeks, trying to talk Becca out of going to Vinita and speaking in Lucas Pell's behalf. They had some heated words about it, but she stuck to her resolve. The more he objected, the more determined she became. When the time came for the trial, she drove over early, nerves snapping like high voltage wires on the rampage.

Parking near the old red brick courthouse with its crumbling facade, she strode across the grass and up the steps, heart drumming in her ears. In the top of a sweet gum a mocking bird trilled its repertoire to the cloudless day.

The public defender Walt Whitman failed to impress her much when he met her inside the courthouse and led her to the elevator. Reminded her of Ron Howard, and who could take such looks seriously?

He punched the button, smiled at her as strains of "Is It Really Over?" by Jim Reeves floated from beyond the closed doors. The plaintive music rode with them to the third floor. She followed him down the hall past a long wooden bench and through a door marked Court Business. Inside, they sat across from each other at a scarred table. Whitman didn't seem forceful enough to be effective, but rather struck her as a man unsure of his own capabilities. Probably couldn't defend Lucas with any alacrity, but what could the boy expect from a public defender?

She tried to concentrate on what he was saying.

"We succeeded in separating Lucas's case from that of the boys who actually robbed the store. A judge will hear our case in about an hour. We need to prepare you for the stand. Go over a few things. The other two boys' attorneys opted for a jury trial. Think they can dude those little punks up enough to play on their sympathy."

"And you don't feel the same about Lucas?" His name grated on her tongue like ashes.

"He's sullen, hostile, and not very well spoken. Even his body language dares you to like him or believe him. All that can go against him in a jury trial."

"Won't it with a judge?"

He raised his shoulders and adjusted his glasses. "It's a touchy situation. When you decided to testify I knew I'd made the right choice to not ask for a jury trial. What Lucas did to you happened when he was a juvenile and those records are sealed. Only the judge can know them. I'm counting on him being impressed that you would ask for leniency for Lucas."

Numbly, she nodded. Would she be able to do this?

Whitman continued. "I'm hoping that the judge can see beyond his tough facade. Depends on his mood. But more on if he believes Lucas and the witnesses Spinner's man dug up."

Odd. Spinner hired someone? She wondered if he paid the bill himself. That went far beyond the purview of his job. He sure must think a lot of this kid.

A court clerk opened the door and stepped inside, causing the PD to glance at his watch. "It's early yet. We're not prepared."

"It's not that, Mr. Whitman." He glanced at Becca then handed Whitman a folded piece of paper.

"Excuse me," he said and opened it, then smiled. "Is she on her way over here?"

The clerk nodded. "You want her in here? She'll be your kid's witness."

"Yes, bring her straight here." Turning to Becca, he grinned, and she saw how he might very well turn a jury or judge to his way of thinking. When he smiled an earnest country boy emerged, honest and true to the core. In that moment, she would trust him anywhere.

"What is it?"

"Seems one of the girls who was in the car has come forward and said that Lucas is telling the truth. She wants to testify for him."

"Does that mean you won't need me?"

"To the contrary. She and Lucas were going at it hot and heavy in the backseat while the robbery took place, and now she wants to talk about what happened. The judge may not believe her. She has a certain reputation. While it can't be brought up because she's a juvenile, it could sway his opinion of her testimony. We need everyone we can get if we're going to free Lucas. That is why you're here, isn't it, Mrs. Kraft?"

He pinned her with eyes that glittered and she saw yet another side of him. He would put up with no nonsense.

She swallowed harshly. "Why I'm really here is to get my life back, Mr. Whitman. And the only way I can do that is to look this monster in the eye and forgive him for what he did. And if part of that means I have to say in public that I think he should have another chance, then so be it. I am not in the least happy about any of this, however."

He rustled through some papers, frowned. "I have to insist that you not refer to Lucas as a monster."

"Of course not."

"Okay. Sorry I haven't had time, but let's go over your testimony. I know this will be difficult, but I have to know everything you're planning to say. There can't be any surprises. I have to know you didn't come here to torpedo this case. To get back at Lucas for what he did to you."

"You have my word on that." She drew her shoulders back. Whatever was to come would not be pleasant, but she was determined to get through it with as much decorum as was possible. And dear God, how badly she wanted a Valium. Or two or three.

After going over her testimony, she followed him into the hallway where he left her sitting on a bench.

A plain girl dressed in a loose dress and white sneakers, her blue-streaked hair drawn back into a ponytail, was escorted by a dour-faced matron into the room she and Whitman had just left.

Becca stared at the wide marble staircase leading up to the fourth floor that, according to the directory, housed the jail. She was nervous and her knees kept jittering till she pressed them tightly together. Soon the girl was brought back out and told to sit on the same bench, the only one in the hallway.

Whitman explained that they wouldn't be allowed in until it was time for each to testify, and that they should not discuss the case.

After a few minutes of silence, the girl said in a whispery voice, "I'm not supposed to talk to you."

"Then you'd probably better not."

The girl nodded, began to swing her feet, vibrating the bench.

"Could you please not do that?" Becca said, after it appeared the girl could continue the action forever.

"Sorry. I'm nervous."

"Me, too." Becca glanced at her. Hard to believe the fresh-faced child was a criminal.

In all her life, Becca had never been in a courtroom. Had never even received a traffic ticket. This was all so foreign to her.

What if she got one look at the boy and couldn't speak? That day she'd come face to face with him on the dock, her entire body had trembled, her vision blurred, her heart raced. It hammered in her ears to the exclusion of everything else. Suppose that happened again? And she started screeching, made a fool of herself?

What the *hell* was she thinking?

Determined to get through this, she cleared her throat, straightened the pencil thin, calf-length navy skirt, and stared at an enormous American flag fastened to the wall nearby.

What if she fainted?

Stop doing this. Stop it now.

The door opened, a man stuck his head out. "Rebecca Kraft."

Her body jerked to attention. "That's me," she said, but couldn't stand. "Oh, dear. I...."

"Take a deep breath," the girl beside her whispered. "Do it and get it over with. That's what I do."

Nodding, Becca touched the girl's hand. "Thank you," she whispered before rising and moving weak-kneed into the courtroom.

She'd expected quiet, but there was a rustling, a murmuring, a general low noise of feet scuffling and someone coughing. The sound of her heels on the polished wood floor echoed in the high-ceilinged room. Morning light slanted through vertical slatted blinds at two windows on one side of the room. No one was there except the people involved in the trial and they sat at two tables beyond a rail and just in front of the judge's bench. To their left, the jury seats were empty.

"Please come forward, Mrs. Kraft," the judge said.

A man in a dark blue suit rose and asked her if she swore to tell the truth and she said she did. Then, somehow, she was sitting in the chair next to the judge.

Her throat had gone bone dry. A glass of water and a box of tissue sat beside her, and she sipped at the cold liquid, set down the glass, and looked up. For the first time since entering the room, her gaze met that of Lucas Pell, sitting at a table beside Walt Whitman.

Saliva poured into her mouth, nearly choking her. She took a deep breath, tried to look away from him, but his smirking expression caught and held her. Why did he do that? Didn't he know it was the best way to alienate everyone? She studied the mass of bruises on his face, a cut above one eyebrow, the orange jumpsuit he wore, the angry jut of his jaw, how he slouched in the chair despite Whitman's nudging him.

She scarcely heard the lawyer's questions, nor her own answers, as she told her story. Briefly, as he'd requested. By the time she finished tears rolled down her cheeks. Would she never be able to talk about Jeremiah's death without crying?

"So tell us, Mrs. Kraft, in your own words. How do you feel about Lucas Pell?"

"I—well, I, uh, I want to forgive him. I want to ask for leniency for him because… because…. Oh, God." She leaped to her feet. "God, I can't do this. He killed my son. How can I do this?"

The judge hammered his gavel. "Mr. Whitman, please control your witness."

"Mrs. Kraft, please." The PD leapt from his chair, crossed the room, and took her arm. "Your honor, could we have a recess?"

The gavel slammed down. "Ten minutes."

Whitman supported her to a chair in the same conference room they'd used before, sat down beside her, and waited. Painful sobs tore from her chest, as if some unknown entity were ripping them from her heart. The young man's hand patted at her arm, but he didn't speak.

Finally, she stopped crying, but continued to tremble. This was no good. It wasn't going to work at all. Jon was right. She should've left well enough alone.

Before she could tell Whitman that the door creaked open and Spinner eased in. "Sorry, just got here. We found a couple of fishermen who think they saw Lucas picked up out by the State Park. I don't know how much good it will do us. Still doesn't prove he didn't know those kids. What's up?" He straddled a chair across the table and eyed Becca.

Taking a shuddering breath, she said, "This was a mistake."

"She lost it in there," Whitman said after a long silence. "I don't know what effect her outburst will have on the judge. I'm trying to understand your motivation here, Mrs. Kraft. Believe me, I am. But I have to consider what's best for Lucas. Did you deliberately sabotage this young man to get back at him? Because if you did, you ought to be ashamed."

The accusation angered her. "I would never do a thing like that. I honestly thought I could do it. I wanted to, needed to." He couldn't know how much she needed to do this.

He took her hand, held it gently in both his and caught her gaze with his. That trust-me look again. "This trial is not for you, Mrs. Kraft. It's not about what you need. It's about what Lucas needs. I think you ought to remember that. His young life is at stake in there. If he goes away for this crime, he's lost, completely and absolutely lost."

"What is it about this boy? First Spinner, now you. You'd think he was a saint instead of a killer." She jerked her hand from his grasp.

"He's neither," Spinner said. "He's a young, lost boy who never had one single chance in his entire life. Don't you think it's time he was given one? If you have to have a personal reason for doing this, then realize that perhaps your conscience would rest easier if you were able to help give him that break. Perhaps then you could go back and live in your beautiful home and drive your fancy car and play at running that business that caters to others just like you. Rich snobs with too much money and too much time on their hands. Why don't you—?"

Whitman came to his feet. "That's enough. This is getting us nowhere. I'll go back in there and tell the judge Mrs. Kraft won't be testifying. We'll go with the girl's testimony."

"What girl?" Spinner asked.

"Walk with me, I'll tell you on the way. Good day, Mrs. Kraft. I'm sorry we upset you."

Still reeling from Spinner's sarcastic diatribe, Becca studied this man who was sleeping with her best friend. His accusations cut her like the slash of knives. She wasn't really like that. Was she?

Before the door could close behind the two men, she came to her feet. "Wait. I want to do this. Please."

Whitman glared at her over his shoulder. "I can't take a chance you'll break down again."

"I won't. I promise. This time I'll get through it. He looks so beaten, so terrified. He's just a baby, barely older than my Jeremiah would be. Let me do this."

The two men exchanged glances. Spinner nodded.

Whitman raised an eyebrow, shrugged. "Okay, fine. But—"

She held up a hand and managed a weak grin. "I know. I'll do it right this time. I will."

Seventeen

He refused to attend Lucas Pell's trial. Jon awoke with that thought uppermost in his mind. All the previous day he'd invented excuses not to go. The kid was a budding gangster. He'd killed Jeremiah. The little bastard. The alarm continued to ring and he fumbled around shutting it off and swung his legs out of bed. Elbows on knees, he rubbed his face.

What was he thinking? Hers was a kinder wish, and she shouldn't have to do this alone. It was the first positive move she'd made to deal with Jeremiah's death. Who was he to tell her she was wrong, even though he was sure she was? The thought of her facing that boy in a courtroom and announcing that she forgave him for killing Jeremiah sent cold shivers through Jon. Hell, he couldn't do that. If she could pull it off, she was braver than him.

With a sigh he called the office and told Celie he wouldn't be in.

Whether Becca could go through with it or not, he wanted to be there. What had he allowed to happen to their marriage? Making love to her the night of the storm had brought back so many memories. Granted, he'd spent too much time with the business, but that was to be expected, wasn't it? While the breakup wasn't all his fault, he carried the burden of abandoning her when she needed him most. It was time he faced his responsibilities and at least stood beside her in this. Things might have gone too far to patch up their broken marriage, but at least he owed her that much.

Because he got a late start, he drove too fast on the interstate, but forced himself to slow down when he exited on old Route 66 and entered the city limits of Vinita. Familiar with the small town after so many hurried trips to the hospital with Becca, he made a left on Wilson and a right on Canadian. Traffic was light and he soon pulled into the parking area around the old brick courthouse. Erected in 1920, the building had seen its better days, but he rather liked the ambiance it presented. Vinita was the second oldest town in Oklahoma, and as such boasted quite a past and a goodly share of historical buildings. Green lawns and stately trees gave the area a neighborhood appearance. Much better than the starkness of some of the county facilities in larger cities.

He parked and hurried inside. A directory on the wall inside the lobby told him that courtrooms were on the third floor, and he took the wide marble stairs two at a time. As he reached his destination, Becca come out of a room to his right flanked by two men.

Thank God, he was in time.

Concentrating on what a tall Indian was saying, she didn't see him until he said her name. A flicker of pleasure brightened her surprised expression. Or was that just wishful thinking on his part? The expressive eyes were bright, and he could tell she'd been crying. Most of her makeup was gone, but she was sober. Tiny lines at the corners of her eyes made her all the more attractive. A look of fierce determination reminded him of the Becca he'd known in college. So much so that he couldn't speak for a moment.

"Hi," she said. "I'm so glad you came."

From her demeanor, he might have been a boyfriend she'd invited to the prom, and he couldn't help but be touched.

She turned to the younger of the two men with her. Had to be the public defender. He'd recognize one a mile away. The tall Indian with his long hair tied back and a stern scowl over his broad features had to be that Spinner fellow.

Becca introduced them. "Mr. Whitman, this is my husband Jon. Jon, this is Walt Whitman. And do you know Spinner Grayfeather?"

Jon shook Whitman's proffered hand, then nodded at Grayfeather, who kept both thumbs hooked in the waistband of his jeans. He'd told Becca to think of Jeremiah not in darkness, but in light. Funny, he didn't look like the type of man to say something like that.

The hallway was strangely quiet with few people sitting on either side of the large doors. "Have I missed anything?"

They all stared blankly at him for a moment, then Whitman said, "I'm afraid it's a closed trial. You won't be able to go in, but you can wait out here for your wife to finish."

Becca reached for his hand before he could react, because she could read his face better than anyone else in the world. She knew he was about to insist they couldn't keep him out. Sometimes her mind-reading pained Jon, but she'd been at it pretty much since the first day he'd spotted her across the table at the library on campus and gone gah-gah as only a young man can over a beautiful girl.

The memory brightened with the touch of her hand on his arm "This won't take but a few minutes. I'm so happy you came to support me. Please wait for me. We need to talk."

He resisted the urge to wrap an arm around her, tell her everything would be all right. Damn right they had to talk, but that could wait. He kissed the back of her hand and let it go. "I'll be right here, on this bench."

Standing on her toes she touched her lips to his cheek, whispered, "Thank you, Jon," and followed the two men into the courtroom.

Stomach doing a flip-flop, he sat down on a bench next to a wan girl who didn't look at him but followed Becca with an adoring gaze. He fingered his cheek where his wife had kissed him. Examined the feelings warring within his heart. A hell of a note, but he might be falling in love with his wife all over again. Or maybe he'd never fallen out of love with her, and had been too stubborn, and even a bit too stupid, to admit it.

After a moment, he went to watch the trial through the window in the door. Becca testified, and he was mesmerized by her courage and his newfound feelings.

Though she sensed it wouldn't be any easier the second time, Becca returned to the witness stand determined to finish what she'd started. With Jon providing moral support, she felt more secure. She glanced at Lucas Pell. He sat straight, wrists crossed on the table in front of him, wary gaze watching her every move.

Whitman must have spoken to him about his courtroom demeanor.

"You are still under oath, Mrs. Kraft," the judge reminded her, and she nodded. "Are you ready to continue?"

"Yes, sir. Your honor. I'm sorry about earlier."

He gave her a reassuring nod and waved a hand as if it were of no consequence. The gesture filled her with more resolve and the belief that this man really did want to help.

The water and tissues had been replenished. Probably in case she broke down again. This time she wouldn't need them.

On that note, she lifted her chin, watched Whitman rise, button his jacket, and stride toward her, wearing his friendly, country boy grin.

"You've already testified that you hated Lucas Pell because he killed your son Jeremiah in an automobile accident in December of Two Thousand Thirteen."

Eyes squeezed shut, she gulped and nodded. "Yes, that's true."

"But you have come to court here today to ask for leniency for him?"

"Your honor," the prosecutor said, rising. "He's leading the witness."

"Sit down, Bob. There's no jury here. I know what leading a witness is. Please tell us, Mrs. Kraft, why you're here, in your own words." The judge waved a hand of dismissal toward Whitman and studied her warm brown eyes.

And so she began. "I want to ask that you consider what this boy has been through, how hard his life has been. I understand he has changed, is working and trying to get his life straightened out. And that he's no longer drinking." She paused. How easy it was for her to relate to that. Sunlight filtered through the twin windows on her right, wove bands of warmth across her lap. She spread her fingers as if to catch the beams.

"It is true he killed my son," she said as if awakening from a trance. "And I can never forget that. My life will never be the same." She stared at Lucas, who was watching her with tears running down his cheeks. "But he didn't do it because he's evil or because he set out to kill someone."

"Your honor," Bob the prosecutor said, again on his feet. "What does this have to do with the charges against this defendant?"

"Not much," the judge admitted. "Mrs. Kraft, I realize that you aren't a witness, but rather have come to ask the court to consider this boy's past before condemning him. I think you have done that. Do you wish to cross?" he asked Bob the prosecutor.

Bob studied Becca a moment, glanced toward Lucas Pell, then shook his head. "No questions, your honor."

"I want to say something else," Becca said.

"You're excused, Mrs. Kraft." The judge's firm voice might have frightened a meeker person into silence. It only strengthened her determination, so she was able to accomplish what she'd set out to do.

Rising, she looked straight at the boy. "I want to tell Lucas that I forgive him." The words sounded as if they'd been jerked from her mouth.

"Counselor," the judge said, beckoning toward Whitman.

He came forward and escorted Becca from the stand. A clerk took her arm and guided her out of the courtroom. She didn't glance in Lucas Pell's direction. If she never saw him again, she would be happy.

Though her knees wobbled a bit, a great burden lifted from her soul. The very air she breathed tasted fresh and clean. She had done what she needed to do. Outside in the hallway, Jon rose and, with a little cry, she went into his arms. Languished in the familiar embrace she'd missed for so long.

"Oh, God, Becky." Taking her face between his hands, he kissed her deeply. "Is it over? Really over?"

She vaguely wondered what he meant by that, but the moment was so precious she didn't want to think about it. She had gotten through the worst time in her life since Jeremiah's death. And felt a certain peace. Nothing was over. Nothing ever would be. So what was he talking about?

"Let's go home, Jon," she said.

"You don't want to wait and see what happens with him?"

"No, I don't, Jon. I did what I had to do. For myself." She hesitated, glanced shyly at him. "For us."

He tightened his arm around her, said nothing.

"Let's go to the condo," she said. "I feel like going out, celebrating. Let's go to that little place where you took me when we were first married."

"Guido's?"

"Yes, let's eat and drink wine, and then let's go home and have some more wine."

He twisted a curl of her hair. "And then what?"

"I'm sure we'll think of something. We couldn't have forgotten what to do after that, could we?"

He arched a brow at her. "After the other night, how can you ask?"

Relief washed through her. It hadn't been a dream after all. She linked her fingers through his.

Walking beside him, listening to the joyful sound of his laughter, rekindled memories of their younger days, when they'd strolled hand in hand on campus, dreaming their dreams and planning their plans, with no notion that anything bad could ever happen to them.

Side by side they left the courthouse, moved through the afternoon sunshine. He walked her to her car, opened the door and, after she was in, leaned down for another kiss.

"I'll follow you," he said, dimples going deep, the silver in his hair catching the afternoon sunlight.

"Good, because I could never keep up with you."

"Surely you haven't forgotten the way."

Their gazes locked, and for a moment both were still, as if to speak or move might break the spell. How this had happened, she was afraid to wonder. Desire to be in his arms flowed through her, warm and entrancing. As if sensing her emotions, he brushed his fingers over the bare skin at the opening of her blouse. Goose bumps raced to her nipples, flowed through her belly, and nested deep down inside. Lurking there, lying in wait for Jon to light the fuse that would send them exploding into a shower of brilliant stars. Making her feel alive again.

She watched him walk to his car, the confident gait so familiar, the set of his shoulders triumphant like a knight following a victorious battle. How she loved that strut, as if he owned the world.

They might not make it to Guido's tonight.

Arriving at the condo ahead of him, she hurried upstairs. In her closet, she found the red peignoir he'd bought her for their fifth anniversary, when they were still making love with reckless abandon. A wonder she'd even kept it, but she had. Much like she'd stored other hopes and dreams in the darkest corners of her existence, in the hopes they'd one day see the light again.

Before he arrived, she slithered out of her suit, letting the skirt, blouse, and jacket drop to the floor. At a sound, she turned to see him standing inside the bedroom door, jacket gone, unbuttoning his shirt, with that old twinkle in his eyes.

"I always did like to look at you in only your shoes and undies," he said.

Smiling, she dropped the peignoir to the floor, crossed to him. "Want to take off my stockings?"

On his knees, he hooked his thumbs over one lacy top and peeled it down, nibbling at her exposed flesh with warm, moist kisses. Off came her shoe and he kissed each toe. Then he moved toward the other stocking, became distracted by the taste of her inner thigh.

She sucked in a gasp of exquisite pleasure the likes of which she'd not known in far too long.

"Oh, God," he breathed. "I'd almost forgotten how delicious you are."

She locked her hands behind his head, held him close, his breath hot through the filmy panties, stirring memories. Such memories.

"Take them off," she whispered, groaned when he pulled the flimsy fabric away with his teeth and buried his face there.

Weak-kneed, she clung to him, his tongue searching for the feast his mouth desired. Hands cupped around her buttocks, he lowered her to the thick, creamy carpet without losing a second of concentration on the work at hand.

An orgasm shuddered through her with unexpected suddenness, blinding in its intensity.

"Becky, my Becky," he said, coming up for air, resting his cheek against her quivering belly.

With one hand he cupped her breast through the lacy bra, with the other he struggled to remove his pants.

She touched his hand. "Let me do that. I can do that."

On his knees, he went so still she could scarcely hear him breathe while she worked to open the belt, unzipped his pants, and reached inside to roll down his underwear. Her fingers closed around his throbbing erection.

No time now to wonder or think or regret what might have been. Shifting, she guided him between her legs.

One deep breath, then another, and he plunged inside her. She thought she cried out. Someone did. Another orgasm rocked her, then another, and in the midst of the chaos, the primal pairing, he came magnificently. Hands wrapped around her hips, he lunged forward, backward, forward again, as if he might never stop, crying unintelligible words over and over.

"Jon, darling. Jon," she whispered. "Don't, it's okay."

"Oh, Jesus. I can't stop. I don't want to stop. Too sudden. Let's not quit yet."

Long after he had gone soft, he continued to move against her and hold on tight. Another orgasm rocked her, as if she might never get enough of this man she'd thought lost forever.

How long could this go on? He continued to want more, mouth suckling at her breasts, hands roving, until he began to grow hard again. Once more she took him inside, and he cried out almost immediately.

Quiet at last, he held her, murmured, "I'm so sorry, Becky. I never meant to—"

"Don't be sorry. You couldn't help it. We couldn't have done anything else." She didn't want to talk about their loss at this very moment. Later, yes, they would have to talk about him and her.

"This was wonderful. I may not walk for a week, but—" Her attempt at levity fell flat. He continued in a serious tone.

"I didn't mean *this*. This—yes, this was wonderful. Too soon over, and so… I can't think of the right word. But I meant about not taking the time to understand, about leaving you. All those years I wasted when we could've been together. I never meant for things to be that way. It was just, I guess, I got so wrapped up in the work, and you had the kids. Everything just kind of unraveled. I saw how brave you were today and realized what a fool I've been."

Odd. She'd thought he'd meant he was sorry about Jeremiah and what his death had done to her. But that wasn't what he was saying at all.

"It's okay," she whispered, and fingered back his mussed hair, stroked his forehead, soothing him like a child. Of course it wasn't okay. It was a terrible waste, like he said. But it was time to face today.

"Those days are gone and nothing can be done but to put it behind us and snatch at every new one. My darling, it was as much my fault as yours. I let us drift apart when we had the kids, and then when Jeremiah—"

"Hush, don't," he whispered, and covered her mouth with his.

If he wanted to start over, she would. They were, after all, alone together like they'd been so many years ago. Each supporting the other, like it should be.

Pulling away from the kiss, he fingered a lock of hair from her cheek. "Let's go out to the island first thing tomorrow. Spend a few days together? Maybe go out on the boat. It'll be like it used to be."

Tears of joy filled her eyes, left her feeling a bit guilty. But it really was all right to be happy. And Heaven knew she didn't want to be alone any longer. This time, they would make it work.

After Rebecca Kraft left, the judge heard testimony from the fishermen and the girl, then dismissed everyone to consider the case. Lucas trailed between Spinner and Whitman to the conference room. They sat, but he clasped his hands together to keep them from shaking and stood at the window looking out across the small town. Hope grew in his chest, but he pushed it back down. He was going to jail, no matter who had spoken for him. What meant the most was that Kraft woman standing up there, looking him in the eye and forgiving him. A calmness settled over him. So even if he did go to jail, maybe the ghost of Jeremiah would not go with him.

They had no more than retired than they were summoned back. The judge asked Lucas to stand and he did, but his knees threatened to buckle and he pressed his palms on the tabletop. The old fart was sending him to jail. Look how he glowered down at him. He wanted to shout at him to get it over with. To stop looking at him like that.

The words, when they came, echoed like he was down in a well or something. He only heard some of them. Probation. Don't leave the state. Stuff like that, but then the tone of voice hardened, and he listened.

"One more step in the wrong direction, young man, you come before me again, I'll bring the wrath of God down on you. You understand boy?"

All he could do was nod, till Whitman elbowed him. Then he said, "Yes, sir. I do, sir. Yes, sir." It was like he couldn't stop, and Whitman again took care of it poking him into silence.

Walking out of the courtroom was like he'd stepped out of his body and into someone who was happy, a condition he'd never known. The air vibrated with an excited conversation between Whitman and Spinner. Walking between them, Lucas wasn't sure exactly how he felt about the outcome. Surely it would come to him soon. He couldn't believe he was free, after being so sure he was going to prison.

"I think the girl's testimony turned it around," Whitman said.

"Nah, Rebecca Kraft made a hell of an impression. If you'd planned it, her breakdown and return couldn't have worked better for Lucas."

"Don't forget your man Keeler did find two fishermen who said they'd seen Lucas hitching. Still, without the girl corroborating his story about not knowing the kids who picked him up, it would've been sticky."

"I don't understand why I'm on probation, then, if the judge believed them all," Lucas said.

The three stood aside, halted. Spinner faced Lucas. "It's not exactly probation. It's more like the judge wants to make sure you don't get in any more trouble, and so wants you released in my custody for six months, just till you get straightened out. He wants to help you. We all do."

"Yeah, but I wanted to go to... I mean, I thought I'd—"

Spinner put an arm around Lucas and he cringed, pulled away. Couldn't help himself. No one touched him. No one would never touch him again. He'd let Spinner know that often enough.

Spinner's arm dropped away. "Not complaining, are you?"

"She did say it was all right, didn't she?"

"Who?" Whitman asked off-handedly, wearing a wide grin.

"Mrs. Kraft. She forgave me, didn't she? For killing her son."

When Spinner reached out a hand, Lucas couldn't respond with his own, but he did try out a silly grin aimed at Whitman, just to let the man know he truly was pleased he got him off.

"Don't worry, you won't see me in this place ever again."

"Well, kid. We did it. Let's go home." Spinner started for the door, and Lucas followed.

He'd dodged the bullet this time. Scared stiff lived in his belly though, all the time. It wasn't the last time he'd get in trouble 'cause that's just the way things were for him. He dare not let down his guard for one minute. Who could think hitching would get him almost tossed in the slammer?

Still in a fog, he trailed Spinner down the courthouse steps.

Strange about the girl, getting up there in front of everybody and telling the truth about picking him up. After the way he'd acted when she started to do him in the back seat. He never wanted sex, couldn't figure out what people saw in doing such disgusting things. Still, when he was drunk, he could please men and women both. The idea of what she did to him, and him not able to stop it happening, made his skin crawl. Like his body was not in his control, no more than his life was. That scared the bejesus out of him, even now when it was over. He'd barely been able to look at her when she sat up there and said all those nice things about him.

He hardly listened to Spinner, who was going on about Hank's Garage and how he could go back to work the following day.

The best part of this whole thing was Mrs. Kraft forgiving him. Now the bad dreams would go away. Her dead son would stop following him around. That's what they'd said in group, so it must be true.

"Whatcha thinking about, Lucas?" Spinner waited at the open door of the Nova.

Startled, he searched for something to say. Wished he could tell Spinner what he was really thinking, but he couldn't. It was too embarrassing, too secret. His own business and no one else's.

"Nothing," he said. "Nothing."

He went around and climbed into the passenger seat.

He was free, and this time he wouldn't mess up. He'd go back to work, and this time he wouldn't fuck up.

Be damned if he would. That little voice kept saying different, though, and somehow he couldn't shut it up.

Eighteen

After Lucas was released, Spinner fed him at a Sonic then took him back to Chota and his shabby room. Reminded him that he had a job to go to the next morning, and left with a silent wave. A gesture that gave him a lonely feeling. Six months, the judge had said. Six months to report to his counselor. Maybe he wouldn't be able to put up with it that long. Maybe he'd run and to hell with it.

After passing an entire night without interruption from the ghosts, Lucas dressed and went to Hank's garage and did his job, careful to be nice as he could be. The woman had forgiven him and now he could go on with his life. Odd to feel the sun on his face and the wind blowing at his spiky hair. Like he was new or something.

That evening in his room, he got to thinking about that woman, that Mrs. Kraft. He couldn't get her out of his head. She'd come back into the courtroom looking so sad, telling him it was okay about the accident. She didn't blame him anymore. It was like a big weight had been lifted off him. He wanted to talk to her, ask her questions, find out stuff about her and her family. Let her know how truly bad he felt about what had happened and how good her forgiveness made him feel. Maybe she'd be up for that now that she didn't blame him for her son's death. Didn't hate him and wish him dead.

So, after a while of sitting on the sagging bed, then standing at the window, then lying down and counting the fly specks and water marks on the ceiling, he gave in to the urge. It was simple, really. All he had to do was go up to her door, knock, and smile at her. Ask if he could come in so they could talk. She'd let him after the way she'd looked right straight at him and said she knew he'd changed. He should be given another chance.

And so what if she told him to go away? At least he would've tried to be friends. He truly hadn't explained to her what had happened and how bad it made him feel to think about it. Spinner had told him that it wasn't enough to say he was sorry.

That just didn't cut it, he'd said more than once.

That decided, he dressed in a pair of new jeans and a clean tee shirt, spent some time on his hair, though all it wanted to do was stand straight out from his head, and took off walking. It was late and there wasn't much traffic along the road that led to the gated community where the Krafts lived. In sight of the iron gates and stone pillars, he waited in the shadows for the best ride. It soon came. A slow-moving Sierra, black and shiny and big. He trotted alongside the SUV, its huge body allowing him to remain hidden in the darkness until it eased past the guard and into Rocky Cove. He ducked into some bushes until his heart stopped racing. Thought about what he would do next.

Was he crazy? Sneaking into this fancy neighborhood so he could have a heart to heart with the mother of the boy he'd run over and killed? He'd done it before, hadn't he? This time he wouldn't lose his nerve.

Being there was kinda scary. Almost worse than facing down an enemy bent on bashing in his head. He didn't know nothing about rich people, how they thought, how they talked, how they lived. All he knew for sure was that life here was different from where he come from.

Since he'd been to the house once before, he spotted it right away, with its tall columns on either side of a door way too big for just normal people. The porch light shone out across the green lawn that looked like a thick rug of some kind.

His knees shook so hard he could hardly walk along the stones that led from the driveway to the door. What should he say to her? Standing there, staring at the carved panels, he forgot exactly why he'd come here. What if she took one look at him and started beating on him? Or cussing, screaming, chasing him away?

Suddenly stricken weak, he leaned on the door, took big gulps of air, listened to the pounding of his heart. They'd taught him in group how to control anger, but not how to stop the jitters. He tried slow breathing, counting, imagining a quiet and peaceful day. If it worked for not getting mad, it might work for slowing down his loping heart.

Standing straight, he hammered on the door, stepped back a pace or two and locked his hands behind him to stop their shaking. He wanted to run so bad he could hardly keep his feet from dancing. Nothing happened. No one came. No lights showed, but there must be rooms inside that didn't have windows on the front.

He knocked again. Still no one opened the door. Disappointed, he scrubbed his feet nervously.

They weren't home. He'd come all this way, worked himself up, all for nothing. Finally, dull with disappointment, he started back down the stone path.

Stopped midway. Give it one more try. Knock really hard. It was a big house, they could be out back. Maybe there was a doorbell. He hadn't thought to look. Squaring his shoulders, he returned to the door. Act brave. If he didn't he'd pee his pants.

Forgot about looking for a doorbell. He'd already pounded on the thick, rich wood panels till his knuckles burned.

Before the sound stopped echoing in his ears, the knob turned and the door eased open.

"Yes?" a man's voice said.

Lucas couldn't make out his face. Felt like he'd swallowed a baseball. Stammered, " I—oh, uh…." Shit, he hadn't expected a man.

"What is it, son? You lost?"

"I, no, sir. I wanted to see Mrs. Kraft, please." A wonder he got the words out, his mouth was so dry his tongue stuck to it.

"It's late. What's it about? You selling something for school?"

"Yeah, that's it. Something for school." The lie fell out, and it was way too late to get it back.

"Maybe I could help you then. What do you have?"

The man swung the door wide to get a good look. Feeling foolish, Lucas locked his hands together behind his back.

"I just need to see Mrs. Kraft." Oh, God, he wanted to run, the way the man stared at him. Trying to decide if he was someone bad sneaking into this safe place to do him harm. Wondering how he got in unless it was okay. Funny how rich people were.

"Come on in, then. I'll get her."

Breath hissed out. He sounded like a tire losing air. He slipped through the opening, waited just inside, shaking hard again.

"Becky, honey. Someone to see you." The man, must be her old man, turned back and winked, nodded at Lucas, as if they had some secret. He sure looked awful happy. Unnatural.

"Coming. Who is it?" The same sweet, soft voice she'd used in the courtroom when she told him it was okay. What he did. Killing her son.

She stepped into the light from another room, her gaze moving from the man toward Lucas. When they lit on him, her eyes widened, her mouth made a big O and she covered it with both hands.

"Becky, what is it? What's wrong?" The man went to her, put an arm around her shoulder.

She was beginning to make sounds like she had the day he and Spinner landed on her dock and he tried to talk to her. This wasn't right. She wasn't supposed to be mad at him anymore. What was wrong? Did she take it back that she forgave him?

He tried to say her name, found he couldn't move from the spot cause she started to scream behind her hands in bubbles and gurgles. The man pulled her close, muffled her cries against his shoulder.

"Becky, honey. Take it easy. It's just some kid wants to sell us some candy for school or scouts or something. Don't, honey."

The man didn't get it yet, Lucas could tell. But he sure as hell did. She didn't want him here, still hated him. She'd lied, lied in court about it being okay. Why did she do that?

"Why did you lie?" he shouted. "You said it was okay. You said you forgave me." Tears poured from his eyes and his throat closed.

"Get that little monster out of here," she shouted, then buried her face once more in the man's shoulder.

"You're Lucas Pell," the man said, his voice harsh and scary. Like how someone talks who is going to beat the shit out of you. And he sure as hell didn't look happy no more.

"You little bastard. Get out of this house now. Before I beat you within an inch of your life. What are you doing coming here, upsetting my wife? Get out. *Get out!*"

Even though the man continued to hug the Becky woman, Lucas felt the fury of the words. Monster. Bastard. He raced for the door, slipped through the opening, fell hard on both knees, off the step onto the stones, but scarcely felt the blow. Scrambling and half crawling, half running, he got out of there.

He ran all the way to the gate like the devil was chasing him, rolled under it and raced away, the guard's shouts fading into the darkness at his back.

Legs pumping, lungs sucking air, he flew down the highway. Didn't matter even if someone came along and run right over the top of him. Killed him deader than hell. Made no difference what he did, everything came out the same. He was worthless and no one would ever want him around. All he'd ever been good for was what his folks had taught him to do, and he could do that damn well, long as he stayed drunk all the time. He ran till he couldn't breathe, then sank into the weeds along the side of the road, gasping for air, tears wetting his cheeks. Behind him the sound of cars whishing by. The drivers didn't care. Nobody cared.

Lying in Jon's arms, sobs subsiding, Becca couldn't stop thinking of that terrible boy coming to their house. Right up to their door and inside, as if he belonged here. As if he ever would. And after she'd told Spinner to make him go away. How could he possibly think she would welcome him into her home? Just because—oh, God, what had she done?

At last, wrapped in her husband's embrace, she drifted into a dream about Jeremiah.

Mama had once explained to her about spirits and the afterlife, about karma and how the things we do can come back on us in another life.

But she'd never believed her. Had rebelled about believing anything her free-spirited parents told her. Mama said that the dead did not rest easy if we refused to let them go. Said they would come back to say goodbye and if we refused, why then they drifted in a kind of hell.

"Jeremiah, my sweet Jeremiah," she said, and reached out for him. "Don't ask me to let you go. Please don't."

He gazed at her, eyes full of tears, then shook his head and walked away, disappearing in a mist that closed about her till she could see nothing. Leaving her lost and wandering, waiting for she knew not what. Maybe Mama was right.

She awoke with sunlight playing across the covers.

Jon brought her breakfast in bed. She stared at the table where her pills once waited. All gone now, swept off into the trash.

Determined not to let that terrible boy's visit ruin their efforts to mend this marriage, she asked, "Who are you and what have you done with my husband?"

An expression of relief softened his features and he smiled. "I think he's with my wife. I brought enough to share. Sit up."

Placing the tray across her lap, he sat on the edge of the mattress.

"Cinnamon toast?" She picked up a slice, took a bite. It tasted like sawdust. "Yummy. Orange juice. Did you make this coffee?"

"I made it all. What do you think? I have a sexy little maid in the kitchen?"

"Sexy little maids don't cook. They do other things."

He snagged a piece of buttered toast as she laid hers carefully aside. "I have this beautiful wife who takes care of the sex. Sure don't need a maid for that."

If he could put the previous night and her hysterics out of his mind, then so could she. She wiped crumbs from his mouth with the tip of a finger. Swallowed her sadness.

"It's a beautiful day," he murmured. "I thought we'd maybe take the boat out. That is, if you're up to it."

The orange juice went down smoothly, and she carefully set the empty glass on the tray, glimpsed a twinkle in his eyes. Blinked to rid herself of dark thoughts.

"What about the office?"

"What about what?"

"The office. You know that place you work and earn scads of money."

"Oh, yes, that place. I called Celie. Told her to rearrange my entire schedule. I'm taking some time off. If they can't live without me for a few days, then I should've trained them better."

"Jon?" She hooked an arm around his neck, pulled him toward her, jiggling the tray and sloshing coffee from the cups. "Jon, is that you in there?" Gazing deep into his hazel eyes, she kissed him playfully on the nose.

For a moment he was silent, then he moved the tray to the bedside table, shoving aside the clock radio.

"My sweet one, I could ask the same of you. No pills, no bottles of booze, no hysterics when we make love."

"What about that boy and last night, Jon? He was supposed to leave. Spinner promised."

"He shouldn't have come here. The little bastard. Made me as mad as it did you. Let's forget all about him. He's not going to ruin this for us."

Dragging in a deep sigh, she held up a hand. "Okay. We'll start over. No more talk of other days or Lucas Pell. How will that be?"

Lowering her head, she nuzzled his throat, breathed in the fragrance of soap and his shaving cream. "Before we dress, how about a little messing around?"

"I'm up for that," he said with a laugh.

And he was. After some time they carried the mood into the shower where he poured liquid soap in his palms and slicked it over her body, beginning at her feet and working his way up. By the time he reached her breasts he was very ready to complete what he'd begun.

But she wanted more and when he tried to back her into the corner, she snagged the bottle of soap, poured it in her hand and knelt. Hot water poured across her back, his erection nudged her cheek.

"Not yet, big boy. Not yet." She worked her way slowly up his legs, one then the other, while he groaned her name.

"Never mind, I'm getting there."

When she raised on her knees, she wrapped her soap-slicked fingers around his throbbing penis.

"Holy shit, Becca."

Through the steam, she peered up at him. Smiled. With the other hand she cupped his balls, squeezed gently.

He let out a sound between a grunt and a gasp, hooked her under the arms with both hands, and in one swift motion pushed her into the corner out from under the hot spray.

One hand pinned her there while the other gripped her buttocks and lifted her right off her feet. He slipped inside, drilling deep, holding on for a long sweet moment, then in and out, in and out. She came at the instant he did, shuddering along with him till they slid to the floor with a thunk.

"Dear God." She breathed out the words like a prayer. Fingers clung to his shoulders. "Whoever you are, I love you."

His lips came down on hers, tongue exploring. Responding in kind, she tasted soap and the man she remembered marrying so many years ago.

They were okay at last. Everything between them would be okay.

"I love you too, Becca. I promise to show you every day from now on. Now let this old man up off his knees before you cripple him."

The sun peeked over the horizon, rays warming Spinner's back. He tapped again on the door. Raine finally answered, barefoot and wearing a disreputable robe. That usually perfect cap of hair stuck up in all directions, making her look like a wood sprite.

Who the hell are you? Where's Raine?" He shoved his way past her to check out the living room.

"Idiot," she said, coming up behind him and wrapping her arms around his waist. "What are you doing here so early?"

"Is it early? I hardly slept last night. They gave Lucas probation and released him to me. He'll have to report to a PO as well, but I think it'll work out good for the kid. I'm too excited to sleep. This is just what he needs."

She slipped around to stand in front of him, looking up into his face. "From that grin on your face, it's what you needed as well. Does this mean you'll be around here for another six months?"

"No. The office isn't real happy with me spending so much time over here. Want me to get my butt back and take care of other business."

"And I can just imagine what you told them." Raine laughed. "Rebel that you are, I don't see how you keep a job."

"Truth to tell, I have a little trouble in that department. I want to help these kids, not deal with office politics." He tilted his head at her. "Did you talk Rebecca into testifying?" He brushed hair from her eyes. He'd never seen her so unmade, and it suited her. Sure as hell suited him. Perfection always made him a little nervous.

"No. You mean she actually did it?"

"Yes, indeed. And it didn't hurt his case in the least. It was clear he really had nothing to do with the robbery. I think the judge decided to give him a chance, even though technically he was outside in the car when it went down. And I think he decided that a lot because of what Rebecca said. She was one terrific and sophisticated lady. She came apart once, then pulled it all together and insisted on going back in and finishing what she started. It took a lot of guts."

Her face grew very serious. "Do you really think I enabled her to go on drinking and popping pills? I'd die if I thought I was to blame, or hurt her in any way. She's a dear friend, and one I couldn't live without."

"Aw, honey. You gave her permission to do it and keep your friendship, but it wasn't your fault. It's hard when we love someone to know how to help them. Believe me, I know."

"Mmm. Come on out in the kitchen and I'll make us some coffee. I think it's time we talked, and not about either of our pasts, but our future."

The words unnerved him. He hadn't thought they actually had a future, him and this refined lady. Better if things stayed just like they were.

Hand in hand Becca and Jon walked down to the boathouse that housed their thirty-foot cabin cruiser, christened *Dream Kraft* so many years earlier. She had aged with grace, the deck a gleaming patina, brass fittings and white bow immaculate, despite recent years of neglect. Each spring and fall Jon had called a service to take care of her needs, but that's as far as her care had gone for quite some time.

As if they'd never been away from her, Becca untied the lines and stepped on board while Jon started the engine. When he turned toward her and grinned, he looked so vital, so much like the old Jon she wanted to throw her arms around him and squeal with delight. Instead she returned his grin with one of her own, and only felt a slight tremor of guilt.

"Good thing I had her serviced regularly. Thought I might be selling her." One arm open wide, he invited her to step into his embrace. When she did, he ran a curved thumb along her cheek. "Okay about last night? The kid and all?"

The concern in his voice brought a lump to her throat and she nodded because she couldn't speak.

"Still know how to pilot her?" he asked.

"I think so."

"Okay, put her in reverse and let's get out on the lake." He moved to the stern to push clear of the wooden planks while Becca steered. After pulling the bumpers aboard, he joined her at the wheel.

A brisk morning wind chopped whitecaps on the lake, but the thirty-foot cruiser handled the rough water with scarcely a waver. Becca balanced on spread legs to regain the feel of being on water after so long a time. The wind fingered through her hair tied back with a white scarf. Seagulls dipped and spun, screeing at each other. She watched their antics with amusement. Amazing how the graceful birds had gotten to this landlocked state to make their home on the massive Grand Lake of the Cherokees.

"I hope you brought your bathing suit," John said. "It's going to be hot today. We can take a swim in the cove."

"You're crazy. The water's got to be icy yet."

"Yeah, but I know a way to get warm after a quick dip." He slapped her on the fanny. "By the way, I like those pants. They look quite boaty."

"Boaty?"

"Yeah, and they hug your lovely bottom so well."

"Lord, Jon. I'm a forty-eight-year-old woman with sagging parts. You can't convince me my bottom is still attractive."

"Not only is it attractive, it's sexy. And you have no sag at all in any of your parts, far as I can tell. You still look just like you did the year we met."

"Now that I know is an exaggeration. But I love hearing you say it. You're not so bad yourself." She deftly heeled the boat to port to meet an oncoming vessel on the starboard side.

"Where do you want to go?" he asked.

"Doesn't matter, just spending a day out here with you is wonderful. Oh, Jon, we came so close to losing this. That boy isn't going to make a difference. I won't let him. Besides, I'll talk to Spinner, make him keep his word." An idle promise or just a deep seated hope she could carry it off? She wasn't sure.

He grunted. "We won't speak of him again. Let's just cruise until lunchtime, then dock at Elmer's and have some of his deep fried catfish?"

If he didn't want to discuss the bad times, then she wouldn't, but sooner or later they would have to.

"Okay. And after, maybe we could anchor in Blue Cove and sort of have a siesta."

He spread a warm hand over her back. "Sounds perfect. Did you let Raine know you wouldn't be in to the shop today?"

"I left a message on her machine. Funny, she should've been home getting ready to go in, but no one answered the phone."

"Probably already left."

A few minutes in the kitchen drinking coffee, discussing Spinner's need to return to DHS in Vinita, and how it wasn't that far over there, and he had followed Raine back into the bedroom, unable to keep his hands off her. The planned talk about the future hadn't transpired, and he was relieved. He preferred to concentrate on the raging, hot desire that burned in him when they were in the same room.

"Is this the way our life is always going to be?" She helped him yank off her robe.

"Just one roll in the hay after another." He ran his palms over the curve of her hips. The satiny, warm, soft skin stirred him as nothing ever had.

"What do we do after the magic is gone?" She unbuttoned his pants, worked the zipper and tugged them down over his erection.

Without replying he kissed one bare breast, then the other. Despite the passion, he took his time working on the engorged tips of her nipples. Had to make this last, this intense, joyous, mindless bliss. For one day soon it would be gone, and they'd both move on.

"When they hang down to here." She marked off her waist, then moaned and leaned into his hot, eager mouth.

He dropped to his knees and began kissing her belly. "You mean, here?" Down lower he went. "Or maybe down here. Or even here."

She cried out and fell back on the bed, dragging him with her.

The phone rang, but she ignored it.

Much later, the alarm went off to tell her it was time to get up and get ready for work. The noise roused her from a sound sleep wrapped in Spinner's arms.

"Gotta get up, gotta go," she mumbled into his chest.

"Me too." But he only held her closer. "God, I don't want to let you go. I'm afraid this is a dream."

"It's no dream, kind sir, and if you don't let me go I'll be in trouble. Imagine all those frantic women lined up outside the shop for their caffeine fix and not getting it. Pandemonium would reign."

"Let that sexy little Cherry handle things." He laughed, kissed her and unwrapped himself, sat on the edge of the bed and rubbed his face.

"Uhm, she's liable to call in the law if I don't show." She massaged the hard muscles along his back. Traced the native symbol tattooed there with the tip of a finger. "Did you ever wish you were doing something that would make a difference?"

"Yep, until I took this job."

"Oh, that's right. You do something that makes a difference. It's me who doesn't."

"Don't sound so sad. Providing caffeine for frantic and bored rich women has a place in this world. Somebody has to do it. It's a perfectly respectable job for a beautiful rich lady with time on her hands."

She slipped from under the covers to sit beside him, regarding him with a slight frown. "What makes you think I'm rich?"

His finger slipped down her spine. "For starters, the way you dress and talk, and this place."

"I'm not rich, far from it. The bank owns this house. They just let me live here as long as I send them some money occasionally. And as for my speech, it took me a long time to learn how not to talk like the little girl from across the tracks." There, it was out. Had to be told, sooner or later. If he only wanted her because he liked his ladies rich, then she'd lose him. Better now than later.

"You're kidding." He arched a brow.

"Disappointed?"

"No, hell no." Stunned, he continued to study her. "It's just, I thought.... Well, that's a load off my mind. I couldn't imagine lolling in the lap of luxury. What a relief. You'll be perfectly comfortable in the lap of poverty with me."

The delight in his voice told her what she needed to know. But his assumption that she was staying with him terrified her. Not yet, not anywhere damn near yet. And that's what she needed to discuss, and soon.

He reached for his pants, pulled them on, then found his shirt in a wad and slipped it over his head. "I gotta get over to Hank's. Make sure

Lucas showed up this morning. Though I don't doubt he did." He pulled on his socks and slipped his feet into worn boots.

"Think I'll take a shower and get myself to work."

Rubbing a hand along her bare thigh and over her butt, he sighed. "Neither one of us is going anywhere if you keep walking around looking like that."

With a laugh, she put a hand on her hip and strutted into the bathroom with an exaggerated swing to her hips.

"Oh, baby," he moaned.

"See you, Spinner." She closed the door and leaned against it to catch her breath. Though the warning little voice spoke volumes, it was way too late to put a stop to this. Heartbreak might be just around the corner, but she couldn't give him up. At least, not quite yet. Might as well stop breathing.

Nineteen

Because they hadn't packed supplies for an overnight on the lake, Jon and Becca returned to the island before dark. After tying up the boat, she held his hand as they walked up the steps to the house. Scarcely two weeks ago she'd had little to live for. Now, the warm, gentle touch of him made her believe that at least some things could be made right again.

His silence matched hers. No speech was necessary. Soon there would be much to say, but not at this very magic moment.

"Want to go out to supper?" he asked, standing in the center of the kitchen looking around at the seldom-used, immaculate room.

"No, I'll fix something." She swung open the fridge, studied the offerings. "Hmmm. Need to go shopping. There's some cold cuts and veggies David left. Sandwiches okay?"

He nodded and rubbed his stomach. "After all that good catfish and hush puppies, I don't need much."

Munching at baby carrots and sweet pepper sticks, they rehashed their day like a comfortable married couple. Later he helped her put everything away, then wrapped her up in his arms.

"I want to shower. Care to join me?"

"What did you have in mind? A repeat performance?"

He took her hand and led her upstairs.

"This should set some sort of record." She pulled his shirt over his head and went to work on the zipper of his Dockers.

"I don't think so. Remember the time we did it on every flat surface in the apartment in a twenty-four-hour period, only stopping to drink water and take a bathroom break?"

"Oh, Jon. I hadn't thought of that in years. Neither of us could get to class the next day." Down came the pants.

He kicked out of his shoes, grinned at her. "Next day? I thought we were out the rest of the week."

"And you wanted to send it to *Ripley's Believe It or Not* and I wouldn't let you." Laughing hard she peeled off her shirt and shorts.

"Yeah, you said it belonged in the *Guinness Book of World Records.*"

Again holding his hand, she followed him into the shower and into his arms.

He kissed her shoulder. "Did you ever get it in?"

"Get what in?"

"Our record. Did you send it to Guinness?"

"Why? Want to try to break our own record?"

"I wouldn't mind."

Much later, wearily comforted, she fell asleep in his arms and dreamed about Lucas Pell and Jeremiah, standing on a hill together, glancing back at her, then looking off. Lucas had the same expression on his face as when he'd come to the house and she called him a monster. As if he'd been totally destroyed. Jeremiah looked pensive, disappointed.

She yelled at him to come back, to stay away from that boy, but he only waved, and then they disappeared over the rise. Together. When she ran to the top, there was only the stillness of green grass in an eerily windless day. Crying out in silence, in the way of dreams, she struggled to awaken. Sat up in the bed and saw her son across the room with his back to her, shoulders slumped forward so she couldn't see his face. Darkness surrounded him and a light shone from above, forming a perfect circle around him. So real, so ungodly real. This only happened in those sappy movies, didn't it?

No, don't. Don't go there. It's a trick. It's not Jeremiah.

Yet she couldn't stop herself. Heart beating so wildly she feared it would leap from her breast, she moved toward him. Had to touch him. Feel the silkiness of that blond hair bleached in streaks by the sun. So much like hers. As she reached for him, he raised his head to look at her, but he couldn't. He had no eyes. His mouth opened, closed, uttering words she could not hear. He lifted his arm, pointed beyond where she stood.

Fear rippled the hair on her neck. She would not turn. Could not. Knowing what she would see.

"Look, Mama. Look. Please, you have to look." His voice, so sweet, so dear, so real.

Like a rusty hinged gate, her head swung around. The other boy, the filthy little dirty little ugly little urchin.

And he had eyes, oh, yes, he had eyes. He'd stolen Jeremiah's eyes, and they gleamed with tears.

"Please, please don't leave me here," he begged, his voice ragged.

Then his fingers clawed at her, plucked at the long, flowing gown she wore, dragged at her so she couldn't move, could only shuffle her feet in place while her heart beat so wildly it nearly burst from her chest.

When she looked back where Jeremiah had been, he was gone, the light fading.

She awoke digging at the blankets, feet kicking, kicking, mouth open but unable to speak. Jon's side of the bed was empty.

Heart battering at her rib cage, a rampant knowledge grabbed her in a hideous embrace. It had all been a dream. Nothing of the last few days had been real. Not Jon, or their lovemaking. Nothing. All had sprung from a drugged mind. All save the death of her sweet Jeremiah. She was alone. Her first thought pills. A big handful of them. This time make it work.

Bereft and feeling so lonely a great hole of blackness opened to swallow her, she cried out Jon's name.

No one answered. "No, please, don't let it be that." Panic reared an ugly head. It was true. He'd never been here. She was going crazy. What if that awful boy came back, attacked her? She peered into the silent, moonlit room, saw Jon sitting at the window staring out over the lake.

Hand spread over her slowing heartbeat, she murmured, "Oh, thank God. But why was he sitting there like that? As if …. "What is it? What's wrong? It's not working, is it?" she asked softly.

"I don't know what you mean."

Relieved to find him there, yet afraid of what was yet to happen between them, she rose, shrugged into a robe, and went to stand behind him. Touched his shoulders. "Yes, you do know. We can't keep walking round and round this. We've got to face it together."

"I don't know if I can." He took her hand, kissed the palm and held it.

If her heart was going to stop, make it be now. Don't let this tear them apart once more. Losing both her son and her husband again would surely drive her over the edge for good.

"Maybe we need to get help," she said, shuddering at the half-remembered dream.

"You mean—?"

"I mean, a professional. I don't know. A psychologist, a psychiatrist. Someone experienced in getting people through loss."

Shoulders stiffening, he remained silent for a long moment, then asked in a hoarse voice, "A loss? Is that what we call this? A loss? It sounds so— so trivial. And not something I could ever share."

She leaned down, put her cheek against his, found it wet with tears. "Not even with me?"

He stiffened. "I can't." His voice broke. "If I let go for even a minute, I'll fly into a million pieces."

She kissed him. "Oh, my poor dear. For so long I didn't think you cared."

The noise that erupted from deep inside him ripped at her soul. Shoulders heaving, he began to cry, great huge sobs like the lament of a wounded animal. Without attempting to stop him, she sank into his lap and held him tight, joined his grieving with her own

At long last, he quieted. After a while, stirring, "Jesus, I'm a mess."

"Me, too." She sniffed and wiped her face against his tee shirt. "But at least we're a mess together."

"What are we going to do?" His hand on her head.

"I don't know. Something. I dream of Jeremiah a lot, but lately the dreams have changed. They used to be horrible, seeing him dying, suffering, bloody. Now he seems to be wanting something of me. And he looks okay, you know? Only impatient, ready to move on. He wants something of me, of us, Jon. And that other boy is there, too."

"Becky, dreams don't mean anything. You can't think Jeremiah is actually coming to you in your dreams? Your parents sure did a number on you."

"No, it's not like that. But I do think that my own, uh, my subconscious—that's what dreams are about, isn't it?—my subconscious wish is to do what's right so I can let him go."

"And what do you think is right?"

"That boy. Lucas."

"What?" A faint whisper when he should have been roaring at her.

"He was with Jeremiah the last time I had the dream. Both of them trying to tell me something. Something my mind needs me to embrace. I think we need to do something for, with, or about Lucas. I keep remembering something I read somewhere. Wish I could remember who said it. He said that forgiveness is a kinder revenge."

"Utter rot. I always hate how people quote someone to prove a point. Whoever said that didn't know any more or less about this than we do. I want to kill the little bastard. Now that's true revenge."

She rose from his lap, wiped her face with her fingers. "I know you don't mean that. It's just not in you. It's just a thing we say when we're so unhappy and angry we can't think of anything else."

"Well, you can't mean we should forgive him, help him. Surely you don't mean that."

"Only if you're agreeable. But listen to me, Jon. This boy, he's never had a chance. Imagine if that were our Jeremiah, abused from when he was no more than a baby, in the most horrid of ways imaginable. Wouldn't we want someone to help him? If we couldn't?"

"Christ, you have some strange ideas. He isn't our son, he never could be. Next you'll be telling me we should take him into our own home."

"Well, I...."

"Absolutely not. What are you thinking?"

"Lucas needs something we might be able to give him. Just till he can get on his feet. All I'm asking of you is to go with me to see Spinner, talk to him. Maybe visit with Lucas, then make up our minds. That's not much to ask, is it?"

"It's the moon, Becky. You're asking me for the moon."

She touched his hair gently. "Once you offered me the moon, Jon. Once a long time ago." Tears clogged her throat. If he refused, all would be lost. For her, for him, for their marriage. She knew that as well as she knew her son was gone and she would never see him again.

He wrapped his arms up and around her awkwardly. "Shit, Becky. How can we do this?"

"I don't know, Jon. I only know we have to try."

He nodded, said nothing more. They remained in each other's arms till dawn painted the windows peach and gold.

The following morning she called Raine at the shop, arranged for her to contact Spinner and set up a meeting between them.

"If you'd like, you can come, too. You're as much a part of this as anyone. In fact, I'd feel better if you were there."

After she told her what she and Jon wanted to do, Raine agreed without offering an opinion, said she would call Spinner and get back to her. "Then everything's all right. Between you and Jon, I mean."

"Yes, I think so. Yes, it is. We're working it out. This is part of it. Something we have to do, or at least I have to do. Jon is reluctant, but willing to try."

"Okay, fine." Her voice strangely flat. "I'll let you know what Spinner says. I'll call you at the lake house?"

Becca told her yes and hung up.

Spinner's cell rang before he arrived back at the motel after leaving Raine. It was Hank. Spinner's hopes did a tumble.

"The kid didn't show up this morning. Came in yesterday, happy as a clam, worked all day. Left. Ain't seen him since."

"Shit."

"That's it, man. I'm sorry. I can't keep putting up with this."

"Hank, I'm damn sorry about this. I gotta go, see if I can find him."

"Yeah, well, good luck. Best thing could happen is he's long gone, you know?"

"For everyone but him, maybe. See you. And thanks for your patience."

Seething, Spinner drove to Lucas's place. He didn't expect to find him there. He'd probably lit out for good. Jumping parole would be the final straw for the kid.

Furious, he busted in the door without knocking, praying the boy would be there so he could read him the riot act. How could he ruin his life this way? With no thought for the consequences. After all he'd done for him. Spinner hauled up short when he saw Lucas huddled in a miserable lump under the window, staring through the murky glass.

"Jesus," he whispered, seeing not Lucas but himself on one of the many days Burke had come looking for him and found him wiped out by something, anything. All it took was one small occurrence. Burke often physically fought him to a standstill. And how many times over the years had the man patiently placed him back on the road to his salvation? Never giving up. He could do no less.

"Aw, dammit, boy," Spinner squatted beside Lucas. "What happened?"

"It ain't no use," Lucas said. "Leave me be. Let me go down my own way. I'm a killer, and a monster. That's what she said, and nobody has use for a killer."

"Who she?" He resisted shaking the boy. "What have you done?"

"Yeah, see that? Always what I've done. Why don't you ask what she done? I only wanted to thank her for helping me, for telling me right out that she forgave me. But it was all a lie. She screamed at me. She don't forgive me, she hates me."

"You went to her home?"

"Yeah. So what?"

"You shouldn't a done that."

"Why? She said it in court. I thought it would be okay."

"Well, it wasn't, was it? But this isn't the end of the world. You gotta learn. This is her problem, not yours. I warned you saying you're sorry isn't always enough."

Lucas raised his head to stare at Spinner, eyes streaming. "Then what is? What is enough to get him out of my head?" He clawed at his spiky hair, jammed the heels of his hands into both temples.

"Don't, son, don't," Spinner said, and clasped the rigid fingers in his own. "I don't know all the answers. I wish I did. You need to take care of yourself now. You're worth saving. Don't let it all be for nothing."

"It is for nothing. I'm nothing. Why you wasting your time? Go away. Leave me be."

Spinner had never seen Lucas in this shape, thoroughly destroyed by someone else's actions. Always the blusterer, he'd fought all life had to hand him to a standstill. Tough little buggar, destroyed by that rich woman's whims. Sure, she'd lost her kid, and he felt damn bad about that. But Lucas had never had anything. No parents, no home, no one to care for him. Why couldn't she see how destructive her actions were, not only to Lucas but to herself and her family?

Sorrow and hopelessness encased Spinner like a shroud. He couldn't explain this to Lucas. Wanted to run from this cheesy place, jump in the Nova and drive. Leave it all behind. Lucas and his constant demands, the desires he felt for Raine and a life he couldn't have, his own broken dreams.

The cell phone in his pocket rang, but he didn't answer, just hunkered there on his heels gazing at his own mirror image and wondering if maybe the kid wasn't right. Maybe it was all for nothing, in the long run.

Damn, how he wanted a drink. The gut wrenching desire stunned him, after all this time. Ten years of sobriety and he still couldn't quell that demon.

The damned phone just kept ringing, and he finally snatched it from his pocket and thumbed the slide.

"What?"

An instant of silence, then Raine said, "Sorry to bother you. Guess you never heard of voice mail. Should I call back later?"

Heaving a sigh, he rose and moved to the other side of the room, turning his back to Lucas. "No, I'm the one who's sorry. How are you?"

"Okay. Obviously the same can't be said for you. Listen, if this is a bad time, you could call me later. I'll be home all evening. There's something. While it's not an emergency, it is important."

"No, it's okay. What is it?" Behind him, Lucas stirred. Like someone interested in what's going on. Good. Take his mind off self-pity.

"Jon and Becca Kraft want to talk to you about Lucas."

"Not surprised. He won't do it again."

"Do what?"

"This isn't about him going out to their place the other night?"

"I don't think so. No, they didn't mention that."

He scratched his head and turned to stare at Lucas who returned his gaze. "What then? He said...." He turned away. "What do they want to talk about, do you know? The mood I'm in at the moment, I could cheerfully choke her."

A beat. "I'd rather you'd talk to them, if you have time."

"Raine, they don't want to make trouble for him, do they? I wouldn't want—"

"Oh, no. Nothing like that."

"You don't sound real happy about this."

"To tell you the truth, I'm not. But it's their decision, and yours and Lucas's. I think I'll stay out of it. You'll be glad to know that I will no longer enable Becca. Especially not for this." Anger colored her tone, rousing his curiosity.

"When do they want to get together?"

"Tonight? Their place, if you don't mind going out."

"Oh, I'd be allowed inside the gates? Me and my beat-up old Nova? Should I dress in black tie?"

"You know what, Spinner. I think I'll just hang up now and let you get over whatever is bothering you. Call me later, if you want."

The click of her disconnecting startled him. "Well, shit. Maybe I will, maybe I won't."

But the phone didn't reply. He stuck it back in his pocket.

"What?" Lucas stared at him.

"Nothing to concern you. I'll be back in the morning, first thing, and we're going to go get you a job. You got that? And when we do, we'll find you a better place to live. This is a goddamned dump. You be waiting, you hear? And without that woe-is-me look."

He stood over Lucas until he nodded, though miserably.

"Okay, then. And you'd better be here when I get back. You got that? Or I'll hunt you down and truss you up like game and deliver you to the jailhouse door myself. Understand?" Without waiting for a reply, he slammed out the door and stomped to the Nova. He'd about had enough of everyone and everything cluttering his life, including this ugly damned car. Damned thing looked like hell. He'd go to the Spot-Not and wash it before he went out to the Kraft's. And he'd dress in something besides jeans and a tee shirt.

"So what is it you wanted to see me about?" Spinner was seated uncomfortably beside Jon and Rebecca Kraft on the deck of their fancy house. Nice evening for a chat. Cool breeze blowing off the lake, a brilliant sunset painting the water's surface in splashes of red, purple, orange, and gold.

Becca bit her lip, glanced from Jon to Spinner and back again.

On the verge of tears, voice quavering, she plunged. "When I sat in that courtroom, I forgave Lucas, because it was what I had to do for me. Not for him, for me, so I'd feel better. All the while, I was imagining the smirking little bastard being beaten, wanted desperately to smash him in the face myself." Sucking in a great sob, she stared defiantly at Spinner.

He didn't rise to the bait, just watched and waited like a cat waiting at a mouse hole.

Jon broke the silence. "You can't forgive someone for killing your child. At least, I can't. I thought how brave she was to do what she did over at the courthouse, because it was something she had to do, but I'll never forgive him, not in a million years. He's a murdering, sick bastard, not fit to walk the same earth that Jeremiah did."

"Mr. Kraft, I...." Spinner broke off, rose and went to the rail to stare out into the fading light, afraid he would say something he shouldn't.

Jon's angry words echoed. After all this time, he had finally vented his feelings. A good thing, but maybe this wasn't the best time.

Waves embraced the shore with soft kisses, and no one spoke for a while. In the gold-streaked ashen sky, stars twinkled like a scattering of diamonds. Far off to the southwest lightning flickered. Brass lamps along the deck rail flickered on.

Becca broke the silence. "It's not like he took a gun and shot Jeremiah. But still that doesn't make our loss any easier."

"Then what do you propose to do?" Spinner asked. "This boy is hanging on by his fingernails. So far, your actions have done him more harm than good. I don't know what you want."

Jon replied before she could. "Becky has this idea that we need to try to help the boy. That in some way, it's what Jeremiah would want."

"Help him in what way?" Doubt filled Spinner.

Eyes gleaming, Becca struggled for words that wouldn't come, reached for Jon's hand, squeezed it.

Still, Spinner waited, studying the attractive couple in the glow from the lamps. They seemed to have come to grips with their troubled marriage, but could they make it through this?

"It's as if Jeremiah's soul is still here, waiting for I don't know what. We need to do something. Something that's right. Not destroy this child with our hatred. If we could've given our son's heart to save another child, we would have. God, this is so hard, I don't know if I can get through it." Her voice caught.

Through sobs she plunged on. "I want to try to give Lucas our son's spirit, if that makes sense. Honor Jeremiah's memory in a way that will do some good. Sort of like a heart transplant. Can we do that?"

A look came across Jon face, transformed the furious hatred that had burned there as he considered his wife's plea. Tears filled his eyes and gleamed on his cheeks. He took both her hands in his and raised them to his lips, and they both stared at Spinner.

Waiting. Hoping for something he was afraid he couldn't give them. "Jesus," he murmured.

Twenty

Both men stared at Becca. Long minutes ticked by, punctuated by the serenade of peepers and the occasional mournful call of a night bird. A breeze from the approaching storm cooled the air, but it remained silent and far away. Neither replied to her offer to help Lucas. What else could she say?

With a sigh, she rose, failure weighing her down.

"Well, I guess that was a bad idea. Could I get anyone coffee? A drink?"

Spinner cleared his throat. He sounded as if he'd found his voice down in a barrel. "Coffee, please."

Jon stood. "I'm going to fix myself a stiff drink." He followed Becca inside. "Jesus Christ, Becky. What was that all about? Spirit transplants. Good God."

"I thought you'd agreed to back me up, at least offer this boy what he's never had. I have this terrible feeling that if we don't do something we won't survive and neither will Lucas." Disappointed, she opened the cabinet, took down a filter and filled it with coffee.

"I know, and I want to, but I'm afraid he'll break our hearts. Besides, I'm not sure I can abide having him around."

"My heart's already broken. And if you'd admit it, yours is too. Don't you see I'm trying to mend us? But that by itself isn't enough." Pot in hand, she filled it with cold water and started the coffee. "Doing it only for our own satisfaction is selfish. I'm broken-hearted to say it, but our son is gone. This is about Lucas. Jeremiah would want this. You know he would."

He only stood there frowning. Infuriated by his stubbornness and her own frustration, she whirled. "You go out there and you ask Spinner about that boy's life. Get him to tell you what he went through since he was a toddler. Then you think of our Jeremiah, our little golden haired boy laughing and playing. Safe from such monstrous acts. You think—"

"He wasn't so safe. If I could've kept him safe he wouldn't be dead. I couldn't even do that much for him, and I'll never forgive myself. Never." The sadness painted over his features brought tears to her eyes.

The strongest man she'd ever known stood before her, beaten and defeated, admitting aloud what had been eating at him in silence all this time. Maybe this at least was the beginning of his healing.

Turning from the counter, she wrapped her arms around him. "Oh, Jon, if only I'd known you felt this way. Things would've been different if we'd had this conversation a long time ago. Shared our sorrows instead of walling them up to handle alone." Under her ear, his heart thundered and she wanted so badly to help him.

"Don't you see? It wasn't your fault. It wasn't mine. It wasn't even Lucas's. If we're looking for someone to blame, things are going to get really complicated. I'd rather...." She caught her breath, swallowed another sob. "I'd rather try to make it right. Somehow. Without more lives being destroyed." She felt her reserves slipping back into the old darkness. All was lost if she couldn't make him understand.

At last, he lifted limp arms from his sides and encircled her. "Okay, honey. Stop this, now. This is supposed to be helping us. Let's go back out there and talk to Spinner, then I guess the least we can do is meet this boy, if he thinks it's okay. We'll try this, but I still have serious doubts about it being the best thing to do."

Unable to speak, she remained in the curve of his embrace for a moment, then drew herself straight, grabbed a paper towel, and mopped the tears from her face. "But you will agree to give it a try?"

He nodded.

She patted his arms. "Well, at least that's something. Thank you, Jon. Thank you."

He followed her back outside without mixing a drink, stood by silently while she presented her idea of letting Lucas live with them for a while. A gap of silence followed. Throats were cleared.

Finally Spinner said, "I'll arrange it on a trial basis, but until this is a done deal, I don't want Lucas coming out here. Hoping for something he can't have. Keep in mind, he's not cute or smart, like in some movie. You can't take him home like a pet to be groomed and sent to obedience school.

"You have to face it. He may rob you, wreak havoc with your family, get back on drugs or booze and trash your home. Please know what you're getting into. And I won't have the two of you playing games for your own benefit. He's been hurt enough for a dozen lifetimes."

In the golden glow from the deck lanterns, Spinner's eyes gleamed with a fierceness that sent shudders through Becca. If she met this man on the street, she'd be terrified.

"There are some things you need to understand. While Lucas's welfare no longer comes under the purview of the Office of Juvenile Affairs, since he is eighteen, the Department of Human Services will do a follow-up. And he is under my supervision for six months as part of that deal."

Becca clenched her fists, excitement crowding her thoughts. This was really happening. She nodded, pushing away a fear of failure. Jon gripped her arm, said nothing.

Spinner continued. "I'll have to clear this, but I think if the two of you agree to counseling, there won't be a problem. If Lucas agrees, he is an adult, and that will weigh in your favor."

"Counseling?" Jon's voice rose a notch.

With a silent plea, she stared up into his features, shadowed by the lantern's light. "Yes, we will. Won't we, Jon?"

"I suppose we can try. I want us to be together. Stay together."

"Oh, thank you," she breathed.

"I can recommend someone. Though I understand the trauma you went through, and I'm very sorry for your loss, you aren't my concern, he is." He held up a finger. "This isn't a done deal. Not yet. One meeting with Lucas, we'll see how it goes. Be at my place around eight o'clock tomorrow evening. And about that counselor."

Becca glanced up at Jon and he nodded. "Leave the name with us. We'll make an appointment," she said.

Spinner wrote a name and phone number on the back of one of his cards, laid it precisely in the center of the small table and crossed the deck. At the door he stopped. "If you change your mind about all this, no one will think the less of you. But do it now, before you meet with Lucas. Just let me know. Don't hold this out to him, then jerk it away. And be ready for him to say no. He very well could. I can find my way out." He left without waiting for a reply.

"Well." Jon stared into the darkness.

"It'll be all right. I promise it will." She went to him, wrapped her arms around his waist and laid her head against his back.

They sat on the deck side by side in silence for a long while, watching the approaching storm. When the clouds blotted out the stars and thunder and lightning started to play tag in the night sky, they went upstairs to bed. Together.

The ringing telephone awoke Becca. She fumbled in the darkness for it. One of the kids? David? Christie? She would never get over the abject fear of a phone call in the middle of the night.

"Mom, it's me," Christi said.

"Honey, are you okay? Where are you? I hear strange noises."

Christi laughed. "I'm fine. Are you okay? How's Dad? And David?"

"We're all fine. David's still hiking the Ozark Highlands Trail. Where are you?" she repeated when horns honked and people shouted.

"I'm in...." Muffled noises, as if she'd covered the mouthpiece to speak to someone else. "In Sydney. Mom, I'm coming home."

"Oh, sweetheart, that's wonderful. When?"

"In a few days. Mom, are you....? I mean is everything okay? You sound good."

Jon raised his head from the pillow. Mumbled, "Who's that?"

"It's Christi, she's coming home."

"Is Dad there? At the house? In the bed?"

Becca couldn't help but laugh. "Yes, my pet. Your dad is here, in the house, in the bed, if that isn't getting too personal."

Christi chuckled. "Mom, you do sound wonderful."

"Well, I guess I am, if not wonderful, at least getting there."

Someone shouted Christi's name in the background. A boy. "Gotta go, or we'll miss our connection. There was this little plane and we were late, and, well, I won't tell you about that till we get there. Love you both."

She was gone.

Becca held up the phone and stared at it, then at Jon. "I wanted to let you talk to her, but she's gone. She's on her way home, I think. Something about a little plane and I heard a boy. She sounds happy. Oh, Jon, you don't think she…?"

"I don't think anything. Christi's always happy." He mumbled something unintelligible, buried his face in his pillow, and went back to sleep.

Waking him in the night had always been an impossible task. The house could blow away and he'd sleep on, yet come six a.m. he would hit the ground running, as if he had an internal clock that wouldn't allow him to remain in bed one moment longer. In the morning he probably wouldn't even remember the call. The telephone in her hand began to blare and she disconnected, placed it on the nightstand and crawled out of bed to go to the window. The storm had passed, leaving the sky bright with stars that swam about in the lake like aquatic fireflies.

Excitement balled in her stomach, sent quivers through her. It would be so good to have Christi home. But suppose she brought someone with her? That boy. She had said we. Oh, dear. Well, nothing would be wrong with that, except what would Christi think of this thing with Lucas? So much happening all of a sudden, she struggled to take it all in.

How wonderful it felt to worry about ordinary things again. Well, maybe not so ordinary, but it felt as if she'd been ill for a very long time and had finally recuperated. Could get back to the business of planning such a simple thing as shopping for food to have when Christi and her friend arrived, and opening up the guest room. And stewing about the possibility that he and her daughter were sleeping together.

A hundred thoughts went through her mind, before it finally circled round to settle on Lucas Pell.

Suppose Spinner was right and this would do harm to her family?

She couldn't have that. Absolutely not. Yet what about this boy? The look on his face the other night when she screamed at him about being a killer and a monster had haunted her ever since. Somehow she had to rid herself of the guilt and the horrible nightmares. But were her motives too selfish to make this work? That young man needed hope for a future. And she and Jon might be the only ones who could offer that hope. What a frightening thought.

Maybe David would call, so they could tell him about Christi. Then he would return too and they'd all be together again. Only this time everything would be different. They'd see she was no longer a pathetic heap of self-pity, that she was doing something positive to make things better for all of them. And best of all, their father had come home where he belonged.

Though it was three in the morning, the hundreds of thoughts running about in her head kept her from sleeping, so she crept into the bathroom, took a shower, dressed, and went downstairs.

Before he arrived back at the motel from the Kraft's, Spinner's cell rang. His skin prickled. What now?

He answered.

"You talked her out of it, didn't you?" Raine asked without so much as a greeting.

"Well, hello to you too. And how are you doing?"

A big sigh he could almost feel blowing in his ear. "Sorry. But I've been pacing the floor waiting to hear. You're not going to let her do this crazy thing, are you?"

"First of all, I'm not so sure it's crazy, and—"

"What?"

"Second of all, I don't think I could talk them out of it."

"Them? Jon is willing to do it too?"

"No so much as her, but he's hanging in there. Why are you so upset about this?" He clicked the turn signal and swung off the highway into the motel parking lot, shut off the engine, but remained in the car.

"Because it's not only crazy, it's dangerous. She doesn't know this boy… what he might do to her, to them all."

The statement fueled Spinner's anger. "And you do?"

Silence for a beat. "I really thought you had better sense than this. You're just playing all the angles for this kid. How nice for you if you can get him installed in their home, all his needs taken care of."

"Nice for me? This has little to do with me. What do you know about it, anyway?"

When she didn't reply, he bailed out of the confining space of the car and stomped around in the parking lot yelling into the phone and waving his arm around. "This is my job and in spite of what anyone might think, even me, I'm damned good at it. You don't know a thing about me or what's nice for me. And I'm not sure I want you to."

Waving his arms some more to rid himself of the fury her words had fired, he disconnected before he could say something he couldn't take back.

What was all that about him being so damned good at his job? Only a few weeks ago he had lamented his inability to help these kids. And this deal with Raine. He ought to tell her to stuff it, or worse. Seems he wanted to leave his options open. Anyway, it sure as hell felt like it. Going into this relationship with her, he'd known the outcome, dreaded it but saw it coming. Goddamned snooty bitch.

Whoa. That must have come from a defiant angry core of self, left from his deprived childhood. Hiding away, waiting to explode as soon as something he couldn't control came along. And one thing was for sure, he couldn't control his feelings for Raine.

Go inside, take a shower, cool down. Maybe go out and find a bar and… no, hell, no. No one could make him get drunk again. No one. Not even a woman who drove him wild with desire, wilder with frustration. Damn Raine Gregory and her wicked, wicked wiles.

Despite himself, he grinned. She was wicked, but in the very best way, and he wanted her at this moment as much as he ever had. Dammit, he didn't have good sense about women, never had, never would. And especially not this one. Maybe he'd just go over there and show her how much he wanted her, how much she needed him. Wipe that smug, self-serving smile off her lovely face.

Yeah, that's what he'd do.

Yanking open the car door, he threw himself inside, cranked the engine and floor-boarded it, tires squealing through the quiet night.

Raine lay awake in bed when the pounding began. Sounded like someone knocking the door down.

"Don't have to guess who that is," she muttered, and hurried to reply before he woke the entire neighborhood. She only wore a tee shirt and didn't bother to put on anything else. Let him see what he was giving up with his bullheadedness.

The lock was barely released when he punched his way in, stopped short when he saw her, backlit by the entryway nightlight. She stood her ground, arms akimbo so he could get a good look.

"Damn you," he growled, and wrapped his arms around her, lifting her feet off the floor.

Heart beating its way out of her chest, she tried not to react, to hang like dead weight, be uninterested, unaffected. Oh, shit. That wasn't going to work. What made her feel good, deep down inside, was that not once had she been afraid he'd hurt her. She'd come a long way from that terrified wife who'd let her husband beat her senseless on a regular basis. This one, well he was a different matter altogether. And she knew deep down inside that he would never lift a hand against her.

His hot breath swept over her face, crawled down her throat, his mouth chasing it into the hollow of her throat. When the tee shirt got in the way, he set her down long enough to snatch it from behind, pull it over her head and down off her arms. So quick, that even had she wanted to resist, there wasn't much she could do before he lifted her again and buried his face between her bared breasts.

Mouth searching, he found a nipple and took it in greedily.

Shot through with a fiery passion she no longer wanted to control, she wrapped her legs around his waist. His mouth went to her belly. She sucked in a great breath, trembled through and through, as if lightning had struck and sent sparks out her fingers and toes. They would have both tumbled to the floor had he not been so much bigger and stronger than her. Staggering, he carried her down to the thick carpet of the living room.

Joining him in the animal-like behavior, she yanked his jeans open and tore down his jockey shorts, releasing his erection.

With a groan nearer to a howl, he grabbed her wrists and rolled her over onto her back, straddling and penetrating her in one smooth, swift movement that ruptured her mind into a million pieces. Conscious of nothing but the intense fire he tended so ferociously, she tightened her legs around him, rose to meet the onslaught and hung on. And hung on, and hung on, until every breath was a gasp for air. Until her vision clouded and she no longer knew or cared where she was.

He had a way of completing the onslaught that excited her almost as much as the action itself.

And this night was no exception, despite the fury with which he'd approached. After he came with noisy and reckless abandon, he kept her close, locked to him, until their breathing slowed and their bodies cooled. He did not move away, leaving her feeling used and discarded. Rather he ran his fingers through her hair, moved his mouth over her skin, tasting here and there as if he couldn't get enough. She experienced yet another orgasm at that moment, shuddering closer to him, crying out, locking her legs tighter and rocking through the pleasure.

Spent. Serene. Sated.

Limbs wrapped together, argument forgotten, they lay still and quiet in the darkness.

"I certainly like the way you get over a mad." She traced his ear with a fingertip. His ebony hair had come loose and spilled out over her shoulders like a silken veil.

If they had children, they would have raven hair and pitch-black eyes.

Whatever had brought on that thought? She ran a hand over her belly, still quivering from deep inside. Did she believe in premonitions? He was her first sexual partner since she'd left "what's his name." And they'd used no protection. Oh, shit! What if they'd—

He raised on an elbow, looked down at her, smoothed her hair with one hand. "What are you thinking about?"

"Me? Oh, uh, nothing."

"You looked so, I don't know, dreamy."

"I guess I was dreaming. But it's time to get back to reality, isn't it?"

He kissed her gently. "I suppose. What were we fighting about? Do you remember?"

Laughing, she rolled over and sat up. "Oh, no you don't. If that's an example of how you make up, we'd better space our fights out or one of us is going to die."

"Can you die of too much sex?"

"Buddy, that wasn't just sex. That was… that was—"

"Fucking outstanding," he said. "Or outstanding fucking."

She laughed, and he did too.

But she hadn't forgotten why they'd had words, and the outrageously satisfying sex hadn't wiped out her worry for her friend. While she might get totally caught up in Spinner's antics where sex was concerned, she couldn't forget the loyalty she felt toward Becca. Spinner had warned her about enabling Becca's irrational behavior. Well, didn't that hold true with this crazy idea of hers to take that wild young boy to her bosom? Replace her dead son with him? She wasn't about to let this go without a fight. For Becca's good, and the good of her entire family. And if it caused a rift between her and Spinner, that was too bad. Way too bad, but it couldn't be helped.

When Spinner left it was nearing daylight. Raine had slept some, wrapped in his arms, napped a bit after he was gone. Prepared for a fight, she dressed and headed for the coffee shop. If Becca didn't come in, she'd have to go see her, talk some sense into her. It wouldn't be easy, once her friend turned those wounded wide eyes on her, but it had to be done.

At RainTree she found a beaming Becca already there, bustling around helping Cherry make all the specialty coffees, and looking better than she had in many months. The tables were clean, supplied with sugar, sweeteners, honey, creams of various flavors, and little wooden pots filled with shiny silver spoons. Fountains burgled, lamps and lanterns glowed, koi swam lazily in their lighted pool.

"Well, you look great," she told Becca.

"So do you. I wonder if we both had a good time last night?"

Raine knew she blushed, the heat ran up her throat to her cheeks.

Becca laughed, pointed at her. "Aha, I knew it. You never could hide anything from me."

"I've never wanted to, but this, well." She shrugged.

Putting an arm around her friend, Becca said, "I'm so happy for you. You have no idea how you've changed since you met that big, gorgeous Indian. I was really afraid you'd never get over your experience with Delahaney."

"Please, don't say his name. It's a curse."

She refused to think of her ex, safely shut away in McAlester Prison, concentrated instead on this situation with Lucas Pell. This was a different Becca, happy, actually joking. She had Jon back and they were planning on taking in that little punk because the two of them felt guilty. If she said what she felt, she would ruin that joy, but how could she not say anything?

"Oh, listen," Becca said. "Christi called last night from Sydney. She, well, I think her and some boy are on their way home. It'll be so good to have her here again. And now maybe I can actually show her how much I love her."

Raine poured mixture into the latté machine. "She knows you love her, honey."

"Oh, Raine, I've accused her of so much. Of not loving her brother enough, of not caring about his death. How could I have been so cruel?"

"You were hurting, honey. She understood."

"Oh, sure, that's why she left. That's why David left too, because they understood. And Jon, as well. I almost destroyed my entire family, and blamed that poor young boy for what I was doing."

Raine turned, took Becca's hand. "Honey, I need to talk to you about that so-called poor young boy. I think you're making a big mistake, this idea of yours. You can't possibly be serious about taking him into your family. You don't know kids like this."

Becca's eyes sparked and she pulled her hand away. "And you do?"

"You know I do. I was raised with kids like him. I've seen the violence they're capable of."

"And just look at you," Becca said softly. "How good you turned out despite it. Don't you see you're the perfect example of what kids with nothing can accomplish with a little help?"

"But I didn't kill anyone." The utterance fell from her lips before she could stop it.

Only by the grace of God had she not done just that. Still, her parents hadn't abused her. Not unless you called poverty abuse, and they did the best they could. Even so, the drugs were there and the booze and the wild, unruly crowd from the wrong side of the tracks. And she'd tried a little of everything, including Russ Delahaney. She'd come closer to getting killed by him than anything or anyone else.

"Raine, don't fight me on this, please. You've been a good friend through all of my troubles. Please understand. I have to do this. It's the only way to heal us and to heal that poor boy."

"Please stop calling him a poor boy." Tears stood in her eyes. Her argument was coming to nothing. She so wanted to help Becca, but this she could not condone.

"I'm sorry if you don't understand. I really am. We're going to meet with him tonight. If you don't want to know any more about it, I'll honor your wishes."

"Then honor my wishes." Stomach churning, Raine went into the storeroom to get another packet of vanilla almond mix.

Twenty One

Jon parked the Mercedes next to Spinner's Nova. Staring at the retro motel, Becca took a deep breath and tried to calm her jittery nerves.

What a ratty place this was. Weeds peeked through cracks in the pavement, and here and there broken glass glittered. No cars nosed up against the other units, a sign the aging motel had plenty of vacancies. Amazing the place had remained open as long as it had. People who came to Monkey Island didn't stay in a second-rate motel. Several resorts along the shoreline handled visitors. Most residents were at least comfortably well off, and had year-round or summer homes along the shore. A good number of people who lived in Chota were either Indians or poor whites. Progress and the interstate to the west had passed them by. Everyone shopped in Vinita fourteen miles away. Except for the convenience store out at the intersection of Highways 60 and 59, all the big stores were in Vinita or Tulsa.

Becca practiced deep breathing, as if she were preparing to birth this frightening moment when she would come face to face with Lucas Pell.

She waited for Jon to come around and open the door for her. Not sure she could stand, her knees were trembling so, she would need his support as they crossed the pocked pavement.

Perhaps reading her thoughts, he opened the door and cupped her elbow. "Don't worry, hon, you look nice." He had watched her change three times before settling on a beige pantsuit and brown loafers.

"Thank you." She tipped her head and smiled tremulously.

Anything Jon wore looked good on him. This evening he'd eschewed his usual suit and tie for casual brown slacks and a pale cream short-sleeved summer shirt. His loafers were much like hers. They probably both had the same idea. To avoid overwhelming the boy.

Already, this meeting was difficult, and bound to get worse once Spinner opened that door, but she'd get through it successfully without making a fool of herself. If only Jon didn't blow it and reveal his lingering doubts. She squeezed his hand when he rapped on the faded panel.

"Okay, it'll be fine," he whispered. "I'll behave," he added as if reading her thoughts.

She nodded, and Spinner swung open the door to greet them, eyes somber. Did he own nothing but tee shirts and jeans? Still, she had to admit, he wore them very well. Not hard to see what attracted Raine. Surely this thing between them couldn't last much longer, though. Nor would Raine's refusal to side with Becca where Lucas was concerned. Both were typical of her friend's wayward personality. She waved like a flag caught by an Oklahoma wind. What appealed one day was gone the next. This wild fling with Spinner would blow away when he came between her and what she truly wanted—RainTree and a peaceful life. Becca only hoped Raine hadn't fallen in love with him.

"Well, come on in, then," Spinner said.

Reverie broken, Becca tried to move forward, for a moment couldn't so much as budge. Jon stepped in and tugged her along by the hand. His fingers tightened around hers when Lucas rose from where he was sitting on the edge of the bed.

An attempt had been made to slick down his unruly spikes of sandy hair, but tufts escaped whatever goo he'd used. He wore a new white tee shirt, stiff jeans, and scuffed blue and white sneakers. His tongue darted once around thin lips, and he stared at her with hooded brown eyes.

Her vision squeezed into a narrow tunnel. If she wasn't careful, she was going to faint. Dragging in a deep breath, she clung to Jon and glanced around the room. Anything to keep from meeting the boy's penetrating gaze that challenged her in some inexplicable way.

"Lucas, you remember Mrs. Kraft, and this is her husband, Jon."

They all nodded at each other like robots, then turned their collective gazes once more toward Spinner.

He rose to the occasion. "I apologize for the seating arrangement. Rebecca, would you like to sit here?" He indicated a chair he'd drawn near the bed. "Jon, I'm afraid you'll have to sit on the bed, here next to Lucas."

The formality with which he spoke threw her off balance. She and Jon hovered in the center of the tacky room, eyeing their assigned seats.

Spinner lowered himself to the floor under the window, crossing long legs in front of him. "Sit, all of you. Sit, Lucas."

Becca did so first, then Lucas scooted to the far end of the bed and Jon perched on the edge, leaving a large space between. Everyone waited, as if it were a game of musical chairs and the music hadn't yet begun.

"Well," Spinner said, and cleared his throat. "I've told Lucas a bit about why you wanted to see him, but thought it'd be best if you got acquainted before we worry much about why you're here."

Becca cleared her throat, then flushed. "Did you find a job, today?" she asked, looking past the boy's shoulder at the wall.

"Uh-huh."

"Oh?" she chirped. "Where?" Lord, help me find something intelligent to say. Anything. Dissolve this lump the size of a boulder lodged in my throat.

"It don't matter. It's just a job."

"He's going to work at Hammer's Boat Yard scraping hulls and fixing engines," Spinner said. "Not much, but he has to start somewhere."

"Besides, ain't no one gonna give me anything important to do."

Jon shifted a bit. "What would you like to do, Lucas?"

Even her comfortable-in-any-situation husband sounded unsure of himself. His tone stilted, he continued to struggle with his feelings toward this boy who'd killed their son.

"Like? What the fu—" His eyes darted toward Spinner who scowled and shook his head. "I mean, what does it matter?" He glared at his counselor. "What I like, I mean."

"We have to know what we want before we can pursue it."

How many times had Becca heard Jon say that to one of the kids? And now he said it to Lucas. Her heart warmed. If he could do this, then she could too.

"You think maybe I could go to work for you?" Lucas sneered, fists doubled at his sides.

Jon glanced quickly at Spinner, then at Becca, swallowed and studied Lucas. "I think you could if you got rid of that attitude, applied yourself, took some courses. Then, yes, you could go to work for me."

Knowing how difficult that was for Jon, Becca wanted to leap up and hug him.

"Oh, well, then. I'll get right on that."

"Lucas," Spinner said.

"Well, shit, man. He thinks I could take some courses?" he

mimicked. "What's this, apply myself? What courses? And what's wrong with my fucking attitude?"

Rather than aim the question at Jon or Spinner, he'd shot it across at Becca. "What'd you come here for, anyway? You told me, you called me a killer. What you want with me, anyhow? Make you feel better to toss me some crumbs, you high and mighty bitch."

He might have hit her, the words were delivered with such venom. She said nothing.

"Lucas. That's enough," Spinner said, but he didn't react otherwise. Obviously accustomed to this sort of behavior.

Jon's body language telegraphed his displeasure and he pivoted to face the kid, shoulders back and arms flexing. Not good. From what she knew of Lucas's past, that would be exactly the sort of reaction he would be pleased to handle.

Before the situation could escalate, she swallowed harshly. "We want to help you, Lucas."

"Uh-huh. Sure, you do."

"Why else would we be here?"

He looked around, like he was trapped and couldn't escape. "Alls the help I want from you is to tell me it's okay, what I did. That you know I didn't do it on purpose. I didn't want to kill no one. No one. Just tell me that, so he'll fucking leave me be." Tears coursed down his cheeks, increasing his anger. He fisted them away, like maybe if he hurried she wouldn't notice.

"Leave you be? Who?" Becca shuddered. Surely he didn't mean Jeremiah's ghost.

"Your son, that's who." He hiccoughed out the words. "Can't close my eyes he ain't there." The boy drilled her with a hard stare. It was as if they were the only two in the room.

It was true. Jeremiah had visited them both in their dreams, a connection of sorts. She had to somehow deal with this hurt, furious child who had no idea what life was all about and probably wouldn't live to find out.

Licking her lips, she tried to say the words, but they wouldn't come out. Just say you forgive him.

Say it.

"Lucas, I know you didn't... didn't...." Damn, she couldn't say it. The words stuck in her throat, choked her into silence.

"See?" Lucas shouted. "I told you. What'd I tell you?" If he were addressing Spinner, she couldn't tell it.

He jumped to his feet, made for the door. Spinner was on him in a flash, pinning his shoulders in a bear hug.

"No, you don't. You're not running away from this. No more running," he hissed in Lucas's ear.

Shouting, kicking out with the heavy shoes, Lucas connected with Spinner's shin bone, still the big Indian hung on.

"Settle down. Cut it out," he soothed, a grimace all that revealed the physical pain of being kicked.

"Damn you. Damn you all," Lucas cried, then was somehow in Spinner's embrace, sobbing on his shoulder.

Though Jon showed every sign of getting out of there, Becca watched the tableau and refused to budge. She shook her head at her husband, remained seated. The boy's shoulders heaved. He blubbered words she could scarcely understand, muffled as they were by Spinner's broad chest.

"Then tell them," Spinner said. "Hush your bawling and tell them."

"I c-c-c-can't."

"You can, and you will. Remember what we talked about. Making a fresh start. Wiping out all the old shit, starting over. This is where it begins, Lucas, or this is where it ends. Up to you."

After a moment, Lucas turned, spread his hands wide at his sides. "I'm sorry I hurt you. I am sorry. It was my fault, all mine. If I live another hundred years, I can never make up for what I did to you and your son. He's dead because of me, and I can't never make it up to you. Not ever." He stopped, gasped, sobbed some more, and Becca slowly rose, her heart aching.

"I never shut my eyes I don't see him dead. I was drinking. I don't do that no more. I promise I never knew what could happen. I can't. Stop. *Seeing*. Him." The words tumbled out in twos and threes. The boy nearly choked on them, but he got them out.

Her heart jerked in her chest as if struck by a mighty blow. "My sweet Jeremiah. Oh, Lucas," she whispered. "Oh, you poor child."

Only a few steps separated them, and she had no idea how she took them, but she had her arms wrapped around him. The heat of his sorrow washed over her, tears poured from her eyes.

For a stunned moment, he remained stiff in her embrace, then slowly, he looped his arms over her shoulders and bent his head so it rested against hers.

"Oh, Jesus. Jesus, I'm so sorry," he said.

Maybe he'd never prayed in his life, maybe he didn't even know what prayer was all about, but he was doing it now.

"I know, Lucas. I know and so does... so does Jeremiah."

They remained there for a long while, both crying and neither saying anything else.

Becca slowly became conscious that Jon and Spinner were talking softly on the other side of the room. Lucas must have noticed too, for he took away his arms and stepped back, looking rather sheepish.

She pulled a handful of tissues from her purse and shared with him. Without a word, he accepted and turned away to dry his face and blow his nose. Both Spinner and Jon sniffed and cleared their throats, then chuckled softly, like men do when they want to pretend they haven't been emotional.

Jon came to stand beside her. "You okay?"

She nodded. "You?"

"I'm all right. What's next?"

"I don't know. Spinner?"

The counselor nodded too briskly. "What we need now is to find Lucas a place to live. He's decided he'd like to work and live here for a while, till he gets on his feet. Then maybe he'll move to Tulsa and try for a better job." He gave her an out, even now. Lucas didn't know about the offer to live with them, and she didn't have to tell him. She could let it go right here and walk away.

She glanced at Jon. "Maybe we could help with that. I mean, if it's okay."

"What'd you have in mind?" Spinner asked.

He knew perfectly well what she had in mind, but she played along. He needed her to say it in front of Lucas to get his reaction, and that was okay. Better out in the open than for him to prepare a reaction that he felt might be the proper one. Not that Lucas had much idea what was proper.

"We have a room and bath over the garage that has an outside entrance. He wouldn't have to... I mean, if he didn't want to, he wouldn't have to come through the house. It would be private, like his own apartment."

"Hey," Lucas said, the angry tone creeping back into his voice. "Tell me, not him. I feel like you're talking about me and I ain't here."

"I'm sorry, Lucas. I didn't mean to do that," Becca said. "If you want to stay there a while, just till you can get on your feet, like Spinner says, and decide what you want to do. Well, you're welcome to do so."

"How much?" Lucas pinned her with sharp eyes.

She smiled, and something went through her heart. Something warm that almost caused her to break into tears again. "I might need you to help out sometimes, nothing big. When Jon's at work, I might need a man's help to carry something, or, you know. Man stuff?"

"I guess I could do that. But how much money? I ain't a charity case. You can't 'spect me to be obliged."

Everyone paused, looked at each other. She wanted to go carefully here. "What have you been paying where you are now?"

"Fifty a week, but I only was making a hundred, so that's tough. I'll be getting, what'd you call it, Spinner? Minimum wage? Out at the boat yard, and working thirty hours. I can do it, though," he hastened to add.

"Well, how about a hundred a month?" Jon said. "Just till you get on your feet."

He glanced at Spinner and both nodded. They'd already cooked this up. That's what the talking had been about earlier, when she and Lucas were wrapped in each other's misery.

"And thirty hours is good," Spinner added quickly. "We'll get you enrolled in some vo-tech classes over in Vinita so you can learn a trade."

"I took some classes and got my GED while I was in juvie. I ain't very good at English, but I like algebra and those sciences. Do they make you do more of that English stuff? Like nouns and verbs and stuff. I never could catch on to that, but I did pass 'cause of liking to read so much. The literature part?"

The boy's turn-around fascinated Becca. His eyes sparkled and his lips curved ever so slightly.

Oh, Jeremiah. My sweet boy. Look what you have wrought.

The thought came unbidden and she turned away, broke down and cried openly. Why did he have to die to save this boy?

Jon moved close, put his arms around her shoulder. "Honey? What is it? You okay? I thought this was what you wanted."

She turned into his shoulder. "It is. I mean, of course, what happened isn't, but look at him, Jon. Why did our son have to die so this boy could have his life back? I don't know if I can put my mind around that. I just don't know."

"I didn't mean to make her cry," Lucas said from across the room, and he sounded so forlorn, she peeked around Jon.

"Come over here, Lucas, would you?" Her voice caught, held.

Though he appeared reluctant, he moved nearer. She freed one arm, held it out. "Come on. If you're going to be a part of this family you have to learn to hug. It's required."

He bounced on the balls of his feet, glanced back at Spinner, studied Jon and Becca. "Family?" His voice vibrated the question, his throat clicking loudly when he swallowed. "Man, I don't know. I ain't never been much for hugging."

"That's 'cause you've never had anyone to hug," Spinner said. "Why don't you give it a try?" The man sounded so pleased with himself, you would've thought this was all his idea.

She wanted to smack him one on general principles. Instead she grinned. "You might as well come, too. You look like you could use a little hug yourself."

Lucas sidled their way some more. Her fingers touched his shoulder. She gently coaxed him until he came closer and she could get an arm around him, his muscles taut as drawn cables. Jon dragged in a huge sigh that broke once, then eased his arm around Lucas from the other side.

"Ah, what the hell?" Spinner said, and joined them till they were all wrapped around each other.

A serene stillness settled over the small room. Heartbeats echoed in Becca's ears. Her's, Lucas's, Jon's, and Spinner's all thumping like mad. And somewhere, like a ghostly echo, Jeremiah's.

"Well, that's enough of that." Spinner backed off with a self-conscious chuckle.

Each one broke away, Lucas shuffling and looking down at his feet. When Becca caught Jon's gaze, he nodded crisply, eyes bright. A done deal. Not that there wouldn't be problems, and plenty of them. She expected at times to not be able to bear looking at Lucas for very long without that old resentment beginning to boil. And Jon had a temper that he held in check pretty well most of the time. He'd cut loose over something and there'd be a bad time for a while. But the first steps had been accomplished, the hurdle crossed. Next week they started group counseling, and that would help them all.

She couldn't have been more pleased at how the meeting with Lucas and Spinner had gone.

Jon's cell phone interrupted. He unclipped it from his belt and connected.

"Yes, hi, baby. Where are you?"

Oh, no. It was Christi. What would she think of this? How would they tell her?

"When? No, your mother should've told you. I took the week off. I'm out here at Monkey Island, but I can come get you."

He laughed. "No, I'm not sick, and yes, I suppose that's silly. You could be halfway home before I'd get over there."

Glancing at Becca, he listened a moment. "Of course we'll wait up for you. Bringing a friend? Yes, Mom did tell me that. A male friend, I take it. She has the guest room ready." A cock of his head, and he said quickly, "I think we'd better talk about that when you get here." A beat. "Sure, honey. Take care and we'll see you soon. Love you."

The phone was back on his belt before he glanced at Becca. "They were in a hurry, something about their bags, I don't know, anyway, she said she'd talk to you when she gets here." He raised an eyebrow. "There may be problems about the guest room for her friend."

"I'll just bet there will be," Becca said. "Don't look so stern. It hasn't been that long since we were madly in love." Only after the words were out did she realize how they sounded. "I mean, before we were married we, oh, well, you know what I mean."

Even Spinner looked embarrassed. "You guys go on. I know you're excited about—it is your daughter, isn't it? Coming home. It'll be a week or so before we can get Lucas situated out there. That'll be okay, won't it?"

Lucas appeared to be disappointed, but said nothing. Silently, Becca thanked Spinner. It would give them time to deal with Christi and get her used to the idea of Lucas being there.

Out in the car, Jon put the key in the ignition, but didn't turn it.

"What?" Becca asked.

"Do you think Christi is going to stay out here?"

"I don't know. She hasn't said. Why?"

"Well, I'm a little uncomfortable having an eighteen-year-old boy, especially one with Lucas's past, living in the same house with her."

"He won't be living in the house, not exactly. Besides, Christi is twenty-one, and not easily impressed, not even by a bad boy."

"Jesus," Jon muttered. "It wasn't exactly her I was worried about. I mean, it is her but it's him mostly. Suppose he gets ideas? He'll come and go, and so will we. She's a beautiful girl, our Christi."

"And a smart one too." She laid a hand on his arm. "Lucas is going to be just fine. And so is Christi. The only thing I worry about is how she'll feel about the idea. Has she ever said much to you about Jeremiah's death?"

"No, not a word." In the darkness she couldn't see his expression, and wanted desperately to turn on the inside lights and get a good look. Know what he was really thinking.

But he started the car and she settled back in the seat. A dart of fear slashed through her happiness over Christi's return and the arrangements they'd made with Lucas. She pushed it away. Too long she'd lived with sorrow and resentment and anger. Time now to let it go.

Twenty Two

Spinner took Lucas back to his apartment. He'd rather let him stay at the motel, but there was only the one bed and he used up most of it. The kid was so hyped he feared what might happen when he came down. When he began to have doubts about the Kraft's motives, the job, going to school. The whole works.

And the doubts would come. It was the nature of the life the boy had lived. Hell, he himself still couldn't handle everything going right. Had to twist and turn it until he found something wrong. Look what he was doing to this relationship with Raine. Going all prickly and treating her like dirt 'cause she didn't agree with his assessment of Lucas.

She didn't deserve that, no more than she deserved him showing up at her door and taking advantage of her vulnerability. He ought to stay away from her, period. But failing that, and he damn sure would fail that, he should talk to her instead of fucking her. Women needed to be talked to, and the two of them had never communicated. He knew very little about her except that what she had she'd earned the hard way and some man had mistreated her terribly. Had tried to kill her, for Christ sake. He hadn't wanted to know details, mostly because if she shared her past, she'd expect him to do the same. He wasn't about to go into that dark place. Not with anyone.

After telling Lucas he'd pick him up and take him to work the next morning, he let the Nova find its way to Raine's place. This time he'd begin a dialogue instead of grabbing her and throwing her down and, Jesus, thinking of it gave him a hard-on, and he wasn't even halfway to her house yet. What was it with her that shot down his defenses? He'd always been able to take women or leave them alone. Since Marty, at any rate. He never wanted to be hurt like that again, though the adult in him was sure that nothing so self-destructive could ever happen again. Mostly because he was no longer that person.

Though he hated to admit it, he had a vague notion what was going on here. As long as he didn't stand a chance in hell for a long-lasting relationship with Raine, he could let all his desires surface. Have a fucking good time with her, then move on with no regrets. Unwise for a psychologist to analyze his own actions, though.

Her house was dark and still, and she didn't answer the bell, so he sat down in the swing to wait. This could not be put off until another time. It had to be settled, now, while he had firmly in his mind what he would say.

Lord, she was so beautiful and he wanted her so much. If he didn't cool it things would get out of hand again and where would all his best intentions be? And why would she want him anyway? Especially once she got to know him.

Fidgeting, he looked up and down the quiet street, expecting to see her little red car at any moment. It must be close to ten o'clock. She was probably out with another man. She was much too smart and chic to spend her evenings alone. Thinking like that made him crazy in a hurry. The idea of another man putting his hands on her soft skin, running his fingers through that satiny hair, kissing those sultry lips, drove him crazy.

The swing creaked. Night critters sang. Somewhere a door slammed, a woman laughed, a kid hollered. The neighborhood was nice—older well-kept houses with big trees and neat yards—but not as snazzy as where the Krafts lived. Still, a hell of a lot better than any he'd ever lived in. What would happen if the two of them got together seriously? Decided to hook up for good? Nah, no danger of that. He wouldn't be here if there was. Would he? He ought to get in his car and leave. Never come back. He and Raine mixed like gasoline and fire.

That's probably exactly why he was here. He enjoyed creating the spark that ignited her flame, turned her from quiet and sophisticated into a lustful, madly passionate woman whose desires knew no bounds. And there weren't any strings because—well, because—

Say it fool. They were like gasoline and fire, and she knew it as well as he. Both just having some laughs.

After a while, he got up and paced, stopping occasionally to check the silent street. Lights went out in all the houses around the neighborhood as everyone turned in for the night, and still no Raine. Once he took out his telephone to call Becca, see if she had any idea where her friend was, but he hung up before it could ring and went back to his pacing.

No use asking why he just didn't dial her cell. He knew the answer to that. If she were out with someone, then he'd know, wouldn't he? Besides, he didn't want to look like he was checking up on her. Keeping tabs. Getting possessive.

Shit fire!

He paced some more.

Surrounded by the silence in the back room and the faint, soothing sound of the fountains out front in the coffee shop, Raine stared at the figures on the computer and rubbed her eyes. Everything brought up to date, gross and net profits recorded. The clock face on the screen read 9:30. Time to go home. After a last peek into the shop to make sure all the lights were off save those in the fountains, she gathered her handbag and opened the back door to utter darkness.

The outside light had burned out and she could barely see the shape of her car nosed against the building, not half a dozen steps away. Would have to replace the bulb above the door tomorrow. She pulled the door shut, bent to lock it.

Something hit her hard from behind, shoved her forward, smashed her face up against the metal panel. A hand screwed at the knob, hot, fetid breath washed over her neck, and both she and her attacker tumbled inside. Terror gripped her like steel fingers. She squawked.

"Shut up, Rainy."

Oh, God. Oh no! *Russ.*

The terror tripled, choked off her breath, threatened to burst her thudding heart.

Gripping her upper arm, he twisted her around, slammed her against a shelf, knocking down an avalanche of supplies. Small bags of coffee burst under his scrambling feet, filled her nostrils with the heady aroma. Forearm locked under her chin, he leaned close, his tobacco/beer breath so familiar she gagged.

He was supposed to be in prison. How did he find her? She'd wished him dead so many times. Imagined him lying in his cell with a knife through his throat. She had come to believe it were true. Now, here he was, plunging her into the dreaded nightmare she'd thought ended when the judge sentenced him to McAlester.

As if reading her mind, he said, "Thought you were rid of me, huh? Thought I'd forgotten all about my pretty Rainy." He tightened his arm until she gasped for air. "Well, I got news. Prison only makes that stuff harder to forget. Gonna behave?"

She nodded, lungs frantic.

"In a pig's eye," he said, but loosened his grip.

Frantic, she sucked in huge gulps. "How'd you get out? How—? Why—? What do you *want*?" She rubbed at her burning throat, gauged the distance to the phone near the computer. Another hung on the wall behind the counter in the shop. Her cell was in her purse, but she'd dropped it when he grabbed her.

All so near, yet impossibly far.

"I was such a good boy, they opened the door and wished me well. I got to missing you, babe." He rubbed his stubbly cheek along the side of her neck so hard her flesh burned. "Took me a while to find you after I got out. Shoulda gone someplace else. Coming here so close to home was stupid. Shoulda changed your name." He laughed. "But I'd a still found you eventually."

Terror squeezed at her insides. He would do whatever he wanted. She'd never been able to stop him. She still couldn't. The thought buckled her knees.

"Hey, now, don't go out on me. Not yet, anyway. I got some stuff in mind for my baby. Won't do you no good to fight."

Oh, how well she'd learned that over the years. Her refusal to play his perverted games only made him angrier, and he'd knock her around until she passed out. What he might have done then was too horrifying to think about. The ultimate slicing her throat, deliberately missing the carotid, but coming as close to killing her as he ever had.

"'Member, baby? 'Member what I told you?"

Panic shot through her, and she nodded.

"Say it," he growled, propping her against the shelving.

"Said you'd kill me. Kill me if I— I left."

"And, so what did you do?"

She would die here tonight. The realization somehow freed her. She glared at him, spat, "I left, you bastard. So go ahead and kill me."

"Not till we play some games." He tightened the scarf around her neck. "I've learned a new one. It's more fun to nearly die doing it. It's more fun to do it while you're dying. So let's give it a try."

Numb and stricken mute, she sagged against him. He ripped at her clothes, growling in her ear. Slammed her to her hands and knees, skinned down her pants, and rammed himself into her over and over while the scarf cut off her breath and blackness closed around her. She shut down, let it all go. Dead was better than *this*. So much better.

Raine awoke slowly, sprawled on the floor. Gazed into darkness. Where was she? What had happened? Her throat hurt, and when she tried to speak nothing came out. Moisture wet her face and hair and naked body. Coming from the koi fountain, its glow visible through the mist. A scarf bound her wrists together at her waist, shoes were still on her feet. A dreadful burning between her legs.

He'd forced himself inside her, like a heated branding iron.

With a moan of pain, she rolled to her side and sat up. He hadn't killed her. Why hadn't he killed her?

Because he wanted to play with her some more. Come after her over and over, each time worse than the last.

Oh, God. She had to get out of here. Run. *Run.*

Using her teeth, she loosened the scarf amid animal-like grunts. Flailed about until she could stand. Almost tumbled into the fountain.

What if he was waiting outside? Be just like him. Do it again. He always got off on keeping her terrified every moment.

Lord help me! She could barely see for the black terror that engulfed her. Managed to stagger through the dimly lit shop to the back room. Unsure where she was going and why.

Her clothes lay in a heap where he'd ripped them off. Unable to stand, she dropped into a chair to pull on her pants, then the torn blouse. Never mind the shredded underwear. Tears and more tears, burning like acid. Soul going dark as a cave.

At the back door, she turned the knob slowly, opened it a crack and peered out. Still black night out there. He was waiting for her. Without a doubt. If not tonight, then soon. Let her think she'd escaped, only to come back again and again.

Turning, she stared at the telephone. Call somebody. But who? Whoever came could walk into an ambush. Russ would hope for such a thing. She could not go through this again with him. Where would she go? He was right, she had no idea how to hide from him.

Spinner. Call Spinner. He'd come. He'd do something.

She picked up the phone, dropped it, fumbled for it again, then couldn't remember his cell number. Oh, yes. She'd put it in the auto dial. Which one? Number two, right after Becca. Finger trembling so badly she could hardly hit the digit, she finally punched it and heard the dialing bleeps. The buzz of its ringing. Once, twice, three times. Answer, *please*! Answer the damn phone. you bastard!

Then there was his blessed voice, and her sobbing, crying out incoherently. He shouted her name, shouted it again.

"Where are you? Just tell me where you are."

"S-s-sh. Rain."

"I know it's Raine. Darling, please, where are you?"

"Rain T-t—"

"RainTree? Gotcha. Be there."

"Wait. Wait." She had to warn him. Warn him about Russ.

"I'm still here, Raine. Keep the line open. I'm on my way."

"Spinner, please."

"I know, it won't be but a few minutes. Have you called 9-1-1?"

"No, don't do that. No, no!." Screams, those final three words. Then, "Look out. He's out there. Be careful. He's sick, he'll kill you."

Exhaustion, terror, relief, warred within her and she sank to the floor, dropping the phone.

He was coming. Spinner was coming.

The moment he heard the panic in her voice, Spinner knew he loved her. Knew that if something happened to her he wouldn't want to live. And that was the way of love, wasn't it? Don't let this happen again. You bastard, not again. Not to Raine. Dear, sweet, gentle Raine.

He shouldn't have loved her. Cursed her because he loved her.

At times the Nova's wheels left the ground as he steered around corners and sailed through red lights. In front of RainTree, he leaped out before the car jerked to a halt, left the door open, the engine running.

He's out there, she'd said. Careful, buddy. Don't make a target of yourself. He gets you, she's got no one.

The sign on the front door read **CLOSED**. He rattled it anyway. Locked. Hugging the building, he slipped around the corner to where she always parked.

Black as the hubs of hell back there. No sign of anyone, but shadows everywhere. Her car. Bastard could be behind it. He bent, looked. Nothing but darkness. Shadows. Might have a gun. Heart racing, mind urging him to hurry, hurry, he hugged the trunk and peered around. The back door stood ajar. From inside a pale slit of light fell out onto her purse.

Son of a bitch. To hell with this.

He made a mad dash, hit the door with his shoulder, tumbled inside and rolled toward the wall. Inched in a crouch into the work room.

"Raine?" A husky whisper.

Someone threw themselves at him, grabbed him around the neck, squeezing out a yelp that nearly stopped his heart. Then she was in his arms, clinging, crying his name over and over, trembling, leaving wet spots on his shirt.

"Easy, easy. I've got you now. I've got you." He held on to her nearly as frantically as she held him.

"Is he here?" A voice so terrified it shook.

"Didn't see anyone. But let's go. My car's out front. We'll leave that way. There's some light, I can tell if he's out there." No time to ask who he was. Just get her out of danger. Fast.

She nodded against his chest, and he picked her up. Feather light, and holding on so tight, shaking so damned hard. He had her now. She was safe and alive. Not dead. Thank God, not dead. He'd kill this son of a bitch. Slit his motherfucking throat. Whoever he was.

"You're safe, honey. Safe."

He struggled a moment with the dead bolt on the front door, threw it open, then slammed it behind them, moved toward the rumbling Nova. Dumped her in the passenger seat, glanced all around and hurried to the other side.

No use in calling the cops. He'd take care of this himself.

He took her to his place, held her while she showered, then curled around her in bed while she slept. A fitful sleep disturbed by bad dreams that tormented her. And he told her he loved her, whether she heard him or not. Promised her nothing bad would ever happen to her again. And meant it.

Christi and her friend, a tall, sunburned young man with a thatch of ginger hair and wire-rimmed glasses, arrived at the house around midnight. They unloaded several duffel bags and two backpacks from the trunk of a rented Toyota and horsed them into the entryway. Depositing the ungainly pile on the marble floor at the foot of the stairs, Christi introduced Kevin Soule to Becca and Jon.

Hugs all around, including the effusive young man, then Becca offered sandwiches and cold lemonade.

Seated on high stools around the breakfast bar, the two youngsters chattered and downed two sandwiches each.

Christi, words tumbling over each other, "And then Kevin says, 'I've had enough of this place. Let's go home,' and since I didn't want to lose track of him, I decided to come back too. We hitched a ride on this bush doctor's plane. What a ride that was. Mom, Dad, you wouldn't believe how big and empty Australia is. What few towns there are. And, well, there's not much to do. Sometimes we'd walk all day without seeing anything but kangaroos and dust and the sun. And snakes." She shuddered, went on before anyone could interrupt.

"Never thought I'd be so glad to see Oklahoma again. Everything's so green and so much water. When we flew in I couldn't get enough of looking out the window."

She wolfed down another huge bite of sandwich.

"You *walked*?" Becca asked. Out of all the chatter, that caught her attention most.

"Yes." Kevin laughed. "Walked everywhere. Sometimes we'd get a ride."

"Wherever did you spend the night?"

"Under the sky mostly," Christi said. "We had a tent and all."

"A tent?" Jon looked perturbed.

Christi laughed. "Dad, don't be a stick-in-the-mud. Of course, a tent."

Kevin had the decency to blush to the roots of his hair and concentrate on finishing off his second sandwich.

Becca hid a smile and glanced at Jon, who dutifully glared at Kevin, then his daughter.

Covering Jon's clenched fist, Becca said, "Well, then I suppose it's useless to offer you the guest room, Kevin."

After a second of silence, everyone chuckled. Jon only a little.

While Becca and Jon undressed for bed some time later, Jon muttered, "A tent."

"She is twenty-one, Jon. We can't dictate her morals anymore. Besides, it's the way they do things nowadays. What do we know?"

"Nowadays. If I recall, your folks were never married. At least they said they weren't. Lived together from the time they were kids. Flower children. My mother nearly had a coronary when I brought you home. The daughter of living-in-sin hippies."

Laughing, she crawled under the covers, made room for him. "But I reformed, didn't I?"

"I like hearing you laugh again." He moved in beside her, snuggled close. "I was never real sure you reformed. I think you married me as much to shock your parents as anything. Oh, I know, we did love each other." He sighed, then finished softly, "Do you think they're in there now...?"

"Jon. Even this hippie child doesn't want to think about what our baby is doing in there with that strange boy. Come here."

Long after they made love, she lay within the curl of his arms. How foolish of her to have almost lost this. Bad enough they'd lost their beloved son, but for the two of them to come so close to letting their love escape, had been oh so foolish.

They hadn't talked about Lucas, caught up as they were in Christi's arrival, but tomorrow they would have to tell their daughter what they'd done, and she wasn't looking forward to it. Especially not with a stranger in their midst.

The two kids seemed to get along well. She supposed they were as serious about their relationship as kids got these days. Still, she wasn't eager to welcome Kevin into the family. It was much too early for that. So he would remain a stranger held at arm's length for a while longer. Maybe she'd suggest they have a family conference and send him out on errands or something.

This night she closed her eyes, certain there would be no more nightmares. She felt at peace, sensed her son's spirit at peace as well. Christi hadn't appeared to still mourn Jeremiah's death. Surely she would be okay with this.

That feeling of peace came to an abrupt halt the following morning when they broke the news to Christi about Lucas.

"How could you, Mom? Dad, how could you let her?" Christi stared over the breakfast table, hazel eyes hard as gemstones. "I thought you hated that boy for what he did. I hate him. He killed Jeremiah." Tears pooled and spilled over her flushed cheeks.

"Honey, this has been so hard for all of us. Hate isn't the answer. We have to heal, all of us. If we help him make something of his life, then Jeremiah's death won't have been for nothing."

"It was for nothing, Mom. He wasn't doing anything wrong. That boy was drinking. How can you think we should help him?"

"Now, sweetheart." Jon was always at a loss for words where his daughter was concerned.

She turned on him. "Daddy, I thought you had better sense."

"Christi, don't you speak to your father in that tone."

"I will if I please. I should have a say in this. I'm sorry, but I think you've both gone off the deep end. I can't live in the same house with my brother's killer, and I don't see how you could either."

Jon put his arm around Becca, when she began to sob. The two of them, united at long last, but at what expense?

"What does David think of this lunacy?" Christi no longer sounded like the lively, happy child who had returned home all bubbly and excited only hours earlier.

"He doesn't know yet," Jon said. "And I would remind you, young lady that this is our home, mine and your mother's. You will not dictate what we do here."

Christi gasped and so did Becca. He'd never used that tone with his darling daughter before, always gave in, let her have her way, even if it wasn't convenient. Not being around her much while she was growing up made that a bit easier, but still Becca was shocked at his stance.

"Then I will not live here."

"You're twenty-one years old, Christi," Becca said. "I expected you to move out one day. I'm sorry you feel the way you do, though. You're our daughter and we love you dearly. Please consider our feelings on this."

"Why? You aren't considering mine."

With that Christi pushed from the table and ran from the room. Her feet clomped loudly on the stairs and neither one spoke until her door slammed.

"I guess, in a way, we should've expected that," Jon said. "She'll come around."

Becca laid her head on his shoulder. "I certainly hope so. I don't want this family to break up over this. Maybe we ought to reconsider. I won't lose my two remaining children for this boy. I can't."

"Let's give her some time. I wish David were here, he was always able to reason with our slightly spoiled daughter."

"Yes, but suppose he agrees with her. Then what?"

Jon didn't answer.

Becca wished that possibility hadn't occurred to her. She wanted to do what was right for all of them, including Lucas, but was no longer sure what that was.

Twenty Three

Tied down in a strange bed, Raine awoke and came up fighting, blindly lashing out.

"Leave me be, get away from me, you bastard."

"Easy, there." He had her by the wrists, holding her down.

She bucked and kicked.

"Raine, it's me, Spinner. Come on, ease up."

The terror had hold of her, the reassurances came like ghost words that couldn't possibly be real. No one could help her. Her dream that Spinner would save her faded into the morbid reality of death's approach. For she couldn't live through another attack.

Heart churning until her vision darkened, she struggled to be free. Found herself bound, not by cords, but by a sheet she'd managed to twist around herself.

Gently, he folded her arms behind her back, gathered her close, whispered in her ear. "He'll never hurt you again, I promise. Raine, I promise. Wake up, come on now, sweetheart."

Tender, kind words, urging her to believe. Did she dare? Was it truly Spinner?

"Stop. Don't hold me, turn me loose. I can't stand it."

Immediately, he did as she asked, and she skittered backward against the headboard, hugging her knees under her chin. She believed him, she truly did, but the fear raged through her like a wildfire.

"Okay, honey. I'm not holding you. Settle down now. I'll sit here on the edge of the bed so we can talk. Is that okay?"

Wildly, she nodded, tried to focus on him, but her eyes jittered around the room, making her dizzy. "Sp— Sp-Spinner Oh, please make it stop."

Clenching her fists, she clung to the edge of sanity, shivering until the mattress rocked.

"Raine, do you need to see a doctor? Did he… did the son of a bitch rape you?"

"No doctor." Her teeth clacked and she couldn't answer his question. "I can't talk about it now. Please, not now." Her trembling increased.

"Okay, it's all right. Take deep breaths. Look at me, breathe with me." Though he remained out of reach, his musical voice mesmerized her, and she matched her breathing to his. In, out, in, out. The pounding in her chest slowed, his face stopped swaying like a pendulum.

"That's better. Now, I need to hold you close. Would that be all right?"

She nodded. A weird humming sound came from her chest as she crawled toward him, curled into his embrace, and sighed.

This was where she belonged, where she would stay. At least for a while, till the strength to stand on her own returned. Even then, this man would be beside her. This she knew without asking.

He brushed back her hair, kissed her forehead, his lips warm and reassuring. "Better?"

Unable to speak, she nodded.

"I have to pick up Lucas, take him to work. It's important, but I won't leave you. Come with me?"

"Yes, yes." This time Russ would not ruin her life. It wasn't something she would allow. Not again. Not ever again.

Spinner gave her a tee shirt because her blouse was ripped and dirty, and helped her slip into her pants. "We'll go by your place and pick up some clothes later. And decide what we want to do."

Without further questions, he simply included himself in the decision of what was to be done. That warmed her as nothing else could have.

Becca's sleepless night dragged to a close with a silver glow at the windows and the low hum of conversation passing along the hallway. Christi and her friend. Becca gnawed at a hangnail. What could they do about Christi's feelings concerning Lucas? She and her daughter had been close until Jeremiah's death. All she needed was time, surely. But, if worse came to worst, then some other arrangements would have to be made for Lucas. Much as she hated to think about that, she would not further rip her family apart.

Beside her in the bed, Jon made a tiny sound in his throat. His closed eyes roamed through what must be a pleasant dream. How good it was to awaken lying next to the man she loved, to know the meaning of serenity. That empty hole left in her heart by Jeremiah's passing would always be there. So would the sorrow. But now there was room for anticipation of the days to come. Room for love of the sweetest kind.

Jon's eyes fluttered open, his languid gaze rested on her, his lips curved. On impulse, she slid close and gave him a long, sultry kiss.

"Mmmm, tastes good," he murmured, moved a warm hand to rest on her bare hip. "When did you start sleeping in the buff?"

"You've made a wanton slut of me."

"Sure, blame me." His thumb circled lazily along her belly, fingers trailing lower.

"I like making love in the morning before my body wakes up. It's like satin on silk when you're inside me. Our parts still sleeping."

He moved to oblige her, taking it slow and easy. Back and forth, heat within heat, in a rhythmic throbbing. Prolonging the crescendo until she cried out, locked her arms and legs around him. Still he moved as the steady beat of a heart. And when he came, he did so as if in a dream. Holding her gently, moaning at her breast. Rocking, rocking, growing within her, bringing her to a peak of utter bliss.

"I've missed you so much," he said against her throat.

Barely able to speak for the emotion flooding her, but needing so badly to answer him, she said, "And I you. Don't ever let us be so foolish again."

In silence, he held her very close for a long while, then, "Guess we'd better shower and go downstairs. I fear we have some reasoning to do with our stubborn daughter. Join me?"

"Be happy to," she said, barely able to cover the irritation and fear Christi's declaration of the night before had aroused.

Obviously sensing her doubt, he said, "Don't worry, it'll work out."

She followed him to the shower, wished she had as much faith as he did. "I hope so. I really hope so. I want so badly to do this. For Lucas as well as our Jeremiah."

"Well, one thing's for sure," he added, adjusting the water. "We've been through worse and survived."

Only just barely. Something she would keep to herself.

Later, downstairs, she and Jon formed a united front, entering the breakfast room holding hands. Christi and Kevin sat at the bar, eating Toaster Pops they'd obviously brought with them.

"Well, gang, what's up?" Jon sounded a little too jovial. "Deciding what you're going to do with the rest of your lives?"

Christi arched a brow and studied him quizzically. "I guess. Yeah, I suppose you could say that."

Becca started to speak, but Jon squeezed her hand. "Want me to tell you what I think you should do?"

Christi lay down the half-eaten pastry. "What's going on, Dad?"

"Nothing. Nothing at all. I decided that since you thought you could tell your mother and I what we should do, I'd return the favor. Oh, and if you don't like it, why then I guess we just won't come around to visit you wherever it is you settle. And we certainly couldn't invite you here, could we?"

Christi gasped and gazed wide-eyed from Kevin to her parents and back again.

Becca squeezed Jon's hand harder, said out of the corner of her mouth, "Jon, what's going on?"

"Well, I just thought, dear, that we ought to get this all out in the open. Don't you agree?"

Swallowing her trepidation, Becca nodded. "I guess."

"Mom, what's wrong with Dad?"

"Why don't you ask Dad?" Jon said. "I'm right here."

"Well, that's a change, isn't it?" Christi said.

"Aha. Aimed right at the heart, huh? I won't apologize for not being a good father. Rather I've decided to try to make up for it. Now, I realize that you're twenty-one years old and free to make your own choices, but that holds true of your mother and me as well. You'll be going on your way, I'm sure.

"Oh, you'll come home for holidays, things like that, I expect. That is, if your mother and I behave as you think we should. Isn't that true? And if we don't and you have babies, I guess you could stop us from seeing them. Would you really do that, Christi? Light of our lives, daughter of our hearts."

"Dad, all I said was—"

"All you said was that if we did something you disapproved of, you'd move out, not come back to this house. How do you think that made your mother feel? Or myself, for that matter."

Large tears formed in Christi's eyes. "All the time mom was sick, I felt abandoned. Like she loved Jeremiah more than either David or me."

"Oh, Christi, I'm so sorry," Becca said. "I never meant to hurt anyone. I just couldn't not at the time, I couldn't handle everything I missed you so much when you left as well."

"Enough, that's enough," Jon said. "We all went through a terrible loss and handled it differently. And we hurt each other terribly. It's time we admitted that none of us are perfect, and moved on from there. Don't threaten us. Your mother and I don't want to lose you, or your brother, but helping this boy is something we need to do to make things right for ourselves and him. If you don't understand that, then I'm sorry. So damned sorry."

Up to this point, Kevin had remained quiet, solemnly staring out the window, but he put his arm around Christi and began to soothe her as her sobs grew louder. He whispered something in her ear that Becca couldn't hear, and she sniffled, nodded.

Becca's heart flip-flopped when Christi and Kevin stood. He took her hand, held it in both his.

"I've asked Christi to live with me for a while. We both want to continue going to school, but haven't decided where yet. I know what it's like to be separated from my family. I don't want that for her. It's hell. Excuse me, ma'am." He nodded toward Becca.

"We need some time, Mom. I need some time. I don't think I can be in the same room with this Lucas Pell. Not yet, not now. Maybe someday. But I guess if it's what you have to do, then I'll support you, even though I feel that way. As for the holidays, well, I'll try to work out something."

"That's all we're asking," Jon said. "This family has been shattered, let's put it back together, not leave it lying in ruins around us."

Christi left Kevin's arms, came into her father's in what quickly became a joyous group hug.

Spinner watched Lucas hurry into the shack at the boat yard, and reached for Raine's hand. "You okay?"

Though she nodded and offered the tiniest of smiles, he knew better. Gray shadows smudged her eyes that darted about as if expecting something bad to come at her. Her usually sleek hair stuck out in tufts. She did not look like his Raine. And it wasn't any wonder, considering what she'd told him on the way to Lucas's. This ex-husband of hers had to be some kind of monster.

"Tell you what. I've got some connections, I'm going to see what can be done about putting that son of a bitch back where he belongs."

Eyes going wide, she shook her head, clutched at him with fingers like claws. "Don't. Don't mess with him. He's vicious."

"I've done vicious before, sweetheart."

"Spinner, please."

He touched her cheek with the back of his hand, heart wrenching when she flinched. "We can't go through life expecting him to show up. I'll take care of it. Permanently. He'll not bother you again."

Fuming with repressed anger, he started the Nova and peeled away from the boat yard onto the highway. He'd kill the bastard if he had to. It'd been a long time since he felt like this, itching to punish someone, make them pay in spades. Once upon a time, years ago, he'd have beat the man to a pulp, tossed him in the goddamned river, without hesitation. Now, it would be hard to do, but by God, for her he could. If it turned out to be the only way. But it probably wouldn't.

"Please promise me you'll be careful. He won't hesitate to kill you." She sucked in a sob, wiped her eyes.

Maybe that would be best. Let the son of a bitch try. Give him a good excuse to take care of him permanently. Either way, the man was done messing with Raine.

"Lucas isn't what I expected at all," she said, dragging his mind away from such dark thoughts.

"He's a good kid. I know that sounds ridiculous, considering some of the stuff he's done, but none of it's been deliberate. He doesn't know another way to fight back, to make himself a place in this world. The Krafts are giving him that chance."

"And so are you." She touched his cheek.

He glanced at her. "Are you still resentful of that?"

"I don't think I am. Everything that's happened and then meeting him, him being so kind to me when I expected a little monster, I think Becca and Jon are right about trying to help him. And terribly brave." She stared out the window at trees dancing in the wind, then laid her hand on his thigh. "It must feel good to help kids like that."

"I'm sure it will have its rewards for Becca and Jon. And certainly for Lucas."

"I didn't mean them, I meant you. There are so many other things you could do with your life. Teach or have a private practice, yet you hold on to this social work."

"Social work? Sounds almost like something dirty, doesn't it?"

"I didn't mean it that way." She patted his leg. "You know I didn't. What I'm trying to say, and not doing a very good job of it. Do you think I could, I mean, is there a place you can go to learn how to help kids like Lucas?"

Her question blind-sided him. "You? You want to…?"

"Well, don't sound so incredulous. I was brought up poor, dirt poor. Little Lorraine from the wrong side of the tracks. We lived in the worst part of Tulsa. My folks were good people. They just didn't know how to make things work for themselves. And so nothing ever did. Mama worked herself to death cleaning other people's houses and Daddy went from one construction job to another. I guess I loved them, but I couldn't wait to get out of there. And then, I met Russ."

Struck speechless, Spinner waited for her to go on, but she didn't. Maybe he would kill that bastard for what he did to her.

He pulled up in front of her house, shut off the ignition. "Are you serious about this?"

"As serious as I've ever been. I want to do something important, not just exist."

"It's not easy and it'll break your heart when you lose one."

"My heart's been broken before. I'd rather it be because I was trying to do something good."

"What about the business? Your house?"

"What about them? I can sell my half to Becca. Who knows, she may want to sell out entirely. I think she only started RainTree to help me out. To keep me from moping about after Russ and all. I was in bad shape, and she's a good friend. She'll want me to be happy. As for the house, it's just a place to live."

"Well, if you're serious, there's always a shortage of good help. You'll have to make some choices. You can go to college, get a degree, and become a social worker, or you and I could open a halfway house for these damaged kids. There's never enough places to send them where they can get a second chance. I've been thinking of doing that for a long while. It'd take some doing, but I think together we could pull it off. That is, if you're interested."

"Interested? You bet I am."

The hope he hadn't dared nurture brought tears to his eyes, swelled in his throat until he couldn't speak. But he had something very important to ask her. Not a way in hell he was going to let her and the life she offered get away from him.

Cupping her face in both hands, he looked down into her shining eyes. Cleared his throat, swallowed. "Raine," he said. "Before we get started on all this serious stuff, will you marry me?"

For a horrible instant, her face clouded over and he thought the answer would be no. Had he read her wrong? Been all kinds of a fool?

Then she smiled and planted kisses over his lips, one cheek then the other, the end of his nose, murmuring "Oh, yes," between each kiss.

"Just promise me one thing," she said after she'd run out of targets.

"Anything."

"Don't kill Russ. Just make him go away."

"That I can do." And he could too. When he finished with this Russ character, he wouldn't dare come near the state of Oklahoma again. Ever.

A week later, Becca stood on the porch of the lake house and waved goodbye to Christi and Kevin. All the arrangements had been made for her and Kevin to return to school. They had decided on the University of New Mexico. Jon had invested money for all three of the children while they were growing up and the market had been kind. There would be plenty for their daughter to finish school and get a good start in whatever life she chose. As with her brother David, Jon and Becca would not interfere, though they might disagree with some of the choices their children made.

Spinner had called, said he would bring Lucas over after lunch. The boy was working a late shift at the boat yard, and they wanted to get him settled in before he had to go to work.

Anticipating their arrival, Becca's nerves had a good hold on her by the time the rented Toyota carrying Christi and Kevin disappeared out of sight down the lane. Jon had left for Tulsa early so he could get caught up on work and return home before Lucas arrived.

Rather than stand on the porch staring down the lane, growing more and more nervous, she went inside. Stood at the bottom of the stairs, thinking about everything that had happened in the past few weeks. Upstairs, there was something she'd needed to do for a long while. Maybe she was finally ready to do it.

Trailing a hand along the bannister she climbed the steps and went to the closed door of Jeremiah's room. The knob was cool in her palm, and for a moment she couldn't turn it. Pictured her beautiful son sitting behind that door, working on his computer, or playing that stupid Doom game. He'd glance up when she came in, grin so a dimple stood out in one cheek.

"Hi, Mom," he'd say. "What's up?"

Oh, Jeremiah, how very much I'll always love you.

Squaring her shoulders she pushed the door open and went inside. The gold and black basketball letter sweater with his number 33 on the back still hung over the back of a chair and she ran her hands over it, glanced at the backpack in the corner, his shoes nearby, one turned on its side, just as she'd remembered. With a sigh and a shake of her head, she went to the closet and began to take his clothes from the rod, lying them carefully on the bed—faded jeans, each paired with a tee shirt, the only thing he ever wore to school unless it was a special day. His navy blue suit, a white shirt with two ties draped over the shoulders. The soft brown leather bomber jacket they'd bought him for Christmas the year he died.

She hugged the jacket to her chest, inhaling the pungent aroma, wondered for the first time why he hadn't been wearing it that night. He'd been crazy about that jacket, and it was cold when he left the house. Tears burned her eyes. He'd paused at the door, raised a hand. What had he been wearing?

"See you later, Mom."

"Be careful."

"Uh-huh." Blew her a kiss and closed the door.

"See you later. See you later, Mom," echoed in the sunlit room.

"See you later, my darling," she murmured.

What *had* he been wearing? Impossible to remember. Just like everything else that happened after that moment. Only the blackness, the blind screaming of her wounded soul.

She sniffed, wiped at her eyes. Had to get some boxes, put all this stuff away. Maybe take it to some charity. Not all of it, though. Not the jacket and the sweater. Save those. Forever. Along with the beautiful memories.

Hugging the soft leather, she sat on the bed and stared at the picture on the table. Jeremiah, grinning at her. Caught forever wearing that carefree expression only the young and innocent have. The way she would always remember him.

"What you doing, hon?"

Her breath caught and she looked up to see Jon standing in the doorway, sorrow shadowing his eyes. At last she understood that hers wasn't the only sadness. A sadness she knew would never go away, for either of them. But he smiled and came into the room. And she smiled back.

"Just putting his things away, and thinking."

For a brief instant, he looked away, cleared his throat. Turned back and touched her arm. "I'll help you finish, then let's get some lunch. I'm starved."

After they ate, she sat beside him on the deck, held his hand and watched boats on the shimmering lake, while they waited for Spinner and Raine and Lucas.

Velda Brotherton writes from her home perched on the side of a mountain against the Ozark National Forest. Branded as *Sexy, Dark and Gritty*, her work embraces the lives of gutsy women and heroes who are strong enough to deserve them. After a stint writing for a New York publisher, she's settled comfortably in with small publishers to produce novels in several genres.

While known for her successful series work—the *Twist of Poe* romantic mysteries, as well as her signature Western Historical Romance *Victorians* and *Montana* series—her publishing resume includes numerous standalone novels, as well. *Remembrance* is her sixth such work, joining hard-hitting previous books like *Once There Were Sad Songs, A Savage Grace, Wolf Song, Stoneheart's Woman*, and her magnum opus, *Beyond the Moon.*

Facebook: Author Velda Brotherton
Twitter: @veldabrotherton
www.veldabrotherton.com

www.ingramcontent.com/pod-product-compliance
Lightning Source LLC
Chambersburg PA
CBHW030935260626
47169CB00002B/484